Praise for *The U*
Laurie Gwen Sha   ...out novel

"Endearingly quirky... Despite the risks, *The Unexpected Salami* winds up being unexpectedly delightful."
—Anthony Bourdain, *New York Times Book Review*

"Shapiro's high-concept premise pays off in a truckload of enjoyable gags, hilarious characterizations, and irresistible non sequiturs."
—*Kirkus Reviews*

"Imagine a novel that tries to combine the spirit of Rob Reiner's classic rockumentary spoof *This Is Spinal Tap* with a coming-of-age novel. Shapiro makes the mix work."
—*Publishers Weekly*

"A charming romantic comedy. Deftly done!"
—*Booklist*

"Laurie Gwen Shapiro's romantic, hyperkinetic first novel trips along with a frank comic energy."
—*Time Out New York*

"Laurie Gwen Shapiro's characters are so quirky, engaging and convincing; they jump off the page and beg to be cast into film. These meats are not exactly kosher, but they are funny as hell."
—Ruth Ozeki, author of *My Year of Meats* and *All Over Creation*

"The language is as crisp and dead-on as the movie *Clueless*, and the action as picaresque as *Moll Flanders*."
—Frank McCourt, Pulitzer Prize-winning author of *Angela's Ashes*

"Packed with energy, attitude and wit, this is an unexpected delight, a madcap journey into the wilds of New York, New Jersey, and the dark side of rock 'n' roll."
—Tom Perrotta, author of *Election*

ABOUT THE AUTHOR

LAURIE GWEN SHAPIRO
is the author of one previous novel, *The Unexpected Salami*,
an ALA notable book. She has coproduced two films on the
brothers McCourt for HBO/Cinemax with Conor McCourt.
With her own brother, David Shapiro, she codirected
Keep the River on Your Right: A Modern Cannibal Tale,
which received an Independent Spirit Award. She lives
in New York City with her husband and their new daughter.
Visit her Web site at www.lauriegwenshapiro.com.

THE
MATZO
BALL
Heiress

LAURIE Gwen SHAPiRo

**RED
DRESS
INK**
™

First edition April 2004

THE MATZO BALL HEIRESS

A Red Dress Ink novel .

ISBN 0-373-25053-3

Author photograph by Steven Ashemore.

Visit Red Dress Ink at www.reddressink.com

Printed in U.S.A.

For my husband, Paul O'Leary, my great love,
a careful reader and very much my comic muse.

And to the little bundle who keeps both of us going,
Violet Frances O'Leary—aka Tziporah Chaia O'Leary.

A huge thanks to:

Mikie Heilbron—my chance encounter with your lovely fighting spirit inspired me to write this novel. Thanks for your blessings to make it all up.

Farrin Jacobs, for her good humor and editorial expertise. And to so many more angels at Red Dress Ink, especially Senior Editor Margaret Marbury and Joan Marlow Golan.

Nancy Yost of Lowenstein-Yost, for her savvy agenting and nurturing nature.

A dynamic duo of film agents, Michael Cendejas and Lynn Pleshette of the Lynn Pleshette Agency, for their constant championing; and Paul Brennan at Sloss Law— every lawyer should be so nice.

Corey S. Powell, friend thick and through—a true *mensch* for the amount of time he took to read the manuscript and the thoughtful feedback he offered.

Joanna Dalin, for her thoughts about haggis as well as heaven and hell, and Nena O'Neill, for her thoughts on workable marriages.

Aron Yagoda, to whom I am indebted for information on the mechanics of matzo making.

If I am not for myself, then who will be for me?
And if I am only for myself, what am I?
And if not now, when?
—Hillel

ONE

That Time of Year

The dread kicks in for me around late February. It's not just the onslaught of my spring allergies. It's also the anticipation of Passover—that unwelcome time of year when I curse my ancestor, Izzy Greenblotz. I couldn't avoid the stupid holiday even if my cousin Jake would allow me to skip my annual obligations in the factory. In my prewar apartment building's elevator, Mrs. Minsky from Penthouse A launches the annual Inquisition as she tugs on her Majorica pearls in glee. "Whose matzos are *you* buying this year?" Every year this is the funniest question she's ever asked, and her powdered face flushes with self-satisfaction. There's no need to answer her. Greenblotz Matzo is not only the number-one-selling matzo in the United States, it's the leading brand in Canada and England, even in Venezuela and South Africa. Wherever there are Jews, there is Greenblotz.

I handle my widowed neighbor with a diplomatic smile.

Even though it's weeks too early—Passover is not until mid-April this year—she wishes me an anticipatory happy and healthy *Pesach* when we stop at our floor.

Soon, someone will ask the question I despise most: "How does the Greenblotz family celebrate Passover?"

Since "Greenblotz, Heather" is the only Greenblotz listed in the Manhattan phone book, when reporters from *New York* or *Hadassah Magazine* can't get through to the factory, they call my home line. I never deny that I'm from *the* Matzo Family, which would be too weird.

This year, when a reporter insists on specific details on our upcoming seder, I'm stuck delivering the family white lies that Jake usually spins from the factory office.

Why haven't I gotten my damn home number unlisted already?

"We have a quiet evening together," I say. "Just family."

How can I ever tell the truth?

Can you imagine the family that makes the millions of artificial trees for sale in Kmart not celebrating Christmas, or the Cadbury family not celebrating Easter with a basket of chocolate eggs? I'm too mortified to admit that come Passover I'm home alone in my apartment, chugging down a liter bottle of Diet Coke and stuffing my face with a Panini 2 from the Italian deli around the corner on Second Avenue. That's prosciutto, red peppers and Swiss cheese—a quadruple no-no as far as the traditional holiday is concerned.

My take on what's kosher has always been a little hazy, but even the most wayward Jew knows that pork is never ever kosher. When I was about training-bra age, eleven or twelve, I asked my father if pigs weren't kosher because they love mud. This made perfect sense to my preadolescent mind: dirty equals not kosher. Grandpa Reuben and Dad were padlocking the metal gate on the factory entrance;

Wilson was waiting patiently by the open limo doors in the late-winter sleet. Dad, who my mother insists is very, very smart, too smart for his own good—she claims he has an IQ of 150—shook his head and said, "No, kid, pigs are not kosher because they don't chew their cud. Only plant-eating mammals with multichambered stomachs are kosher. Ruminants do not carry as many diseases."

"What's a ruminant?" I asked, but Grandpa Reuben interrupted.

"Some say that God didn't want us eating animals that eat other animals. Some say that God didn't want us eating the more intelligent animals. I say a bunch of people made up a bunch of rules to give a desert tribe something to believe in." Grandpa and Dad had a rare shared laugh. They forgot that my follow-up question was left hanging, and I quietly climbed into the black limo, so out of place on the (then) low-rent Lower East Side.

Secondly on the kosher affront, eating ham and cheese together is mixing meat and dairy. Such a combination is strictly forbidden to the observant, because, as Grandpa continued his religious lesson in the limo, "If you didn't watch what you ate in the desert without a Frigidaire, you got sick."

Then there's the panini bread itself, which our customers would call *hametz*. Bread is not allowed for the entire eight days of Passover. This custom honors the Jews that didn't have time to wait for yeast-leavened loaves to rise the day Moses rushed them the hell out of Egypt and away from the Pharaoh's rule.

Observant families prepare for Passover by burning any *hametz* that may still be in the house, every last crumb. It's a curious sight to see the handful of remaining religious Jews on the Lower East Side carrying their half-finished loaves and frozen waffles to a communal bonfire raging in a Grand

Street metal trash can. Sometimes when I speed by in a cab, I spy a happy teen stoking the *hametz* fire with a broomstick, smiling broadly at the joy of tradition.

The plate my sandwich rests on is my fourth sacrilege. A properly observant Jew would have one set of plates for meat, one set for dairy, and a third Passover set to use once a year. But this is a dish from the same Mikasa "Tulip Time" dinnerware I bought at Bloomingdale's my first year out of college and I still use all year long. Somewhere in my mother's colossal apartment on Park Avenue is a set of special Passover dishes given to my parents as a wedding gift. They were by Rosenthal, hand-painted a gorgeous pastel turquoise blue with open-petal fuchsia flowers. Wasted beauty. Now the dishes are bubble-wrapped and tucked away in a closet. Or maybe Mom gave the dishes to charity, since we only took the set out once or twice for company when I was really young. For keeping up appearances.

As long as I can remember, the Greenblotz Matzo factory has been kept kosher under the supervision of Schmuel Blattfarb, a devout rabbi with a sweaty forehead and startlingly wide hips. I had heard about him for years, but I first met him in the ground-level office of the factory the day I got my final marks for the first half of ninth grade. My mother and I waited patiently across the desk from my father and the rabbi as they completed the paperwork for the pre-Passover inspection.

As Rabbi Blattfarb got up to sign off, his chair rose with him. He then awkwardly prized it from his hips, lowered it back to the ground and announced that his fee had just gone up to ten thousand dollars a year.

After the rabbi sheepishly said goodbye to all of us, Dad

raised the window and called to our handsome Portuguese driver, Wilson, that we would be right out. We were Brooklyn bound. My mother and father were in one of the better stretches of their marriage, and she had uncharacteristically telephoned Dad with the news of my exceptional marks. Dad uncharacteristically responded with spur-of-the-moment reservations for a congratulatory communal feast at Peter Luger's Steak House right across the Williamsburg Bridge.

"What does Rabbi Blattfarb actually do to deserve that kind of money?" I asked Dad at our artery-clogging dinner.

"Just ridiculous!" my mother marveled.

"Long answer or short answer?" Dad asked me.

"Short," Mom said.

"Long," I said.

"To begin with," Dad said, "the flour and water going into the factory must be certified one hundred percent kosher, which basically means a few phone calls. Then, since Moses and his followers had no time for leavening as they left Egypt, the matzo that's specifically kosher for Passover cannot be baked longer than eighteen minutes, which is the longest time flour and water can go without self-fermentation. It's not Blattfarb's time we're paying for though, it's his name."

Although the factory still more than meets the strict standards, and has the all-important Blattfarb stamp of approval, no one in my family has been kosher at home for two generations, let alone kosher for Passover with that scrubbing-the-house-for-all-crumbs business and that bothersome third set of plates.

Even though my family's dietary habits may raise eyebrows among those who care about these things, I don't think we're alone in eating whatever we want. From my observation, the majority of Jews in America are culturally, not observantly, Jewish. Except for a High Holiday or two, they haven't been to synagogue since their symbolic ascent into adulthood, a *bar mitzvah* for a thirteen-year-old boy, a *bat mitzvah* for a twelve-year-old or thirteen-year-old girl, supposedly spiritual events, but these days more about the gifts and party one-upmanship. The *bar* and *bat mitzvahs* I've attended over many years have featured an inexplicable Italian theme with an ice sculpture of the Coliseum and a Leaning Tower of Pisa cake; fifty decorative doves flying around the room who shat all over the white-and-blue table settings; multihued cheese cubes laid out on a table so that they formed an approximation of the *bar mitzvah* boy's face; the same *bar mitzvah* boy's triumphant entrance into the reception hall wearing a crown with a Star of David orb; three hundred primarily Jewish guests doing pharaoh dance moves to "Walk Like an Egyptian"; and most recently, a reception at the Times Square ESPN Zone during which the rabbi and the cantor from the morning's services drove arcade bumper cars.

Unlike today's *bar mitzvah* extravaganzas, the typical American Passover centers around a toned-down ritual meal that is on par with Thanksgiving in terms of family must. According to my father, it is the most celebrated Jewish holiday in the world.

Passover is a week long, but the first two days are the big communal seder days, the ones that you're supposed to spend with your extended family. True, as far as Jewish holidays go, *Yom Kippur,* the High Holiday when you fast to mourn the dead, is up there. But it's too morose for a lot of people. Passover is different; it's happy-household time.

But what does the Greenblotz family do for Passover? The folks who cater Passover for the Jewish masses?

For the past five years, specifically to avoid Passover, my mother, Jocelyn Greenblotz (née Kaufman), has sent herself on a variety of impossible-to-reach-her escapes that involve snorkeling, an odd new hobby for one of the world's great shoppers. These high-end adventure tours attract the richest of the rich, like the man who invented polyester and several family members of the Roosevelts. Two years ago Mom took an $18,000 expedition cruise to Micronesia, which included snorkeling in Yap—an island, she wrote cheerily on a three-line postcard, that has currency made of huge circular stone. Last year, she joined three girlfriends from the Yap trip on a journey to the Pitcairns. This time, she cheerily wrote on another three-line postcard, she snorkeled, and nearly every islander is a descendant of the mutineers from the HMS *Bounty*.

You won't find my expatriate father, Sol, at a seder dinner either. Almost ten years ago, Dad legally transferred his Greenblotz Matzo family board of directors vote to me, his only child, when he left the U.S. for Bali in a sudden rush to find himself. The last time I heard from him was after the terrorist bombing of the Sari Club in Bali; he was bidding good-bye to his villa and his two teenage servants (one girl, one guy) who got paid the equivalent of $25 a month. (Apparently a good wage for Bali.) I attacked Dad's bad handwriting and chronic abbreviations, working backward like a hieroglyphics expert, and still it took me twenty minutes to fully decipher the one-paragraph letter on light blue airmail paper. (I was as proud as the guy who broke the German code when I worked out *abbre* was his abbreviation for *abbreviating*.)

Server down. Thought I'd let you know I'm abbre my stay here.

I'm spook by the rise of milit Islam in Indon. Have new luv, and we've decided to move to Amsterd. In touch shortly.

He wasn't.

As my cousin Jake Greenblotz now heads the matzo factory, he must pass himself off as a kosher, dedicated Jew. But even he leaves a day of Passover-week media tours to go home to his longtime Irish girlfriend, Siobhan Moran, and they order in spareribs and chicken with jumbo shrimp.

If word got out what really goes down in the Greenblotz family, it would be a religion-wide scandal. To me, it's already a personal tragedy.

two

Sell, Sell, Sell

A frantic but jovial call from Jake starts my day. "Hello, Sunshine. You free later this morning? I've got a double media booking."

I eye the clock. Nine-fifteen already! Didn't I set that alarm? "I'll grab my datebook," I say sleepily.

"You don't have a PalmPilot? You, with all your technological know-how?"

"God, no. I had one, but it crashed before I backed it up. Never again. The thing was ugly anyhow."

"I'll wait," he chirps.

There's the damn Filofax, by the microwave. I open it to the right day. "So, it looks pretty light. A phone meeting I'm sure Vondra can cover. Sure, okay, what time do you need me to be there?"

"You're the best," Jake says after a bite of what sounds like apple. "Eleven o'clock is when your guy from the Food

Channel is coming. I'll be at City Hall for a presentation to Jewish purveyors." Despite his money, Jake says *purr-vay-yahs* with that special Jersey accent that could land him continuous character-actor work.

"Is that a big deal?"

"Guss's Pickles will be there. And Second Avenue Deli of course. Mayor's having a full-blown Yid press conference. It's black-*yarmulke* time."

"I don't get you."

"Every politician in New York has two *yarmulkes*, black for daytime luncheons, and white for fancy dinners. Trust me. I'm the one who gets photographed with them."

"What happened to Schapiro's Wines? How come I saw a For Rent sign when my cab drove past?"

"I didn't tell you? I heard this direct from Norman Schapiro. They cashed in on the Lower East Side real-estate boom. They closed the factory and opened a little stall in the Essex Market for the nostalgic customers. But the family moved all their manufacturing to Monticello. Norman asked me why we're not doing the same."

"Did you tell him about Izzy's proviso?"

"Why give anything away in this business? Norman may be wine but he still goes to the kosher-food conventions."

"So much for the old neighborhood. Probably you'll see condos pop up in their old factory with some cutesy name like the Winery. I just can't believe we're the only ones left downtown." I sigh and say, "You excited to meet the mayor?"

"He's been by the factory already. Twice. Even if he wasn't Jewish, it's a regular pitstop for every mayor when he decides it's time to court the Jewish vote. I'd rather tour the Playmate of the Month and give her any Greenblotz macaroons she wants." After I laugh weakly, he says, "So, I'm glad you can do the Food Channel thing. I don't trust anyone else from our staff with the TV interviews."

"Anything special I have to know?"

"Nah. Their reporter's doing a special on food pioneers. Mostly want to know about Izzy. You'll know what to give him. The business is recession-proof because we're in the Bible, families get together whatever the financial circumstance, that kind of bullshit. Have a pen?"

The first one I pull from the drawer is the one with Heather Greenblotz printed all over it in different cheery colors and sizes; it came in a cheery pitch letter from a new charity called the Tumor Society. "Uh-huh, go ahead."

"His name is Steve Meyers."

I size up my interviewer. "Meyers? A Jew. Easy as pie."

"They still have to ask the same questions for their segments."

"But I won't have to give him the whole spiel. Last year I spent fifteen minutes explaining the significance of the shankbone in the seder to the WCBS *lite* reporter, like I know anything about it. I even printed a page about it off your computer and we read it together. He still couldn't get it. And he wouldn't start in on the matzo until he got it. Then when we started taping he kept calling the factory a cracker factory."

"Oh that old fart, I've seen him on TV. Did a segment where he asked Carnegie Deli what part of the cow pastrami is from. Why do the schmucks always succeed? What's his ridiculous name?"

"Talbot C. Kelton. That bow tie and seersucker suit is part of his 'I'm a funny WASPy guy' shtick."

Jake snorts a bit. "Generally speaking, men with bow ties should be shot. Anyhow, I'm not so sure you're right about Meyers. Look at Springsteen. German names can go either way."

"Beck's Jewish," I say. How long can we keep up this amusing departure from our usual conversation? I usually talk to Jake about matzo and matzo alone. Occasionally his former days at the dog track filter in, or his yummy-yummy thoughts about how slutty the latest pop kittens are. What is it with grown men and Britney Spears?

"Who's Beck?" Jake says after another crunchy bite.

"Rock star. Critics' darling. C'mon, you never watch the Grammys?"

"If it's not Springsteen or Billy Joel, I want nothing to do with it. Look what time it is. I really gotta go already. My day is already packed with or without the mayor. We have three million orders to fill."

"Okeydoke. I'll be by at eleven."

"Thanks again. I won't be here, but the place will be in full gear."

Jake and his brother, Greg, who has stiff bleached hair that stands up like wiry grass, and lives in a fancy condo in South Miami, are the sons of my aunt Elsa and uncle Nathan, who died in 1991. They were skiing without their boys and were both decapitated during a six-car pileup outside Casey's Caboose, a family restaurant in Killington known for its happy service and lobster tank.

Of the two of them, I'm much closer to Jake. Despite the brutality of his parents' accident, he finds it in himself to treat other people with kindness. Plus, he's a lot funnier than Greg.

The best sound I've ever heard in my lifetime was the laugh that came from Jake's mouth the year after the big car accident. Jake and Greg had each received reminder postcards from the cemetery that unveiling headstones was the Jewish tradition on the anniversary of death. They jointly called my house to remind their father's brother, my father—Dad in turn asked me to find my way back into NYC from my dorm at Brown so I could be an extra source of emotional support.

At the cemetery, Greg and Dad had to pee. Not wanting to desecrate anyone's ancestor, uncle and nephew drove back to the office before any prayers were read. Alone with me for the first time in years, Jake said in an unreadable voice, "Did they have to be so showy?"

"Showy?" I said nervously. I wasn't sure what emotion Jake needed from me to get him through this sorrowful day. Unlike Greg, Jake had steadfastly refused therapy.

"A *double* decapitation?" After his year of unhealthy stoicism, an unbridled guffaw was an unlikely event. But there it was and God bless it; it paved the way for his first honest weep and a pledge to me that he would see my father's famous shrink.

The three of us—workhorse Jake, flaky Greg and booksmart me—are three of the five Izzy Greenblotz descendants with voting power in our privately held company. Mom has never had a vote on Greenblotz Matzo's family-run board of directors because she is not a full-blooded Greenblotz, although she wouldn't want a vote in the first place. She'd consider it a curse. Mom hates "the fucking holiday" that she is convinced ruined her marriage. Maybe the fact that she married a mostly gay man has more to do with their early break than Passover stress.

None of us talk to Marcy and Rebecca, my two other first cousins who also hold board votes. They are the estranged, backbiting nutcake kids of my backbiting nutcake aunt Shara Fishbein (née Greenblotz) who died in 1994 from cancer my branch of the family had not even known about. I was not invited to Aunt Shara's funeral, nor was my father, her only living sibling. Neither was Jake or Greg as Aunt Shara had always felt that her two nephews hated her (they did), and thought that they were my father's allies in our family warring (they were). Jake and I were notified by Shara's lawyer after the burial. Dad had just moved to Bali and I had a phone number for him then. I called to tell him about his sister's passing and the funeral situation. Dad was flabbergasted (breast cancer!), and distraught, and pissed off. Surely he had a right to be there even if he hadn't talked to Shara in the year since he'd told her that she was a public nuisance for writing irate letters to the Museum of American Folk Art about their continued refusal of her "masterpiece" fruit-themed quilt festooned with Granny Smith apples, lemons and mandarin oranges.

My mother and father may have major differences, but not about that branch of the family. Even during the final cold freeze in their disintegrating marriage, they drew together in a shared revulsion over Shara's and her daughters' mad rush to Grandpa Reuben's house in Jersey after a vague stipulation in his will was read: "Divide personal items as the family sees fit." By the time my immediate family and Jake and Greg walked into the three-story house in West Orange— the so-called "good" Orange as the real-estate agents say— the cedar fur closet was threadbare. Mom thought Shara's posse must have carted away Grandma Lainie's old minks the previous day. Shara's daughters apparently weren't through with their booty hunt, because when Jake and I opened the guest-room door, we came upon my dear cousins crawling around like lice, double-checking if there were any secret hiding places under floorboards for Grandma Lainie's lavish jewelry that hadn't been doled out after her own death. (Marcy had a small Tiffany lamp in her hand, which she tried to inconspicuously roll under the bed when she spotted me with mouth agape.)

Now all communication with Marcy and Rebecca, such as dividend discussions and financial decisions, is through their new lawyer, Mortie Altman, who carts along a tarty female associate we all think he's screwing—or *schtupping*, as our matzo customers like to say—to serve as the other proxy during big votes.

We licensed out our name to other product lines in the 1960s for buckets of money. Jars of gefilte fish, chicken consommé and borscht, tins of chocolate and plain macaroons, and plastic-wrapped boxes of multihued half-circle candied fruit jells carry the Greenblotz name. You have to keep current in the Jewish-food business. In 1985, our family board voted to phase out Greenblotz prune juice, and phase in dark chocolate-covered matzo. That was my aunt Shara's one brilliant suggestion during her lifetime. She had taken a weekend quilt-buying trip to Lancaster, Pennsylvania, with her youngest daughter. They'd seen tourists devouring salted Amish pretzels covered in chocolate. Later that week, Aunt Shara argued with my dad that if the Amish can update their food, why not the Jews? Dad may have a high-genius IQ, but he was wrong, and Shara was right. After potato-pancake mix, chocolate-covered matzo is now our biggest-selling auxiliary offering. Last year's addition of white chocolate-covered matzo (a product I jokingly suggested to Jake) is doing almost as well.

We stock these "extra" products in our tiny store in the ground floor of the factory on Attorney Street, but we don't really manufacture them; our licensees do. We do make the plain matzo for Passover, and the Passover egg-matzo variant. The chocolate matzo is egg matzo we make, and then ship to a candy factory. There's also egg and plain matzo for year-round use, matzo that hasn't been under the militant Passover eighteen-minutes stipulation. But God forbid we should sell the Manhattan factory. Izzy Greenblotz was smart enough to envision a day when his pride and joy would be in jeopardy, and he legally saw to it that we would have to keep the original factory going. If we sell the matzo factory, resulting revenue must go to charity. We're talking a many-multimillion-dollar business we would walk away from. Three hundred million dollars, cool. Even my soul-searching, gadabout father depends on his payouts. Izzy's son, Reuben—my father's father—put the same dopey clause in his will to be true to Izzy's vision. Now five of us are next in line: Jake, Greg, Aunt Shara's brats and me—a motley quintet fettered together in a loophole-proof fate.

Whenever I start feeling too sorry for myself, I think of a TV documentary I saw last year about a Polish American family in South Dakota. For generations the family has been collectively carving a statue of Chief Crazy Horse out of a mountainside deep in the Black Hills, not far from the Mount Rushmore monument. Except the entire Mount Rushmore carving—all four of the presidents' faces—would fit in Crazy Horse's forehead. The Crazy Horse carvers are going for a three-quarter portrait on horseback. It took me a minute to process the magnitude of this project—Mount Rushmore is seen only from the front! Their first carver, their Izzy, insisted way back in FDR's day that the family never accept government money or assistance from federal laborers. Even though he was about as Indian as Izzy Greenblotz, he detested Uncle Sam for carving white men's faces out of a sacred Sioux mountain. With government millions and manpower, Mount Rushmore was finished in a matter of a few years. With a policy that limits workers to family members and funds to public donations, if your fate is to be born into the Crazy Horse family, you must carve and fundraise until you drop. This is their family mantle. I feel the grandchildren's pain: by their standards, I have it easy. And I don't have to gear up with drills every morning.

When my cousin Jake first volunteered to oversee the factory year-round, I gladly gave my yea vote. Surprisingly, there was no backlash against Jake's rise to power from the Aunt Shara branch of cousins. But then who else would have the inclination to run a matzo factory these days, while we lucky descendants get enough money from dividends to never work? Things are continuing the way Izzy wanted. Money and family. Dad once told me that Izzy wrote our slogan before he even had offspring or a business going. With only slivovitz and fellow cardplayers for company, he was the sole immigrant in the new land from his Polish *shtetl*. But perhaps he imagined the fruit of his loin, the joy his offspring and their offspring would bring him, as he optimistically scribbled a slogan into his penny notebook: *Buy Greenblotz—Because Family Is Everything.* The scribble stuck; it's the slogan printed on every one of our many products.

Since Passover falls late this year, I'm still in the safe zone. Last year, when Passover popped up in March, I was caught off guard with no game plan. I had been seeing Daniel Popper, an intense Jewish on-the-rise associate editor for the *New Republic* who sports a luscious head of black curls many women among New York intelligentsia would love to unfurl.

I met him at a work-related party I forced myself to attend. During a group conversation about disturbing baby trends, Daniel held the floor with his description of a baby girl he'd seen at an adult Halloween party. The infant had been dressed as a sexy cat; she had on lipstick, furry ears and baby fishnets.

Later I was feeling tipsy on an empty stomach and searched out the Pringles. Daniel had the same idea. My confidence boosted by two vodka sours, I told him about how every time I see someone with great curls I think of one of my favorite kid's books, *Ramona the Pest*.

"I don't think I remember that one," he said after a munch.

"A girlie book. Ramona Quimby got in big trouble from her kindergarten teacher for pulling a classmate's perfect curl."

Daniel smiled seductively, bobbed his head toward me and said, "Go ahead and pull it."

Daniel was thrilled that he was dating a Greenblotz—his grandmother would be ecstatic! He pushed me to get together with him as often as possible. On the fifth date in two weeks he handed me a syrupy poem (written in scarily robotic handwriting) comparing the seder family tradition to a garden of orchids, each vibrant bloom representing a cherished family member. I was so grateful to have someone in my life during the month of March that I let the bad poetry go and tried to follow Daniel's tortured analogy. "My family would be more like a garden of moss," I said, and then went out on a limb and admitted that there is little love in my clan. When I added that the Greenblotz family has not held a seder since I was a small child, he chose not to believe me.

"You're so deadpan," he laughed.

It was as if I said the House of Windsor doesn't really drink tea. He laughed harder when I repeated my confession. I held his elbow hard and said, "Daniel, please take this seriously. This is so hard for me to tell anyone."

During our awkward foreplay that night, Daniel maneuvered over my body with the subtlety of a moon rover. I had mentally broken up with him even before the condom tip made an accidental, ludicrous shadow puppet on his wall. It looked like a mini court jester was about to enter me.

"It's over," I said the next morning from a bright yellow wooden stool in his blinding-white kitchen. Of course it dawned on me that I would be alone on Passover, which started the very next night, while one of New York's very available single ladies would undoubtedly snap him up in a flash. I don't think this "catch" had ever been broken up with. His lips opened, and then shut with considerable effort. He grinned awkwardly and gave an almost imperceptible nod.

The bonehead called a week later to see if I had calmed down. "I know what started this. Was it because I didn't want you to wear my 501's so you wouldn't get lady smells in my crotch? I wasn't singling you out. Every girl I've ever dated has stunk up my crotch."

Yes, I am dateless this year, not that Passover is my Valentine's Day. But it would be nice to have someone special in my life to get me through this awkward month. I've never made it past six months with anyone though. If I don't get dumped, I usually do the dumping just before the *seder* season. I can't trust just anyone else to understand my fractured family. I'd rather be alone than with a man who thinks I'm being histrionic.

At least I have my documentary producing in full gear to distract me. I don't work because I have to, I work because I need to or I'd go crazy like Aunt Shara or my grandmothers. Idle money breeds dementia; look at history. Has there ever been a well-adjusted prince? It's hard to be normal when your first jar of Gerber apple sauce is served off priceless porcelain. Documentary-making forces me to leave my world of privilege and squeeze myself into someone else's Payless shoes.

The new film I'm working on, a biographical look at pioneer women in the sex field, is the lucky recipient of a $30,000 Guggenheim fellowship as well as major HBO funding.

My producing partner and closest friend, Vondra Adams, is a grant application genius. She was the one who wanted us to team up after we separately produced a number of segments that got considerable attention from the top of the PBS ladder. Vondra was convinced that, cynical as it sounds, a production company helmed by two women, one black, one Jewish, would be magnets for funding. I was worried that they would look at my personal finances. If so, we wouldn't have qualified. But they didn't, and she was right on the money: we've received grants from the National Endowment for the Arts, Women Make Movies, Sisters in Film and B'nai Brith.

Since our entire production company is an office of two, we're lucky our sense of humor is almost identical. Our only roadblock so far was the initial tension we had on who gets first billing on our films. From Vondra's tone of voice, it was going to get ugly. Because of my hatred of family bickering, I've never really been able to stomach conflict. So before it could turn into any kind of meaningful fight, I bit the bullet and suggested listing ourselves alphabetically, so I always come last. The deal was sealed in the Parthenon Coffee Shop, still our favorite Flatiron-district coffee shop. (Nikos and Mike, two of the twelve waiters from last year's *Neo-Gods of Greek Diners* calendar, work there.) In a buoyant mood after the credit order was settled, Vondra insisted that we flip our names every other film if our newly christened company, Two Dames Productions, took off. That hasn't happened. She's obviously forgotten or regrets her promise. I don't want any ugliness to reemerge, so I've let it slide. Just as well. Since that salvaged afternoon in the Parthenon, we've only had one other fight: who first came up with our running joke imagining tofu "haggis" showing up in natural-food stores next to textured "chicken" and "pork." Why would this be so important to her? Yet Vondra went ballistic when I said that was my idea. I have a great memory and was able to pinpoint the exact moment I first made the crack, but she wouldn't let it go at that. I finally said "Fine. Let's agree to disagree." (But it really was my joke.)

On the whole, though, I admire and adore Vondra, even if at times I'm jealous of her magnetism to pretty much the entire male population, and even more resentful of her fantastic relationship with her family. I'm grateful we have gone into a most productive partnership. My career is the one thing that's right in my life. Another three shoots on our current documentary and I'd say we're ready to edit. Then, it should be an easy trot to the production finish line, as *The Grand Ladies of Sex* is already prebought by Cecelia Neville, vice president for documentaries over at HBO. Cecelia is the most important person in the nonfiction-film industry. She knows her demographic: once she's contracted enough films about environmental treachery, triumph over disease and inspiring disadvantaged youth for her award quota, she'll buy anything with the word *sex* in it, even if it's about a bunch of elegant old women saying the words *gonorrhea* and *erectile difficulty*.

Despite our solid working relationship and close friendship, I haven't let on to Vondra what I'm worth. I'm amazed that Vondra has no idea what I'm worth. After all, there's a lot of media coverage of the factory, and Vondra's not dumb. But she thinks my family factory houses a nice-size cottage industry, and I prefer it that way. What Izzy Greenblotz didn't count on while visualizing an affluent future for his descendants is that no one really likes anyone with serious dough. So I just never mention my finances to anyone except my accountant.

Vondra's family, Southern Baptist Alabamans, branched out to the predominantly black neighborhood of Fort Greene, Brooklyn. And as Grandma Lainie used to say, "How is she supposed to know from matzo?"

I would love to have scheduled a Passover shoot to speed up our documentary, but I have to be available to keep up appearances for the media on the matzo beat. For the next two weeks, my surname comes first, and I must put in time at the factory store. Jake's request, of course, because this gets lots of media coverage for the company. A prominent story on CNN or MSNBC about the family still baking and selling the matzo is worth more than a year's worth of advertising. I cab it down to the Lower East Side Greenblotz factory every other day and will get behind the counter and *sell sell sell* with the cameras clicking; or I will lead curious folk on a factory tour, the way my father did before he'd had enough. Some families come back year after year with their children and grandchildren. The veteran shoppers pinch my cheek like I'm a favorite niece.

What staggers me about our current family power structure is that my cousin Jake treats running our factory as a gift not a burden.

I'm not completely guilty about my conspicuous absence from daily operations. There's some help, in addition to my meager once-a-year contributions. Jake's brother oversees Florida. The Sunshine State is our second-biggest market. Despite my misgivings about Greg's fun-comes-first nature, he does do a decent job despite his minimal effort. After the 2000 election, Jake kept joking with me that Greg is our Jeb Bush. "He delivers Florida for us." I've rarely seen Greg in the past decade, at board meetings mostly, and when I have, he's sunbaked and talks nonstop about game fishing. Jake is amused by his "playboy" (I'd say "misogynist") brother who's had six girlfriends in three years. I heard Jake talking about him to a Midwest distributor who brought his vacationing family on a factory tour: "My brother is a real character, a real ladies' man. Tell me, how many Jews you see game fish?"

Although Jake is only thirty-four, three years older than I am, he has the kibitzing voice of the shuffleboard players on retirement cruises. That manner and his rapidly receding hairline often get him mistaken for a middle-aged manufacturing maven.

Beyond our joking, Jake and I have little in common, but I thank the heavens for his existence. He's more family to me than my parents are. After his parents were killed in the car crash, Jake had a few wild years, living off his large dividends. He spent many weekdays whittling money away at Belmont Track, and through even seedier locales, like the jai alai arena and dog track, both in the blue-collar areas of Connecticut. Now he pays the big dues in our lot, but he genuinely gets a kick out of running the factory. Appropriately enough, Jake has the lion's share of the press. He's a focused man. Focused on matzo. Focused, but I'm betting never truly happy, as he still won't marry Siobhan. You bet this is an issue that hovers over their bliss like a circling vulture.

Siobhan and Jake have been shacking up together for ten years, since he was twenty-four. They first met in Jake's senior year at SUNY Buffalo, when Siobhan was an exchange student. Jake's good-natured mother was still alive then. Elsa Greenblotz was the one who pushed a school for her son where how much money he had was less important than how likable and smart he was. Jake wore ripped Levi's and kept a run-down car on campus to disguise his true financial worth. Then he brought Siobhan around to his parents' gargantuan house with three floors and a pinto bean–shaped pool, a block away from my grandparents' own minimansion. Jake once told me that until Siobhan saw how big his home was, she thought he was just another adorable American attending a state university. He said she was never after his money, she was after his accent. As a preteen in Ireland, she'd plastered her walls with magazine posters of young American TV stars like Scott Baio and Michael J. Fox. She wanted an American, and any good-looking one would do. Jake was much cuter than he is now because he had a full head of curly, light brown hair. As fate had it, Jake was the first American man to point out to Siobhan where the main shopping street on campus was. He chatted a bit with the pretty Irish exchange student, and then he walked her to a good spot for Buffalo wings, his treat. No one ever expected their relationship to last so long, least of all Jake.

On his deathbed our grandfather extracted a promise from his favorite grandchild: if Jake moved in with Siobhan, he would do it discreetly, and would never marry her. Grandpa Reuben was a dour man with a deli belly from eating too many tongue-and-corned-beef-combo sandwiches, who flossed his teeth with his favorite "girls" from a pack of nudie cards. He was sure the marriage would get top coverage in the Sunday *Times* style section: *Jacob Evan Greenblotz of West Orange, matzo heir and Siobhan Moran of Jersey City and Cork, not Jewish, were wed today by Father Seamus O'Flanner…*

"Bad for business!" he croaked at Jake hoarsely. "All the customers in the Northeast, *oy* would they talk! If a Greenblotz can't find a Jew to marry, what is the world coming to?" His life is hours from over and my grandfather worries about matzo sales?

But Grandpa Reuben never delineated between love and money. Just a few years before, as we waited in the rain at my grandmother's funeral in West Orange, Jake told me Grandpa Reuben's most shocking offense. Jake had been in the factory earlier, the day Grandma Lainie broke her hip and had her heart attack—she'd slipped on an especially long shoehorn meant to aid her in her battle with arthritis. While one of our bakers called 911 to get an ambulance, Jake tried to resuscitate her with mouth to mouth, but there was never any hope. And here's the kicker: when the emergency workers covered her up, Grandpa Reuben tried to give Jake a hundred-dollar tip for "his good honest effort."

Thirteen years together and no ring is embarrassing for anyone who knows they are a couple. Jake and Siobhan should follow their heart and get hitched. She was there for him after his parents' deaths. But it's not just that. Jake *adores* Siobhan. He's told me more than once that he loves her meek little voice, adorable elfin ears and quick asides. But Jake is still saddled with guilt about crossing my grandfather's last wishes.

Strangely, Siobhan has come to accept Grandpa Reuben's fascist decree. She even helps out in the store, introducing herself as Jake's wife, Shoshanna Greenblotz, a name used exclusively in the factory. (Jake's cockamamy idea, no doubt.) I guess Siobhan's fiery hair can be mistaken for the redhead tresses that show up in many Jewish families, but doesn't her slight brogue give it away? Yet Jake happily swears that every once in a while when Siobhan lets out a colleenish "to be sure, to be sure," most of our customers think she's Israeli.

I have to grin. Jake is such a lovable screwball. Lately he has taken to wearing a white coat during the Passover season as if he is a Doctor of Matzo; he claims it doubles sales in the same way cinnamon and other baking scents do when piped through the ventilation system in shopping malls. Customers seem to think the matzo is more kosher when there's a man in a white coat inspecting the halls.

But white coat or not, Jake can't erase the ugly truths about America's most famous Jewish dynasty.

I suspect matzo means money and disconnection to

everyone in my family. Even to Jake, who puts up the best front. I can't be the only Greenblotz who stares at a dividend check with ambivalence.

THRee

Interview with a Matzo Heiress

The interview! I can't just lounge around in reverie. After a quickie shower, I put on my stripy blue-and-green silk blouse that I snapped up at Language during their August sample sale. I'm nearly out the door went it hits me that this is TV and a stripy blouse makes the screen go crazy, so I change into a dark red cashmere sweater I bought the same week at Barneys warehouse sale. During the cab ride downtown I pick off a few red lint balls on the sweater and ponder what new tidbits about Izzy I can give this Steve Meyers of unknown religious persuasion. There are stories amusing to Jake and me, like the time Jake removed the back drawer of his desk to give it a good clean. Along with three dimes so old they had portraits of Mercury on them, he found a set of false teeth. "Whose teeth are they? Izzy's?" he laughed hysterically into the phone. The thought of the anonymous dentures amused me for weeks. But by my first traffic light

I come to the conclusion that I ought to stick to the historical angle.

Ben Franklin didn't invent electricity, but as every schoolkid knows he took a lot of credit for reshaping it. The same goes for Izzy Greenblotz regarding matzo, but even though his legend was passed down through our family, somehow Izzy's name hasn't made it to the history books. Until Izzy Greenblotz came into the picture, matzo was mostly made the traditional old way, by hand, as it had been since the days of Moses.

When Izzy Greenblotz started making matzo he baked with the help of simple machinery that didn't do much to speed things along. He'd apprenticed at a traditional matzo baker, and was a quick study: he was manager of the shift workers within a few years. A young man with no family to support, he squirreled away his earnings. In 1915 he was able to buy a Model T that he hooted and tooted all over the Lower East Side. The baker was upset that his manager was upstaging him. Izzy had a brainstorm on how to leave this irritant boss behind.

He looked to America's most famous industrialist for inspiration.

If I could rewrite family history, I'd have my great-grandfather's moneymaking "Eureka!," or whatever the Yiddish equivalent is, come one day at the epicenter of Lower East Side intellectualism: the East Broadway Garden Cafeteria, where Emma Goldman and John Reed plotted cultural revolt and slurped borscht. (I saw the campus film board's presentation of Warren Beatty's four-hour *Reds*—with an audience of two—and read Reed's *Ten Days That Shook the World* during my brief obsession with Lyle Finkel, my twenty-one-year-old anarchist resident counselor my freshman year at Brown.) We'd all like to reinvent our roots; even Alex Haley did some tweaking.

Alas, I know my great-grandfather was way too much of a brash entrepreneur to be involved in Goldman and Reed's leftie lot. I know from family lore that even though he managed to save money, he was big on cards, especially pinochle. And he was also big on whores from Allen Street brothels. Imagine his kosher-factory inspiration hitting there. Wherever the breakthrough came, Izzy Greenblotz soon became the Henry Ford of Matzo.

It's ironic that the famously anti-Semite Ford was the role model for this aspiring immigrant Jew. According to a PBS *American Masters* special I helped research with Vondra, by 1916, the time the Greenblotz factory was up and running, Henry Ford and his $5 daily wages that allowed for worker satisfaction and rapid assembly of his automobiles were folklore. Henry Ford's big year was 1913, the year he launched assembly-line production of the Model T. Izzy Greenblotz's big year was 1916, the year he launched his factory. Izzy— gung ho about mass production after reading a newspaper article about Ford—enlisted an engineer and showed him drawings he had sketched that are now under glass at the factory. You have to wonder where the hell he found a backer. Or for that matter, a suitable engineer. In any case, the engineer he found to bring his ideas to fruition did a top-notch job, because those very same machines are still used in our factory. Outdated, but functional. Who the hell makes modernized matzo machines? With so few companies in the ring, there's no money in it.

Primitive matzo machinery had been around for almost fifty years when Izzy put his mark on it. They probably used it in the bakery where he apprenticed. So Izzy wasn't de facto the inventor. Henry Ford didn't invent the car either. But

Izzy and Henry both perfected what others had done, and made their families rich in doing so.

As my cab zigzags through the streets close to the factory, I eye the new Lower East Side with ambivalence. It's sad if you're the nostalgic type. Every month an old stalwart like Schapiro's Wines closes and a new boutique or trendy bar opens. The old Kedem winery on Norfolk Street is now the nightclub Tonic. The owners have turned the old wine kegs into booths for groovy customers like Sean Lennon and the aging hipsters from Sonic Youth.

My cab also passes Lansky, a restaurant in a former speakeasy named after Jewish mobster Meyer Lansky. When the restaurant had just opened, in a red-hot incarnation called Lansky Lounge, it was ridiculously hard to find. It was hidden in the ass end of Ratner's, the legendary dairy restaurant where generations of my kin ordered cherry and cheese blintzes.

In those embryonic days, the gossip columns often ran beautiful-people shots of Madonna at Lansky Lounge, slumming it downtown, sipping a pink cosmopolitan. Lansky Lounge's popularity soon eclipsed Ratner's and for maximum profit, Ratner's has shut and the bar has taken over, graduating into Lansky, a swanky place that fills both of the old spaces. For a while, the new owners tried to keep the two establishments going so that the older customers would still come to spend money. They changed Ratner's menu, from kosher to "kosher-style," a fuzzy hyphenation that means they shed rabbinical supervision. Dairy-only Ratner's is, or should I say was, a BIG tradition, and no one who cares about such things was pleased by the bastardized version, not even my usually apathetic mother. She called in shock when a neighbor told her about the changes: *Ratner's is selling steaks!* I had to laugh, considering that she's not even remotely kosher. A presidential election determined by faulty polling machines, a mayoral election bought by a billionaire and a war that in my humble documentarian opinion was more about protecting our oil source than securing human rights—none of that elicited even a grunt out of her. But you would think they tore down Yankee Stadium the way Mom carried on about the addition of meat at Ratner's.

The cab lets me out in front of our factory, and when I put away my wallet I stroll over toward Upsy Daisy, a vintage boutique a few doors down. An adorable keyhole-neckline polka-dot dress in the window display has caught my eye. Behind the glass, a salesclerk in blond pigtails and a faded Madonna T-shirt ("Like a Virgin" era) is desperately trying to catch my eye through the glass door, pointing at a brown disco boot. She looks panicked, like she's been held up—but I don't see any customers inside.

I push open the door to check. "Are you okay in here?"

"Ohmi-*gawd*. Help me, please!" My grandfather's lingo, of the *Dem bums* and *Toidy-toid and Toid* variety, has largely gone the way of Ye Olde English language, but so far the new century has brought little change to the mall-girl lilt that first reared its cartoonish head back in the mid 1980s.

"What's wrong?"

"A rat's in, like, one of the Gucci boots. Crawled in when the last customer was here."

"Why don't you tip it out?"

"Are you kidding? What if it bites? Rabies!"

Rodents have never agitated me. When your family owns a food factory, an encounter with a furry visitor is no big news. I'd place a sure bet that the rat crawled over from the factory and into the boutique. I say a silent prayer to the Rodent Goddess (M-Isis?) that Steve Meyers doesn't see any critters when we do our interview. Greenblotz factory rats are especially robust from the abundance of flour to feed on. Dad used to call them "Elvis" rats: they've got such heft that their hips sway from side to side. The factory has two fat and happy cats helping in the crusade against rodents: pitch-black Moses, and the tabby, Elijah.

"Open the door," I say authoritatively, and the terrified girl gladly complies. Or is she a woman still peddling cuteness past the age of twenty-five? With those pigtails, it's hard to tell.

I grab the boot, run out to the street and tip it by the lone oak tree in front of the store, the one with a painted-green wooden-plank border that my grandfather planted as a sapling in 1950. (Grandpa Reuben was given the hard sell by a Jewish charity to fund a forest in the new State of Israel; the oak was his defiant I'll-plant-whatever-damn-trees-I-want gesture.) Out of the Ultrasuede flies a terrified black squirrel that immediately runs up the bark.

"Ohmi-*gawd*, a *squir*-rel!" The cutesy salesclerk laughs. It amazes me that nobody ever thinks of cuddly-looking squirrels as the disease-carrying vermin they are, but the clerk is so much mellower now that I'm not about to go into semantics and whip her into a frenzy all over again. Beneath her blond, the girl-woman has dark roots that are fashionably meant to be there. With her exotic face, I'd venture she's half Japanese and half Anglo. "I'm Sukie by the way."

"I'm Heather."

"Take a blouse or skirt, any one that you like. I'm soooooo grateful."

"You don't have to do that. Really. Besides I have to head over to the Greenblotz factory right now for a meeting."

"No, you were *so* great the way you picked up the boot. You were, like, fearless."

"Tell you what instead. Give me a good discount on that polka-dot dress in the window, and I'll snap it up."

"You've got a deal. I *knew* someone happening would get that dress. Don't you love polka dots? So *Valley of the Dolls*."

"A knockout. I have a launch party coming up that it will be great for."

"What kind of launch party?"

"For a digital-film magazine."

She pauses, and decides to continue her thoughts out loud. "You're in marketing, something like that? Those matzo guys need a community-relations lesson, they don't give their neighbors the time of day. Any store that is new is garbage to them. They keep to themselves, those people."

"I'm a film producer. Heather *Greenblotz*. One of *those* people." I'm taken aback by Sukie's prejudiced comment, but I know what she's saying has some truth to it. Jake doesn't get the young boutique owners at all, and got into an argument with a prose poet over Jake's meager ten-dollar dona- tion to *Phlegm*, a failing e-zine published in an apartment around the corner from the factory. The factory workers are also outright annoyed by the funksters. Their presence has jacked up neighborhood costs, so there's no longer a dollar hamburger at the corner joint. In fact, the restaurants in the surrounding blocks have some of the hottest tables in the city. You have to wait a month to get a reservation at both 71 Clinton and even longer at über-chef Wylie Dufresne's newest restaurant, WD-50.

"Oh! I didn't mean to insult—"

"We're a bit old school, Sukie, but we're not so bad once you get to know us. I'm sure my cousin Jake would love to give you a tour. If not I will. I only work there around—"

"I really wish I could take that back—"

I check my watch. Almost eleven. "No problem, trust me, but I got to fly. I'm taking over a media tour today for my cousin. I help him out when there's too much going on.

Don't think twice about what you said. My cousin *is* brusque if he doesn't know you. And I'll be back for that dress after my meeting is over."

"I'll put it *aside*," she says, the last word an octave higher than the rest of her sentence. She decides on a spur-of-the-moment hug.

I gear myself up for the task ahead and open the front door of the factory, a sprawling five-story building with eye-straining industrial light. There's not an iMac or track-lighting rod to be found—we're one of the last Age of Manufacturing holdouts in downtown Manhattan. If a developer could ever talk my family into breaking the no-sell wills that are kept in the factory strongbox, he or she would be hard-pressed to remove the musty scent of ninety years of flour caked into the walls and floor.

There's a chorus of "howsits" from the staff as I walk toward the back area where Jake's office is. The majority of the thirty or so workers have known me since I was a tot. The newer employees are Dominican and they call out *Shalom!* with a heavy Hispanic accent. I wave back. The din of machines, and the pulsating, rhythmic Latino music on the soundspeaker makes it hard to hold a conversation. This time of the year everyone and everything is in overdrive, as ninety percent of our annual business will transpire in the next month and a half.

The small factory store adjacent to Jake's office is a mecca for Jewish tourists, both observant and those simply nostalgic for the Lower East Side in its Jewish heyday. It brings in minuscule profits, but we keep it open because its raison d'être is the same as those tony Fifth Avenue boutiques that give cachet to mall spin-offs in mid-America. (Our true big business is in the supermarket chains, like Florida's Publix and New York's D'Agostino's.)

Greenblotz has employed Gertie, the elderly sweetheart who runs the store, since the forties. Gertie is bent with arthritis and has such a gaunt bloodless face that I always think she might pass out any second. She refuses to sit, even though she is thin and frail, and may be eighty, even ninety. No one dares to ask her exact age, because she will work here as long as she wants to. Gertie is as much of a lure for the tourists as the specialty macaroons.

She lights up when she sees me and beckons me in with a crooked finger.

"Ess, kindele." She says: "Eat well, my child" in Yiddish.

The smattering of Yiddish I know includes the words and phrases I picked up from Gertie talking with customers, and the expressions I've gleaned by listening to New Yorkers talk in supermarkets and department stores. This includes *schtickel*, which means a piece, as in: *Give me a schtickel of pickle.* My favorite Yiddish word is the one that pretty much sums up my life, *farblungett*, which roughly means *lost without a damn clue how to remedy the situation.*

Gertie hands me an open tin of chocolate-chip macaroons and I poke my fingers in, grabbing the two top ones. Three or more and my Lotte Berk trainer would kill me. It took nearly a year to rein in the bulging tummy and thunder thighs I was gifted with after my scary bout with depression.

I give Gertie a kiss on her rawhide cheek and tell her I have an interview and can't talk until afterward. I enter the office that has been Matzo Central for almost a century, where Izzy Greenblotz would sit, and then his sons, and then his grandchildren, Uncle Nathan before the car crash, and then my dad and Aunt Shara who hated each other so much they installed a wall to divide the space.

When Jake got ahold of the reins, he took down the "Berlin Wall" and put in a new couch and an Ansel Adams print. I would have gone with a contemporary Jewish artist to reflect the newly hip Lower East Side; maybe I'd frame a Ben Katchor cartoon original or perhaps I would shell out serious bucks for a painting by Eric Fischl. But Jake is the man in charge and he "loves mountains," even if the same mountain print graces half the insurance firms of the United States.

I'm a snob, true, but a private one. I never tear into anyone publicly about taste. I'm exceedingly well mannered to both him and Siobhan, because despite the misgivings my other relatives have about her—mainly to do with her religion, and a misguided view that she's a gold digger—I think Siobhan has a great heart, genuinely loves Jake, and for heaven's sake, she puts up with our bag-of-nuts family. Jake's made it a point to thank me for not ostracizing Siobhan the way Aunt Shara's daughters have. They have hardly ever met her, yet they claim to hate her. God knows what those two witches think of me. The last time Siobhan and I saw my female cousins in the flesh was at Grandpa Reuben's funeral. Marcy, the nastier and eldest, was glaring at me most of the service—perhaps because Siobhan was out of her view, sandwiched between Jake and myself for protection.

I give Moses a scratch behind his black ears, and then eye the factory-office walls. The framed letters to my forbearers from former NYC Mayor LaGuardia and President Eisenhower would be choice archives. But for what? The right corner of my mouth turns up in amusement. A treatise on dysfunction? My mind wanders back to the impending interview. I call in the matzo foreman to ask him to change the salsa tape to our Jewish folk-song tape. Jake's purchase—he pulls out all the stops for media.

In the middle of "Zum Gali Gali" there is a knock on the door, from an extremely good-looking man with wavy dirty-blond hair. My interest is immediately piqued. I am jonesing for a boyfriend lately, and making a film about older women isn't too good for on-the-job prospects.

"I'm here for an interview with Jake Greenblotz," the man says with a confident manner that gets my pulse going.

"Are you Steve Meyers from the Food Channel?" I ask hopefully. He nods. At closer range he's even better-looking. He's tall, about thirty-five, with cat-green eyes that sear.

"I'm Heather Greenblotz. My cousin Jake asked me to take you around."

"Do you know enough about matzo?" Steve Meyers sizes me up with a critical squint.

"Beyond expert," I assure him.

"Okay then. We're up against the clock. You mind if I get my crew stationed in here? There's three of us. I double as producer and host. I'm rather excited about today. I don't usually go on camera, but every once in a while, for a special program, I get the chance."

"Not a problem. You can rest some cases on the couch if you like."

Steve returns with a strapping cameraman in faded Wrangler's who sports a neat brown beard, big brown eyes and an attractive aquiline nose. He's holding a very expensive and huge Beta camera under his arm. Vondra and I are all for the husky cameraman when we organize a shoot. I'm a proud feminist most of the time, but bottom line, men are much more willing to carry their equipment than women DPs— directors of photography—who divvy up the backbreaking camera packs like they're handing out squares of fudge at a pajama party.

The soundman turns out to be a soundwoman, who's also a gaffer, i.e., the lighting expert. She's Britney-blond with a perfectly symmetrical face and light brown eyes, and is painfully thin. I instantly assume the worst, that Steve and Skinny Minnie are hot and heavy.

"This is Jared and Tonia," Steve says with a wave to his crew.

Husky Jared is cleaning his lens with a cloth. He stops and extends a hand. "Nice to meet you." Jared's grip is tight and warm, like the assured squeeze my favorite manicurist gives me after finishing with my last cuticle.

Tonia gives me a small harried smile.

"While they unpack I can get us started," Steve says. "Your cousin probably told you that we're doing a one-off special on American Food Pioneers and we'd like to include a ten-minute segment on Israel Greenblotz."

"Change that to Izzy Greenblotz. Everyone called him Izzy."

"You'd like to use that name for broadcast?" Steve checks.

"Definitely. Who have you already covered?"

"Well, Ray Kroc from McDonald's of course."

I nod. "Of course. Frank Perdue?"

"Frank Perdue," he says with a nod. "And Clarence Birdseye."

"Izzy Greenblotz in that company? Wow. Those are the really big boys."

"We thought your product history might add a little old-world flavor. One of our interns clipped an article from the *Daily News* about your family's factory. She was intrigued that your Izzy invented machine–made matzo."

"To be fair, he perfected matzo machines, not invented them. I don't want to misrepresent Izzy. I have to watch what goes into the media, or vitriolic letters can fly from the Streit and Manischewitz families."

"Who are they?" Tonia asks. As Jake says of non-Jewish blondes, including his own girlfriend: *Shiksa*-city. If you have to ask who these families are, you're not a Jew.

"Rival matzo companies," I explain to her. "Here's the plan," I say in Steve's direction. "I'll tour you through the factory and then we can come back here and I can answer anything else."

"Terrific," Steve says.

"I'm going to have to mic you," Tonia pipes up. "The way it works is—"

"Actually I'm in the business myself," I interrupt, a shameless attention-seeking ploy for Steve's benefit. "I'll save you the hassle."

Tonia shrugs.

"You're in the business?" Steve asks. "Our business?"

"I don't usually work here except to help out with the seasonal interviews. My cousin runs things but sometimes he gets overloaded. The rest of the time, I'm a documentary filmmaker."

Steve seeks out the ballpoint pen behind his ear. "Anything I've heard of?"

"I do cable specials mostly." I slide the wireless mic under my red sweater, facing Steve just enough to give him a little peek at the top of my black lace bra. "For the past few years, I've codirected and coproduced with my business partner, Vondra Adams. The biggest doc we did was an insider's look at the women's prison at Riker's Island—we followed the story of four women who were incarcerated there."

Jared sets his camera down. "I saw that on HBO. I thought it was going to be bleak viewing, but you really captured the humor in their lives."

"Thank you," I say. "They need to laugh to survive."

"Wasn't that narrated by Susan Sarandon?" Steve says.

"Isn't everything?" Jared calls out.

"It could have been Glenn Close," Tonia says with a smile back to Steve.

Dorky documentary humor. I smile too. "No, it was Susan who did it." As soon as I say that, I realize how pretentious it sounds.

"And how is Susan?" Jared teases. "Is Susan difficult?"

Despite my extreme wariness of beards, Jared's looks are growing on me. Those big brown eyes are teddy-bearish, and they crinkle in nice places when he smiles. But I'd like to see his lips without any facial hair above them to complete the picture. Lips are a big turn-on for me. I like them dark and puckering like a 1960s London rock star. My answer lags a bit as I mentally shave his beard. "*Susan* was very nice, actually. In and out of the studio with a big warm smile. Very professional."

"You won an Emmy for that, didn't you?" Jared says. "A friend of mine was up against you."

"Yes, two," I say a bit too quickly. "But not alone," I quickly add to tone that big brag down. "Of course I shared them with my business partner."

"What categories?"

I pretend to think. (Ha, like I don't remember.) "The News and Documentary awards, for, um, Best Investigative Special and for Best Directing."

"Impressive," Jared says.

Tonia, inches away, slips a wireless through Steve's blue oxford shirt.

"Well, the most coveted awards are televised while the documentary awards are presented at a special ceremony. You know when they say, 'Earlier in the evening, Regis Philbin presented the following awards...' One of those was ours."

Mic in place, Steve talks for his audio check. "Check, two, two, check." Then he faces me again. "Don't diminish your achievements. Barbara Walters, watch out. Although you're a hell of a lot cuter than Barbara Walters."

"Can you say something?" Tonia asks me rigidly. Is she miffed at the attention Steve and Jared are giving me? "Just keep talking until I say stop."

"Two. Two. Two. My name is Heather Greenblotz."

Tonia rolls her hand to indicate: *Keep going.*

I nod and say, "For the past year I've called the same restaurant for lunch delivery at least three times a week. I want a Greek salad with no salad dressing. The same person answers every time and says, like she's shocked, 'No salad dressing?!'"

Jared chortles a bit. When Tonia gives me the okay, I say to Steve, "I have a matzo joke if you'd like to hear it." Jake always tells a matzo joke to loosen his guests up, and I try to do the same thing when I'm giving important tours.

"Yeah?" says Steve.

"The one about the man who eats his matzo in the park."

"I don't know that one," Steve says.

"I'm going to have the camera on you," Jared forewarns. "No tripod, handheld."

Jared's *filming* this joke? "It's dumb. You probably don't want to broadcast it."

"Go on," Steve insists. "We can make sure Jared's camera is working properly. He just got it back from our repair department."

I look toward Jared's camera. "A man sits down on a bench and begins eating a sheet of Greenblotz matzo in the park. A little while later a blind man sits next to him. Feeling like a Good Samaritan, the Jewish man passes half the sheet of matzo to the blind man who holds it for a few minutes, looks puzzled and finally says, 'Who wrote this garbage?'"

"Funny," Steve says without a laugh. Maybe he doesn't get that matzo is covered with pinprick-size airholes so the matzo doesn't leaven while baking—holes that look and feel like braille—or his Food Channel editor doesn't like him to laugh while they're taping so it's easier in the editing room to cut and paste voice snippets. Or maybe he thinks I'm dopey.

I can just make out that Jared is grinning behind the camera, though. "Camera's hunky-dory," he says.

I tug a loose piece of thread inside my skirt pocket. "I hope you three have comfortable walking shoes on, because this place is huge. We have five floors here. The factory is actually four conjoined buildings."

"How many square feet?" Steve prods, as we start walking out of the office and into the factory.

"Well, each building is twenty-five by a thousand. There's four of them. So that's five hundred thousand square feet because it's twenty-five thousand times five floors times four—"

"Five floors? Why do you need so many floors?"

"Izzy figured out that the easiest way to set up a matzo factory was to have it gravity fed. The flour is dumped from the top and moves on down, the way they pour concrete in a foundry. It's one of the reasons we could never move. We'd have to figure out our business from scratch, we wouldn't have a clue how to do what we do in a one-story building."

"So interesting," Steve says with an on-camera, very enthusiastic nod.

I start walking and talking: "Long before the Jewish people fled Egypt, Passover was an ancient springtime ceremony of renewal. There was a pagan early-harvest feast and a pagan feast of unleavened bread. Somehow both got swallowed up into Judaic tradition."

"Really?"

"Yeah, but, wait, can I start again? You shouldn't put that

last bit on air. Jews get worked up if you tell them a version of this holiday existed *way* before Moses."

Jared laughs loudly behind his viewfinder.

"Tell us again, without the pagan stuff," Steve says neutrally.

"Long ago, matzo was very thick, and each piece was baked by three women—one to knead, one to roll and one to bake. It had to be made fresh daily. During the Middle Ages, the thickness of matzo was limited to the width of one finger, and it became thinner and crisper as time went on. Thin, crisp matzo could be prepared in advance for the entire Passover celebration. Then, a little over a hundred years ago, matzo machinery was invented." When I talk about matzo I can sound as if I went to an orthodox Jewish day school. But ask me about anything else in Judaism, like why there's a huge party when boys get circumcised, or why a Jewish groom stomps on a glass at a Jewish wedding, and I'd just be making it up.

"Tell us more about the matzo machines," Steve says.

"There isn't a magical do-it-all machine like the one in *Charlie and the Chocolate Factory* that will produce a chewing gum that tastes like a five-course dinner. We need nine machines to make our matzos, because there are nine steps to production, ten if you count shipment."

"Walk me through them, one step at a time," Steve says.

Dad taught me the ten steps before I knew how to read. I take a theatrical breath: "Well, in step one, we start with flour, two we add water, three we mix, four flatten, five stipple, six cut to size, seven goes on conveyors for eight, the cooking. Then, eight, bake in the oven at 910 degrees for fifteen minutes and twenty seconds. Nine, package it and ten we ship it out to the world."

I'm done explaining the matzo-making steps by the time

we reach the oldest machine in my family's factory, the oven, which is connected to cutting devices. I love to start tours here because with its many knobs and motors from the turn of the century, the machine looks straight out of a Jules Verne novel.

"Tell us about this one," Steve asks.

"This is the oven, the most important piece of machinery in our factory. The matzo comes out of the oven in huge prescored squares, which will make eight sheets in a packaged box. Because they are prescored, workers can break them by hand. It's as easy as tearing perforated pages from a notebook."

"How come I can never break them evenly by hand?" Jared asks in the background. Steve looks annoyed that his cameraman is asking questions, even rhetorical ones. I would be annoyed too. It's a big no-no for anyone other than the designated producer to ask away, but the question was not only a cute one, but also quite valid. Even though the matzo you eat at home has lines of dots on it like graph paper, if you try to break a sheet in a straight line along the dots, you end up with jagged pieces. According to my father, it's one of the great mysteries of Judaism.

"The perforations must run deeper on the megasheets," I answer in Jared's direction. "I never even thought about that." Steve motions for me to look back at him and away from Jared.

Now I'm certain that Jared is Jewish, or *in the tribe,* as Jake likes to say. Not that I factor in religion when I want to hook up with an attractive guy. I'd put available and funny over Jewish any day. I'm agnostic to the bone, but oddly, I do daydream about landing myself a nice Jewish hipster. He's someone who knows all the latest foreign flicks but who can also guide me through the parts of my religion I don't have the foggiest idea about. I can never see my fantasy man's face, but he's hugging me in public after our first son's *bris* and we're feasting on potato salad and corned beef with his parents, who are alternating bites of celebratory deli with beams of approval at their newest "daughter," and their newly circumcised grandson. Where this embarrassing reverie comes from mystifies me. But I have it a lot, as much as some people fantasize about a thousand bucks on a horse with impossible odds.

Jared isn't done. "You know that matzo joke about an aerospace engineer who—well, that joke is really long."

"Stop the camera," Steve says in exasperation. "Go ahead, Jared, you obviously want to tell it. We'll pick up after you're finished."

"You sure?" Jared asks sheepishly. "I'm sorry. I couldn't help myself."

"Yes. Tell us," Steve says.

"It's long. I shouldn't have interrupted."

"Go ahead already."

"Well, my uncle tells it the best, but I'll give it a go."

"Begin the damn matzo joke already, for Christ's sakes," Steve demands, although it's obvious from his face that he's not really mad, and that these two guys have a friendship outside of work.

"This guy Avrum is a gifted Israeli aeronautical engineer who launches a company in Tel Aviv to build jets. Everything looks terrific on paper, but when he has a pilot test the new jet, disaster strikes. The wings can't take the strain, and they break clean off the fuselage."

"So the pilot is dead?" Tonia interrupts. "He's responsible for his death?"

"No, no, the test pilot parachutes to safety. Avrum is shattered. His company redesigns the jet, but the same thing happens—the wings break off again. Suicidal, the engineer goes to his synagogue to pray. His rabbi asks him what the matter is. After hearing the sob story, the rabbi tells him, 'Avrum, all you have to do is drill a row of holes directly above and below where the wing meets the fuselage. If you do this, I absolutely guarantee the wings won't fall off.' The engineer mumbles thanks to the rabbi for his advice. But the more he thinks about it, the more Avrum realizes he had nothing to lose. Maybe the rabbi had some holy insight. On the next design of the jet, they drill a row of holes directly above and below where the wings meet the fuselage. The next test flight goes great! Avrum tells his rabbi, 'Rabbi, how did you know that drilling the holes would prevent the wings from falling off?' The rabbi says, 'I'm an old man. I've lived for many, many years and I've celebrated Passover many, many times. And in all those years, not once—*not once*—has matzo broken on the perforation!'"

Steve and I snort in unison. Steve hits an imaginary *boom, boom, cha* drumroll.

"Worth stopping for?" Jared asks.

"No," Steve says with a smile.

"Oh c'mon, Steve, it's a classic."

"When Shecky Green told the joke in the Catskills, it was a classic," Steve says. "When you tell it, it's just sad."

Jared takes the put-down with a good-natured laugh.

"I don't get it," Tonia says.

"*Oy,*" Jared says with an old-Jewish-man accent. "No matter how you try, matzos never break on the perforations. So the wing could never break off if it has a stippled matzo pattern."

There's a touch of confusion still in Tonia's forehead. "Oh, okay."

"We ready to continue?" Steve's tone is impatient.

I smile at Jared and he winks at me.

Since breaking it off with Daniel I have spent the last year in the spinster desert; that is except for one laughable date with a guy whose real face and personality didn't match his online profile, a sparkling profile that certainly didn't say anything about his halitosis. After a very long, supposedly ironic hour together at the new Manhattan branch of Madame Tussaud's Wax Museum, this sad sack decided that he had finally found his soul mate, the one who would love to hear the many, many adventures of his cat named Mama over an "ironic" blue-plate special at the Times Square Howard Johnson's.

I feel a bit silly getting such a charge from an interview. Flirtation must be all in a day's work for Steve and Jared. I can only imagine the number of beautiful women these handsome men meet behind the scenes at New York's trendiest restaurants. Even so, now I have two handsome guys with clean breath winking at me. Both intellectually involved with their careers and charismatic.

"And this monstrosity over here is the packaging machine," I say quickly. Am I actually blushing? "Working this thing is probably the worst job in the factory because it's a repetitive hell. Not to mention that the person who oversees the machine has to have *very* fast hands."

"Does that person know it's the worst job?" Steve asks.

"Hopefully, Braulio won't watch the Food Channel special or he may find out it is."

Braulio, a short Dominican with a considerable beer gut, a constant smile and a never-ending repertoire of Sinatra songs, returns from a bathroom break and gives me a bear hug. I haven't seen him since last high season. His Yankees shirt smells like a mix of flour and Tide that wasn't completely rinsed out. "You want to be on TV, Braulio?" I ask.

"We're from the Food Channel and want to see what you do," Steve chimes in.

Braulio nods enthusiastically. He flicks a switch and demonstrates how fast the packages move on the conveyor. "Like Lucy, no?"

"Lucy?" Steve says.

This time Tonia knows the reference. *"I Love Lucy,"* she whispers toward Steve. "The chocolate-conveyor episode, when everything got out of control—"

"Oh right!" Steve says.

When we start to move on, Braulio happily sings us off with a bit of Frank Sinatra's "I Got Plenty of Nothing."

"See," I whisper to the camera. "I don't think he knows it's the worst job."

"I'd say the next stop for this baby is the Smithsonian," Steve says when we're standing over an aging machine with a queer array of gadgetry. "What is it?"

"I have to admit even I don't know exactly what this one does. It's old and it's been here for eternity. I'll have to ask my cousin and get back to you on that. But I can tell you that whatever it is, it works. Everything here works because of our in-house mechanic who likes to do things his way. The factory will buy him any tools and parts he wants but he'd rather use what works best. Aesthetics be damned. We couldn't find the right tubing to match an old machine and he brought in a garden hose that fit perfectly. Our matzo-cooling fan broke and we weren't going to get a fan for a week from the supply company, so he brought in his house fan. He uses a ski pole to get gears moving again. If he doesn't want to weld, he uses a clamp. Big on duct tape too."

Steve is clearly amused. "What's that machine over there?" he prods.

"That's our polypropylene machine. It's our newest machine, from the fifties."

"What's it for?"

"To put the plastic wrap over the boxes of matzo. Predates shrink-wrap."

"Where do you get a polypropylene matzo machine?"

"You don't. We adapted a basic model for our needs. You could use it to package baseball cards if you set it up right."

Steve gives me a broad smile as we turn the corner: "Our editor will love you. Adorable. You're going to get fan mail, mark my words."

"Especially for those eyes," Jared says from behind the camera.

I am doing an interview, but now the attention is bordering on embarrassing. It's not as if I'm wearing some miracle musk guaranteed to draw them in, this is plain old me we're talking about!

"Your eyes *are* incredible," Steve says.

I'll concede that my eyes are my best feature by a mile. "It's the recessive Greenblotz Blue that shows up once or twice every seventy-five years. Apparently old Izzy had them."

"Sounds like a new lipstick color," Jared cracks.

I grin and pan for Jared's viewfinder: "Greenblotz Blue. New from Max Factor."

We come upon the huge and weighty silver-colored fire doors. "These doors are required by law." I grunt and push the one on the right side open. "We're near the matzo ovens again. This is the most likely place a fire would start, and the heavy fire doors would isolate the flames."

Antique-looking gears are attached to each door, rusting hardware which I hope the camera doesn't focus in on. You're supposed to have regulation weights, but instead, our thrifty mechanic dredged these heavy gears up from the basement.

I curse to myself. I told Jake the last time I saw these doors that *you can't screw* with the fire department. If someone from the New York Fire Department is watching the Food Channel and sees these rusty gears, we'll get called on a violation. Jake knows the local hook and ladder isn't too crazy about our factory to begin with. After September 11 and several Code Orange terrorist scares, they've had bigger fish to fry, but now things are returning to normal in New York and we could get closed down on a moment's notice if the fire department resumes spot-checking Manhattan factories.

"You ever have a fire here?" Steve asks.

"Three years ago a matzo caught fire and the smoke was streaming out the windows. A science-fiction writer who lives in a walk-up across the street called 911, and in a minute ten guys from the fire department burst in wanting to ax open the oven. But Jake knew that if the burning matzo could be kept in the seventy-two-foot oven, it was safe. In an oven that big, a burning sheet of matzo is likely to be contained. He wouldn't let them hack Izzy's oven, so he was arrested for obstruction of the fire department." I have second thoughts about the information I've just let loose. "Steve, maybe you better not let that on TV either."

"You mean about how long the ovens are? Is that a trade secret?"

"No, about Jake's arrest."

"I'll get that edited out if you want. We'll have more than enough for the Izzy Greenblotz segment. Let's get the last of it to be sure."

We continue the tour for another half hour, continuing to the machine that heats wax paper and seals it on the boxes with no glue. I end up showing them some of our collected mementos from the early years of the factory, including Izzy's penny notebook of ideas.

Steve says, "You're a wealth of knowledge, chickie."

"To paraphrase my father, how badly can you screw up flour and water?" Okay, I fucking love how Steve called me chickie so casually. A slick style, that's working on me *big-time*.

"Is your father still active in the business?"

"Uh, no, not really."

"Oh, I forgot to ask. Do you have a slogan?"

"We do. *Buy Greenblotz—Because Family Is Everything*." I force those words out. How could my visitors know how humiliating that phrase is to say and what a joke it is, given our crumbled family connections.

"Perfect. We'll put that on air." He starts undoing his mic. "I'll say that in a voice-over. Where's the best place to call you if we have to check our facts?"

"I can give you my regular office number at my production company. And I'll add my home number in case you can't get me there."

"Super."

I hand him one of my business cards and scrawl my home number on the back.

Steve opens his wallet and hands me his producer's card from the Food Channel.

"Can I have one too?" Jared says to me. Steve gives Jared an indecipherable look.

"Sure," I say, and Jared hands me his card that reads *Jared S.—Camera* and only lists his cell-phone number.

Tonia does not ask for one, nor do I give her one. She packs away her equipment. "We're so near Chinatown," she says to Steve, loud enough so I can hear her. "Can we stop the van and get my sister some imported pimple tea?"

Steve shrugs his shoulders. "I've seen your sister, she doesn't have pimples."

Jared whispers in my ear, "That's because she drinks the pimple tea."

Steve sees Jared leaning in close to my ear and ups the ante with a slightly lingering peck on my cheek on the way out. "You were awesome. I'll call you about when this segment will air."

"Bye!" I call out libidinously. Which one to choose? Bachelor Number One or Bachelor Number Two?

After they've packed up and gone, I remember Sukie and the dress I planned to buy at my Good Samaritan discount.

I take the short stroll down the street and try to open the door to Upsy Daisy, but it's unexpectedly locked. Sukie comes out from a back section cordoned off by a maroon velvet curtain. When she spots me she breaks into a big smile and lets me in.

"Sorry," she says. "Yogurt break. I packed up that polka-dot dress for you. The one from the window. Remember, you don't pay a thing. If it doesn't fit, bring it back for something else you like."

"No, no, I said I'd *buy* it from you at discount. Sukie, you can't stay in business giving your merchandise away."

"I wasn't sure if you meant it about buying it."

"Absolutely I meant it." I can afford it, and I feel bad for these microshops. They have gushing plugs from the in-the-know shopping pages of *Time Out* and *Paper*, but I never see anyone shopping in them. Trust-fund vanities, I think, but then I remember who I am and feel guilty for passing judgment.

"You've got a deal then. How was your meeting at the factory by the way?"

"Fine. I led a production team from the Food Channel on a tour of the place. Actually it was more than fine. Two very cute guys on that crew."

"Send one my way. I just broke up with my boyfriend."

"Sorry to hear that."

"Congratulate me! He was seeing two other suckers 'exclusively.' I can't even, like, think about him too long without getting nauseous. So, wait, how did you get to tour two hunks if you don't work in the factory?"

"My cousin would normally do the tour, but I step in for him from time to time. Jake's over at City Hall, being toasted by the mayor."

"The mayor? Isn't that a huge deal?"

"It's Passover season, which means Greenblotz season. We get serious attention this time of year."

"My last name is Cohen. My dad's Jewish, but we never celebrated anything."

Cohen? With her Asian face and that "those people" comment Sukie had made about the factory, I didn't see that coming.

"My father met my mother when he was trekking," she continues. "Mom's from Tibet, and was raised Bön."

"Raised what?"

"Bön. It's a Tibetan religion."

"The first I've heard of it."

"No one in America has. And believe me, there aren't too many Bön houses of worship in Sacramento. So we were raised in Sacramento like blank pages. I may be the only Tibetan Jew you ever meet!"

"Probably! I thought Sukie was Japanese or something."

"No it's an old nickname for Susan. I got it out of a baby book when I was fifteen and reinventing myself."

I grin and say, "I went the other way. Years ago my mother told me they were dithering on my name before I was born. Dad wanted Joan after Joan of Arc and Joan Crawford, and Mom wanted a prettier name, a bird name or a flower name. They flipped a coin—Mom won. But during the semester in ninth grade when all the jiggling bimbos on TV were named Heather, I made my friends call me Joan."

Sukie laughs, and sighs. "Maybe it's fate that we met. My mother thinks everything happens for a reason. I've been telling my family I'd like to know more about my Jewish side, and along comes a Greenblotz who can fill me in. Can you believe I've never been to a seder? Even Jesus got to go to a seder." Her joke hits a chord with me. I'd like to be friends with Sukie Cohen, but I am sure she is foxing for a possible invite to a Greenblotz seder that doesn't exist, so I quickly feign delight at an off-the-shoulder gold lamé eighties shirt.

"You can try it on if you like." She points to an Oriental screen with hand-painted butterflies, next to a vintage rack of seventies sunglasses with *Polarized!* tags still on them.

When I emerge, Sukie claps silently. "Perfect on you."

"How much is it?" I ask.

"Forty," she says with a whiff of embarrassment that suggests she scooped it up at a vintage buying spree at a Salvation Army or Goodwill for two or three bucks.

"I'll take that as well."

She wraps the lamé shirt in white tissue paper and tucks it in with the dress. The shopping bag is matte white with a silk-screened logo—daisies woven into the words *Upsy Daisy.* She hands me a card with the same design.

I'm about to put it in my Filofax, when I remember our first conversation. "Hey, when's a good time for my cousin Jake to show you the factory? I really meant that."

"Cool! Mornings are best. No one shops in the Lower East Side in the mornings. My customers crawl out of bed at, like, noon maybe."

"Then I'll give you a call sometime soon. I'm usually here several times a week this time of the year. Maybe I can even do it myself."

Sukie smiles, retrieves the business card from my hand, and writes her home number with a little *h* next to it.

FOUR

Getting Off My Bum

Tuesday afternoon, Jake calls me again at my office. "You might like this favor. It's up your alley. It's exotic."

What can this be?

"There's a busload of retired Jews from Argentina touring the factory at four. I don't see how I can lead it seeing as I have ten faxes from irate supermarket managers in Texas to answer."

"Texas?"

"Our trucking company never made it to Houston, and their customers are already stocking up for Passover."

"How can I lead the tour if I don't speak Spanish?"

"Not a problem. They come with a translator from their charter company."

Vondra and I are between shoots, so the tour happily delays the accumulation of paperwork I was set to tackle. Are all Argentines big on matchmaking, or just the Jewish ones?

"You move to Buenos Aires, we need Jewish women. My nephew is perfect for you."

"My son..."

"My grandson..."

A Latino-Semitic mix is intriguing, but I can't stop thinking about my flirtation with New Yorkers Steve Meyers and Jared S.

Tour over, I hail a cab to my place and collapse into my beloved cushiony couch. There's one message. *Heather, Steve Meyers. You never gave me your cell number. Call me ASAP. I have a question I hope you'll like being asked.*

The call plunges me into a rare state of delight. This could be about a date. Maybe he was too uncomfortable asking me out in front of Jared and Tonia. Maybe Steve and Tonia have never had even one date, and Tonia's simply gaga on him, too. Vondra would put up a confident fight for a man; I should take a page out of her book. After watching a few dozen cars go by out my window, I nervously make the return call.

"Just who I wanted the call to be from," Steve says. "I had a *terrific* time yesterday."

There's a skip to my voice I haven't heard in years. "I have to confess I wasn't looking forward to it before I met you, but honestly, I had a blast."

"I'm glad to hear that. Listen, I know how busy you are, so I'll get straight to the point. Would you meet me for dinner tonight? Micro notice, but I'm dying to see you as soon as I can."

Micro notice? I pause, and think, *I'm dateless. I'm horny.* "Sounds fun. I'm actually free tonight."

"Excellent. How about Union Square Café then?"

"That sounds great. But will you be able to get a reservation there on such short notice?"

"Not a problem for me."

"What, you're related to—what's the owner's name—"

He laughs. "Danny Meyer? No. He may have a restaurant empire, but I've got that *s* on him. We did a segment of Great Restaurants of America there and I'm friendly with the maître d'."

"More power to you."

"Would you like to meet at the bar?"

"If you don't mind, can we meet outside the Union Square Barnes & Noble bookstore?"

"Sure," he says. "But why?"

"I want to buy my accountant's book. It's her first novel. Tax day is coming up and we're supposed to meet—"

"It would be nice if you had read her book, right?"

"Exactly."

"What is it about? Should I ask?"

"An accountant in the 1930s who was taught magic by Harry Houdini."

Steve laughs. "I've actually heard about that. I can't think of the name—"

"Hyman's Hocus-Pocus."

"Yeah," he laughs again. "It got a nice write-up in the daily *Times*. That's your accountant?"

"Irma Zimmerwitz. One and the same. She's sold the film rights already, she's amazing. But she's not giving up her day job. She loves numbers too much." I omit the other half of the truth. I never meet a man inside a restaurant anymore, since I was stood up on a blind date two winters ago. Mr. Mama-the-Cat-lover from Matchmaker.com pales in comparison to the awful feeling of being stood up by the guy I "met" on nerve.com. The no-show's self-description via e-mail was vague enough (science writer, brown hair, occasionally wears glasses) to make me look inquisitively at every man who entered our coffee bar. I did an image search on the Internet to see what he looked like, but all that came up was a picture of a black hole. The real guy was a black hole as well: the memory of waiting there with all those people looking at me still fills me with horror.

As soon as I hang up with Steve, I spend a thousand hours picking out the right outfit, finally settling on a hopeful purchase I made at Fred Segal during a business trip to Santa Monica last April—a romantic soft sheer dress in muted pink—unworn to date. The weather doesn't know what it wants but I decide on a mauve pashmina shawl instead of a coat for a sexier effect.

When it starts to drizzle I realize meeting a date on the street is a bad call. I'm thankful that my mascara is waterproof as I run back and forth from the bookstore lobby to the curb.

As Steve crosses from the north corner of Union Square Park and Seventeenth Street, he spots me and waves. He's dressed in a hip dark gray suit, tapered so it fits his slim and tall build. I don't know if I've ever been on a date with a man in a suit.

"Hey, you look beautiful," he says as an opener when he's close enough.

Lightning illuminates the dark skies. It's followed by a loud rumble of thunder that lends the short stroll to the restaurant a slightly kinky ambience.

Safely dry inside the Union Square Café, Steve lifts the shawl off my shoulders, folds it neatly and hands it to the coat clerk. According to city lore, this is one of the hardest restaurants in town to get a last-minute reservation. So when the maître d' comes over to say hi to us with a broad smile, and then insists on a dozen iced oysters on the half shell as a complimentary appetizer, I am duly impressed.

After I've decided on my dish, Steve flags a striking waiter to order the Atlantic salmon for me. As he talks out the merits of his two final contenders for his main meal, the steak frites and the yellowfin tuna burger, I sneak another look at Steve's own striking face. The only flaw I can spot is a little scab on his chin from a tiny razor nick. What would happen if I ran a finger down the edge of his pretty nose?

We're left alone again to talk. "Nice suit, by the way." What a dull thing to say in the company of major charisma. Could I be more nervous?

"Thank you. I actually wore this to work today. A memo went around last month reminding us that in the office there's a dress code. For men that means slacks or a suit."

Inwardly, I'm disappointed that Steve Meyers hadn't raced home to the wardrobe for Heather Greenblotz. "How did it go over in your office?" I say.

"The code wasn't heeded at all until a second memo came the next week telling us that black jeans are not slacks."

The salmon is outrageously delicious and the expensive pinot makes my head swim.

Steve leans forward toward my side of our candlelit table to ask, "So why are you a filmmaker when you could sit pretty on your family's matzo laurels?"

I answer honestly. "There's something about filmmaking that really turns me on. Its excitement, its novelty, its emotional pull. Most of all its unexpectedness."

Steve nods his head enthusiastically and tells me about the last time he truly loved his job, the two years he spent in the Peace Corps stationed in Lesotho. "I switched my religion major to television management in my senior year.

The Peace Corps recruiter, who loved my résumé, confused a television major with a telecommunications major. He thought I could wire poor towns with fiber optics. It was too late to get a new recruit when I arrived, so the field manager put me to work building a schoolhouse instead."

I laugh. "Was the Peace Corps your first job?"

"No." Steve smiles. "My dad always made me work so I wouldn't grow lazy. My first job was at an Adirondack resort. I was a security guard on Lovers' Lane. It was difficult to break people up."

I laugh again and Steve feels comfortable enough to make a deeper confession: "I'm good at what I do now, though. It's fun, but I'd love a bigger challenge. My boss thinks I could host my own show in a year or two. I love to talk, and I *love* to eat."

The scent of the hot chocolate dessert at the next table wafts over, a cruelly pleasant smell that inspires Steve to call our waiter over again. I agree to a shared serving of blueberry cobbler with lemon ice milk, and an after-dinner sherry. I never diet on a date. Steve seems pleased that I didn't put up a fuss.

"But you know what really turns me on?" Steve says.

"What?"

"You."

"I have to admit, Mr. Meyers, you really turn me on too."

Steve smiles, a beautiful ferocious smile. He leans over to lick my arm of fallen blueberry-cobbler topping. He swirls his tongue suggestively with the prize crumb on its tip. "Does this evening end here?"

I'm nicely drunk. "Not if you don't want it to."

The taxi pulls up in front of my building's green-and-white awning. Tito, my always drowsy night doorman—a third-year marketing student at Columbia University—is sound asleep when Steve and I walk past him.

Since my co-op management crew has modernized my building's elevator, we no longer have an elevator operator. This is the latest cost-cutting move by Westin Drimmer, the new head of our co-op board, a type-A man who lost his job on Wall Street last June. The changes to our building are coming fast and furious—Drimmer is practicing his management skills while he searches for another position for an unemployed fifty-something used to a high six-figure income.

Steve and I ride the shiny new elevator to the upper floors alongside a dogged real-estate agent with pink-tinted glasses and a triangular face who's been showing a three-bedroom apartment one floor below mine for the last two months.

The agent and I nod hello. "Isn't it late for you to be here?" I ask her.

The agent fixes the flounce of her black skirt stuck halfway up her ass from static cling. She speaks as if confiding a secret. "I have the perfect buyer coming tomorrow. I'm making sure the place is swept."

"Good luck," Steve says.

The agent smiles and turns to me. "Is the B penthouse available yet?"

"No, Mrs. Leventhal is on life support," I say.

"Are they going to pull the plug? Isn't she in her nineties?"

"She told her son not to pull the plug. She got her request notarized."

The agent passes me her card. "Would you be a dear and call me when she dies?"

Steve shakes his head in disbelief.

"Sounds awful, but that's what you have to do to survive as a businesswoman in this city." The elevator door opens at her floor and she scurries out.

Seconds later the door opens on the seventeenth floor, and

Mr. Kleinman, my other elderly neighbor, emerges from penthouse C with his fly open and the tip of his penis peeking out.

I wince.

"Good God," Steve says.

"You need to go home, Mr. Kleinman," I say.

"Is the girl here yet?"

"Your nurse is here in the morning."

He offers me a hollow stare. "It's nine o'clock. She should be here."

"Oh, but it's 9:00 p.m." My heart goes out to this poor man. His pants are soaked in urine. His bare feet are browned with toe rot. I lead him back to his apartment by his wrist. "Back to sleep, Mr. Kleinman. Do you understand? Tomorrow morning. It's nighttime now."

"Yes," he says. His look is grateful, desperate. Has a flash of awareness broken through his Alzheimer's?

I close the door on my neighbor. "You're a good person," Steve says. "Not many people can handle that kind of scene with such grace."

"I swear he was sharp as a tack when I moved in. I heard he was a senior vice president at Chase Manhattan Bank once, but with Alzheimer's he's a shell of a person. His kids have two homes each but they won't foot the bill for an overnight nurse—so I keep an eye out for him."

"He's hard to miss."

Can I recapture any of the romance from the restaurant? Is it kind of sick trying? My guest makes no indication that he's changed his objective, so I turn the dimmer to a seductive level of light. Steve compliments my modernist black-and-white decor, which I proudly already know is in very good taste, not too trendy, not too decorated. He also admires my one collection I chose to add subtle color to the room: twelve cat's-eye paperweights. I put on a Nina Simone CD that Vondra swears by as an aphrodisiac and join him on the sofa.

Steve pats one of the seat cushions. "Is *this* comfortable. I could sleep on this."

Nina sings about being misunderstood, and Steve drapes his spiffy suit jacket over the nearby chair. In moments he's beside me stroking my hair. It's been so long since I've been in this scenario that I have to think about what comes next. Should I pull off my dress or ask him more about his job?

"I love how you smell," I say finally.

"And how's that?" he asks in a velvety voice.

"Musky. Manly."

"That's a relief, because it sure ain't cologne."

I laugh.

He looks at me and the stars line up as he leans toward my lips. No awkward saliva, no dry tongues. We kiss each other for at least five unbelievable minutes.

"Man," I say when we finally come up for air.

"Can I make a confession?" Steve whispers again.

"Yes?" I pant.

"I can't say this—"

"Don't hold back on me now." I smile.

He grins like a bandit in a bad John Wayne film. "I had a hard-on all through your interview yesterday. You're so damn cute. You must know that."

"Really?" I breathe harder.

"I haven't stopped thinking about you. I even dreamed about you last night." I graze his fingertips and Steve leans over and unbuttons the top of my dress. He kisses between my breasts. "What did *you* dream about last night?"

I think, which is very hard in such a state of arousal. "You really want to know?"

"I do."

"I was floating like a magic carpet over the matzo factory."

Steve kisses my neck and says, "Elevation while sleeping usually means the penis is rising, so it's not that. But it could be the clitoris rising. Maybe I slipped into your consciousness."

"Could be," I say, stirred and damp.

He slips his hand into my gray cotton Calvins and with one-handed dexterity slides two callused fingers between my legs. He works his long fingers so fast it feels like a hummingbird is inside me. He's already a champ in my book, but he ups the ante by sucking my right breast until my nipple is rock hard.

I come with a yelp.

When's the last time I did that? Steve holds me until my pulse lowers. Nina Simone finishes her last note and Steve bites his lip in triumph.

Steve guides my hand to his fly. He's hard and hot. I smile knowingly and guide him to my bedroom and work open the buttons of his shirt. A three-inch silver cross is draped around his neck. Whoa. Not that I have a *Jews Only* policy—but man that cross is intimidating straight out of the gate.

"You must be German-American?" I whisper nervously as I caress his light chest hair.

"Why do you ask that?" He smiles.

"That cross. With your last name I wasn't sure you if you were Jewish."

He smiles again even more enigmatically. "I believe in time. Time is infinite—if you imagine it, it will occur."

"What? Why the cross?"

"Why do you think it's there?"

"Uh—you've got me stumped."

"Maybe it's an amulet. Maybe it's a shield."

Okay. What's going on here? Why is my sexy romp turning into a cloying Hal Hartley art-house film?

He kisses my nose, his cock still fat with expectation. "I'm so excited by the special," he coos.

I'm considerably less hot and bothered. "What special?"

He kisses my ear. "I thought I mentioned it."

"No—"

He strokes my cheek and mutters, "We'll talk later. I can't wait to hear your family's reaction."

My family? The idiot should have waited for the blow job.

"Tell me now," I insist.

"I'm sure you'll love it," he says nervously. "We'd like to broadcast your family Passover celebration. Live. Great press for the Food Channel, great press for you, right?"

I sit straight up. Was this date on a tactic list to get my family to allow a live broadcast? "Is *that* what this night is about?"

Despite being stared at by an angry half-clothed woman he has just finger fucked, Steve anxiously plows on with his brainstorm: "No, of course not."

"What the hell are you talking about then?"

"I ran the idea by our vice president of Original Programming and he loved it. I showed him the footage from our food pioneers special. You're very photogenic."

I fake a hacking cough for the moment's camouflage it offers.

"You okay there?" I can see him thinking: *the girl or the hosting gig.* The gig apparently wins. "I know you might think our target audience would be eating their own meal at that time, but I assure you the show would get repeated later in the week for those other folks. And many Christians are curious about Jewish customs, especially Passover because of the Last Supper. I think it would be a history lesson for America. My boss loved it, thought it was a solid idea for ratings, and good PR for your family, too."

"I have to talk to the family. We make group decisions." My voice needs defrosting.

"I understand. I'm sure they'll love the idea. After all, your family will be immortalized! If it goes well, we can show the program every year."

"Gee." Minutes ago I saw an Adonis on my sheets. Now I want to crush a bedbug.

"You'll consider it then?"

"Promise." As in, *no fucking way.*

"Could you tell me tomorrow if possible? I want to map out the rest of my shooting schedule."

"I said I promise. But right now I think you need to go." I'm having a hard time masking my anger.

"I hope I haven't insulted you, because I'd love to continue where we left off, if you know what I mean. I hope I haven't muffed it up." He smiles, kisses the front of my thong and says, "Perhaps muffed is a poor choice of word."

I may have laughed at bawdy humor an hour ago, but now I feel as if I've been intimate with a sicko.

"Listen, chickie, can we rewind to five minutes ago? I just thought you might be thrilled that my boss was behind my idea."

My arms hang limply as I search his face for any sort of understanding. Is he mean or merely a dim bull? I gird myself for the massive low that's sure to come. I feel like a *chorus girl,* my grandma Lainie's vintage term for an easy woman. "It's time for you to go. *Really.*"

"Heather, I was only kidd—I honestly didn't mean to insult—"

He gets the message and rebuttons his dress shirt.

"Can I call you tomorrow?"

"Maybe," I say.

After I lock the door, I stare out my window until enough time passes that Steve emerges onto the dark street. He flags down a cab. As it rides off in the dark, I feel like turning a deadly ray gun on anyone in range.

I pull out the Nina Simone CD and shove it out of view. I press play on my favorite Aretha.

If I have to wait any longer for someone to love me I'll sprout old-lady chin hairs. The phone rings. I look at my watch. Half past eleven. Is it Steve on his cell, with genuine regret over his amazing lack of tact?

"It's me," Jake says, only slightly apologetically. "I know you stay up late."

"Is there something wrong?" I sniffle.

"No, but there's something important I forgot to ask you when we spoke last."

"Yes?" I barely manage to say. *Don't tell me. A busload of Jews from Liechtenstein is in town.*

"How did the Food Channel thing go?"

This is what's so important? I'm not going to make a laughingstock of myself with my cousin who loves to laugh. I force back the tears. "The filming went fine, but—Steve Meyers from the show called me for a follow-up."

"Want me to handle it?"

"I've taken care of it. I met him for dinner."

"That was his follow-up?"

"Well, he wants our family on TV celebrating Passover. And get this, *live!*"

"Ooh," Jake says, as if he's been punched in the groin. "What did you say? And who'd watch anyway?"

"He says curious Christians would tune in live, and 'those other folks' a few days later. Then I think they want to make it a holiday perennial like The Grinch or *It's a Wonderful Life*."

"That's just nuts. What did *you* say?"

"Well *of course* we're not going to do the *seder*, but I said I'd get back to him. I figure you'd help me out with an excuse. I'm rather pissed off, to tell the truth. I thought he was interested in me. I was sorely mistaken."

"You're *gorgeous*, don't worry. And you know—I'm just thinking out loud here—maybe we should consider the broadcast, Heath."

"It's unpleasant to even joke about such a foul idea."

"Seriously."

"Seriously, what? We don't have a family celebration, remember? No one in our family even knows how to read Hebrew."

"Except your father."

"Lot of good that does us. Jake, let's get this over with. What should I say to Meyers?" I've demoted the dipstick to a last name.

"No, let's talk this out. Maybe we should do this. I'm thinking like a businessman here." There is a long pause before Jake picks up again. I can hear him breathing as he collects his words. "I don't want to getcha upset, but our market share is going way downhill this year."

This is out of left field. "We're the bestselling brand. Recession-proof, in the Bible, remember?"

"See, Heath, the other brands spend big bucks on advertising now that they're out of family ownership and in big conglomerates. They have corporate muscle behind them. We rely on word of mouth for our sales. Advertising is hardly budgeted. And you may not have registered this fully, but our profits have been sinking steadily."

"Well, you didn't exactly highlight this before."

"I didn't want to alarm you."

"You're alarming me now." My turn to pause. I'm somewhere between shocked and furious. "Think it through, Jake. Where are we going to get the family? There's you, Siobhan and me. God knows I'm not dating anyone. Greg's reeling in the marlin and chasing tail come Passover. And your appalling other cousins, what are you going to do—send them an invite through their lawyer? This is a deranged plan. This is not the way to address an emergency. We could hire a real advert—"

"Maybe if I asked Marcy and Rebecca straight out, gave them the truth, they'd say yes. If I tell them we need to get out there to avoid being eaten by the competition, they'd have to help us out. They want to keep this company profitable as much as we do."

"You want our nasty relatives who abhor us on television with us? That's a great image to get out there. And who the hell would lead the *seder?* It would be a group humiliation. We'd have to use English *Haggadahs* to read from, because no one will pull off the Hebrew prayers. This is the traditional family picture you want to put forth?"

"You're probably right about Marcy and Rebecca. On second thought, I don't think they'll come."

"If you're drumming up fake family members," I practically yell, "then I might ask my mailman. He's from Russia, studying Hebrew, now that he can. Has a wife and a toddler here. He can be our dear uncle Oleg. You'd like that?"

"How old is he?"

"Jake," I hiss, "I'm not inviting my mailman. That was sarcasm."

"Why don't you ask him anyway? An accent sounds authentic in a Jewish setting. And mailmen deliver thousands of porn magazines to their residents. They know how to keep a secret."

"Jake—"

"Siobhan will be Shoshanna, of course. We'll get books out of the library to prep her. I'm sure we have one or two others who might want to come."

Yeah, Sukie from Upsy Daisy would, she was that adamant about wanting to attend a *seder*, but I'm not giving this hare-brained plan any more ammunition.

"Look," Jake says after considerable silence on my part. "The Food Channel gets great ratings. This is free national television advertising. Advertising we couldn't afford, and here's someone who wants to give it to us."

"Jake, can't we drum up some cyberbusiness? What about a snappy Web site like Matzo.com?"

"I looked into it already. Somebody already has it."

"Who snagged it? Streit's? Manischewitz?"

"Not sure. Just says *Under Construction*. Could be either of them. Another nail in our coffin because our Web site is hard to load—"

"Since when do we have a Web site? What's the URL?"

"Greenblotz.com."

Despite my Level-Ten Misery, I can't help an unlikely burst of laughter.

Jake joins in with a loud hoot. "Not quite Amazon or Yahoo!, let me tell you. A lousy money waster that some shyster talked me into. I don't have time to overhaul that piece of crap right now. Not until after Passover."

The world is starting to look more crazy than evil. "There must be other ways to save the day than by airing our dirty laundry."

"If people see our family they'll think of us as an extension of theirs. We need this edge in the market. And if the show gets repeated every year, listen, I'm not sure this is an opportunity we can pass up. Hey! Maybe if you get to your mother now, before she makes her plans—"

"My mother? Not going there. Out of the question."

My date with Steve, momentarily forgotten, comes back in a flash. I hurry the call to the end, and when I hang up with Jake, I moan like a goalie who failed to stop a puck in a championship match.

Five

The Request

At the stiflingly awkward dinner with my parents at the Russian Tea Room that followed my college graduation, the topic mercifully turned to professional mental help. Shrinks have always been a common denominator in my immediate family. Relieved at this bright turn of conversation, my parents waxed nostalgic about the multitude of analysts, psychiatrists, psychologists and certified social workers they'd seen. I chimed in with: "I can remember all the way back to Dr. Schwartz."

"You're kidding?" Dad laughed, after a quick look at Mom.

Dr. Schwartz was a kiddie shrink. I was dragged to his office after I wrapped myself in our curtains for a day after witnessing my parents fighting in our kitchen with large and dangerous kitchen utensils. Going to Dr. Schwartz's candy-colored office usually meant me playing with Barbies and

Kens under his watchful eye. At my graduation dinner, neither of my parents believed that I could remember that far
back until a cross-examination in which I mentioned his
drippy nose and huge poster of the Eiffel Tower. Dad stole
another glance at Mom and laughed. Apparently Dr.
Schwartz's final analysis was that they were the ones who
should seek therapy.

Maybe my parents should have listened and left me
alone with my garden-variety angst. But when you have
money, surely a little of it thrown someone's way could
fix things. You keep spending and hoping. So I'm just past
thirty and I've sampled the entire smorgasbord of neurotic Rx. There are, for example, the ultraprofessionals
like my college psychologist, Myrna Bernstein Callahan,
who play anthropologist and never cross the line of dis-
tanced observer. This cold fish silently listened to my
New York rants like I was explaining tribal rituals in
Vanuatu. If I'd told her that I was addicted to Dial-a-
Prayer or that my grandmother bought panties from Vic-
toria's Secret, she wouldn't have batted an eyelash. No
matter how great my pain she would stare at me, neutral
as Switzerland.

The flipside, equally distasteful, is the overly sympa-
thetic therapist, like Patty Zipsky, the one I fired eighteen
months ago when I was truly out of control. I was missing important work meetings, I was eating everything in
sight, and instead of crying just at Passover, I was crying
myself to sleep every single night. Patty was useless during this crisis. She is too soft for her profession. She said,
"I know, I know" every few seconds, and never let me cry
without wiping my tears with her thumb and stopping the
session to sprint to the kitchen for a glass of water. She's
the kind of woman whose kid falls at a picnic and she's

still comforting the child on her lap two hours later. I knew I needed a hard-ass who would scare me into a respectable life. I wanted someone who would talk back to me. It took me six months after I let Patty go to find my current therapist, Bettina Henderson, who I first laid eyes on when I had a nasty flu and was watching *Oprah*.

The topic that day was "Therapy of the Stars," and the second guest after a sinister-looking hypnotist was Bettina, a long lean Aussie with a clear voice and a mass of coiled brown hair. Oprah gave a brief introduction to Bettina Henderson's *"Get Off Your Bum"* approach to the woes of the famous. Then Bettina read from her book, *Get Off Your Bum Therapy.* She dropped huge hints about who made up her clientele. "A household-name cover girl—whose weight has caused heaps of controversy—came to see me. We tackled her fear of losing her modeling contract if she ate a full meal. You might have noticed her healthy weight gain lately—"

"Kate Moss?" Oprah asked waggishly.

"Oh, I can't tell." Bettina said, smiling. "Anyhow, I could've just listened to this model explain why she shouldn't eat. But I walked her out of my office and down to the nearest restaurant. I talked her through a serving of chocolate cake forkful by forkful. I insist she has one treat a day. Life is not worth living without chocolate cake, right, girls?"

An out-of-work child actor that I'd never heard of before came out to join Bettina on the set sofa. His father invested wisely, and now the former child actor had tons of money but nothing to do since the phone stopped ringing. He had no sense of self. The actor explained to Oprah how Bettina sat him down, talked through options with him and helped him translate his acting experience into new skills. "Now," he said, "I head a volunteer agency for new immigrants, and have my *soul* back."

There were so many hoots and hollers that Oprah had to call for quiet.

"You probably can't afford me," Bettina announced, proudly beaming to the viewers at home, "but maybe you have a friend who can play the role of taskmaster. Ask yourself when you're down and out not who's the most comforting to call for help, but who'll be harder on you, to command you to 'get off your bum.'"

Bettina Henderson sounded like a royal pain in the ass, but with my temperature rising and my sinuses congested, I seethed about the ineffective Patty Zipsky years. Bettina's forceful methodology of pop psychology sounded like a godsend. When Oprah said Bettina was New York–based I felt a jolt of excitement: *I* certainly would be able to pay her fee, and why get a substitute taskmaster when you can have the real thing? That's one of the nicer aspects of having money. You want, you get.

Using skills I've gleaned from ten years of finding the right people to appear on camera, I tracked Bettina Henderson down. Like an exclusive new nightclub, her office was unlisted. Still, she made me wait more than two weeks for a callback. "You sound like a very lovely young lady. But I'm *terribly* expensive."

When I insisted it was not a problem, she was thrilled to fit me in. She charges $450 an "hour," the steepest fee a therapist has ever suckered me out of, and she insists all of her clients pay up front. I wouldn't dare tell anyone how much I pay. I know it's recycled self-help claptrap, but Bettina's encouragement has done me some good in the past year. When I was bitching about gaining weight and feeling isolated except for my work encounters, she reached over, handed me the Yellow Pages and commanded me to call her health club. I countered that I was too dumpy to exercise in front of the svelte set, and maybe plastic surgery is the only way, even though I have no tolerance for physical pain except for my yearly blood donation. (My dad and I have rare blood, B-Rh negative, which only two percent of the population has, and ever since I turned twenty-one I've followed his example in generosity to the Red Cross. But even this good deed always gives me the things-entering-my-flesh willies. My mother is exactly the same when it comes to pain. As a result, she may be the only Park Avenue bitch with wrinkles.)

Bettina assured me surgery wouldn't give me the self-respect that exercise would. I insisted no coed workouts for flabby me, so she called the Lotte Berk studio, an establishment that caters to Upper East Side women, and handed me the phone. The program there stresses movement and strength via an exercise program like Pilates, and costs a fortune if you stick to it as religiously as the trainers recommend. But I stuck to it, and I took those inches off. Bettina sometimes verges on Quack City, but at least I have a rudimentary control of my life now, like a songwriter who has a chorus going but the verses are still in temporary bullshit form. My professional life is good, and I've kept off those twenty-plus pounds I'd packed on after I gave Daniel Popper the heave-ho. For a while there it was open slather on the buttered bagels, the home-delivered pizza and, of course, the glutton's ice cream of choice: Häagen Dazs Dulce de Leche. God. How many halves of grapefruit have I eaten this year alone? Grapefruit is punishment food. It's like taking pills. But I get a lot more wolf whistles these days than I did pre-Bettina. My pricey Medicine Lady has fixed my tush and flabby arms but, alas, not my self-loathing and loneliness.

★ ★ ★

I am so rattled by my slutty night with Steve and the seder dilemma that I ignore the onslaught of traffic when I'm crossing First Avenue at Eighty-sixth Street, headed for my therapy appointment. I make it a third of the way across when a taxi comes flying at me, and just misses knocking me down. At the other curb is an Asian teenager wearing a baseball mitt on his head like a hat, and an elderly nun in her habit, sporting white tennis socks and black Reeboks over her hosiery, pushing a blue metal shopping cart full of groceries. The nun wags her finger at me for crossing too soon.

The never-ending Gotham obstacle course: now a BBC documentary production, one with a sizable budget by the looks of things, is blocking my path. As a seasoned producer I can approximate budget size in a glance. The giveaway on this film is the permit to stop traffic, and the "B" cameraman focused on pick-up shots of passersby. A tall, thin producer with a pale face stops me with his hand until the reporter is done grilling a hip-hopper perched atop a homemade motorized scooter fitted with a milk-crate seat. Next in line for the reporter is a man in a chicken suit that has become a fixture of the neighborhood: he hands out samples for the Ranch 1 franchise on Eighty-sixth Street.

I'd go backward and cross Eighty-fifth Street to get to Bettina on time, but a young production assistant who is probably being paid peanuts while scoring a free flight to New York from London has crept up behind me. He's on the use-it-when-you-have-it power trip of the low-paid in the entertainment industry, and theatrically stops anyone with the misfortune to get somewhere in a hurry. "Miss, we're shooting a film for the BBC," and "Sir, I'm with the BBC. You can't walk yet." I'm not claustrophobic, but today I'm almost as tense as the time I tried to get out of a packed Aretha concert at Madison Square Garden with an iffy stomach. "I have to get to an appointment," I plead to the older producer who first spoke to me.

"Won't be a second," he says with a plum-in-mouth accent. "We have a permit."

"For what? Disruption?" I say.

"We're making a film about average people during an average day in post-9/11 New York."

"In March? Wouldn't September make more sense?"

"We want an average day, not one with ceremony. You look like you might have some interesting things to say—"

"As opposed to the chicken?" I say.

The producer smiles. "Brilliant. Keep the chitchat up and you'll get right into the film. So would you like to tell us your thoughts?"

My wavy hair is out of control from the humidity that's been plaguing the city; it's almost in fright-wig territory. "Please don't film me. I'm having a bad day. I just want to keep walking."

"But we're from the BBC," the pretty, redheaded female interviewer cuts in, finished with the chicken. Her accent is the uppitiest of Upper Class, just like the producer's.

I shake my head no. "My hair's too messy to be on air."

The interviewer sneers. "A great tragedy like 9/11 occurred and you're worried about your hair?"

"Yes," I hurl back.

"You're as indifferent as those barracudas that sell souvenirs down by Ground Zero," she sniffs.

"Francesca," the producer hushes her.

"And you're not?" I spit right back at her. Normally I would've just walked on, but lucky for Francesca, she cornered a woman who was just duped by an asshole.

"And how is that?" Francesca says with a start.

"You make documentaries. I do, too. We try and make a buck or two off other people's ideas and emotions."

The veteran producer can't help himself. "If you're so concerned about hair, what did you make a film on—how to shampoo?" He has a good chuckle with Francesca while I gather my thoughts, knife-faced.

Memories of September 11 flash through my brain. I could say a hundred different things. But what I actually say to the BBC crew is: "I'm damn glad someone's down there selling souvenirs."

"You're glad?" the talent, Francesca, says after a sharp click of her tongue.

"Glad. New York is functioning when there's a buck being made. If we think too much about danger and tragedy we'd never get out of bed. I saw Tower Two explode. But what am I supposed to do with that hideous memory? I just don't want to talk about it anymore, okay? And by the way, if someone doesn't want to be on camera whether their mother just died or they are having a bad hair day, I respect their individual right to say no. That's what a release form is for, mutual consent. Making a film is a privilege, not a badge."

Francesca quails at my reproach, turning slightly pink.

"And p.s.," I spit out, "the only shampoo in my films were in the shower room at Riker's Island. I have two News and Documentary Emmys for my frivolity."

The producer turns to the main cameraman. "Did you get all that?"

"No," he apologizes.

"I did," calls camera B.

The producer touches his anemic face nervously, and turns to me with new determination. "Brilliant. One hundred percent heartfelt. Darling, will you fill out a release form?"

"In your dreams."

"Please—" Francesca begs me with her eyes "—it's so hard to get real emotion on film. If you make documentaries you understand."

"Sorry," the producer adds. "We all have our methods."

Now I get it. They were deliberately trying to provoke a reaction from me. I angrily snatch the paper on the clipboard and the producer hands me a pen. I am their peer after all, and I *do* know damn well how hard it is to get a release.

"Greenblotz?" he says when I hand it back to him.

"Yes."

"Like the matzo company?"

"Yes."

The producer looks at me in such a way that I can tell: one more *in the tribe.* Funny, the producer looks about as Jewish as Christopher Robin. But as my father has always pointed out, there are Jews of all skin tones and eye colors. My blue eyes and my cousin Greg's blond hair are proof enough. "Didn't you just give the Food Channel a tour of your factory?" the producer says.

"Yes," I say, confused and still cooling down. Do they know about my sordid night with Steve? Does word spread that fast in this town?

"Jared filmed you," he says. "We went to film school in London together. He was very impressed with you. Do you know your prison film aired on the BBC?"

Of course I know that. I'm still sorting through my emotions. "Yes, we had a lot of e-mail from there."

"Didn't Susan Sarandon narrate that?" he asks with a twinkle in his voice.

"Yes." I soften. But not much softer: the way my week is going, Jared probably just wants my Emmys to open some doors for him. This time I *am* a whit wiser. Every time I think I have chemistry I can later chalk it up to schmoozing. I've had half a dozen "Let's be friends" get-togethers from new acquaintances who seemed genuine but then tacked on a "Can you do me a small favor?" at the end of brunch or coffee. Maybe Jared even suggested the live *seder* to that bastard Steve. "Well, good luck with your film. I'm very late for my appointment."

As I rush to Bettina's, once again the memory of my September 11 washes over my brain in a thousand broken bits.

I didn't lose anyone; I never endured that level of pain. But when I turned my head back momentarily, I saw the second tower crumble in the far distance as I fled my office on Twenty-second Street. It's an image I'll never forget. Vondra was safely holed up with her sisters in a B&B in Vermont, so there was no one with me with whom I could contemplate the tragedy that had a world in shock.

Because Manhattan phone lines were overloaded, I was connected to my other friends only by e-mail. The only person I knew who worked at the Trade Center was a friend I'd partied with at the Los Angeles Film Festival; she had won the special critics' citation for her insider look at her banking firm. On September 11, my festival friend mass e-mailed that she was alive. She had been late to work. Even though her offices were on a low floor and all of her coworkers were accounted for, she was understandably devastated. I sent her an empathetic e-mail saying to call me if she wanted to talk to anyone. Later that day, another e-mail popped up, this time from Dad in Bali.

R U and your m both OK? I love U both 2 pieces. Jake and Siob? Email/call SOON as U can.

I e-mailed him back and printed the original message out for Mom as she didn't know how to use e-mail then. When the NYC phone system was still overloaded at 10:00 a.m., I walked the short distance to her apartment building. I rode up with the elevator operator and a shaken lady who hadn't heard from her husband yet. I walked down Mom's hallway like they taught us in a self-defense class required in high school, keys between each knuckle, I grasped down for grit, a warrior. I keyed open my childhood apartment, but Mom wasn't there. I figured it was best to stay put at her place. I sat in her apartment glued to CNN, occasionally weeping with the rest of America.

I peeked in Mom's refrigerator. It was packed with pricey aged beef her cook always buys from Lobel's, Madison Avenue's upper-crust butcher, and costly fruit and vegetables from the Vinegar Factory. Some rich women love to cook, and can bore you with recipes they clipped from *Food and Wine*. But my mother, whose own snooty mother never taught her to cook, is a throwback to those turn-of-the-twentieth century women who never touched a dishpan but supervised the help as their main job.

Around 11:00 a.m. Mom opened the door and saw me horizontal on her steel couch that took first prize at the Chicago Furniture Show, crying at the CNN coverage.

She said, "Come here, honey. I was having a breakfast date at the Stanhope with Pamela Levine."

Mom had said "of course" to a rare request by her live-in cook, Angela, to leave Manhattan for her mother's nursing home in Yonkers. Angela had wanted to check on her mother's emotional state after such a tragedy. Mom asked Wilson, still handsome and her chauffeur after all these years, to bring along a stash of improvised sandwiches in the Lincoln Town Car in case he and Angela got stuck in traffic.

"Have *you* eaten?" Mom asked when her two employees

had left with a shopping bag full of turkey and romaine baguettes. "The pantry is plenty stocked."

It was. I'd peeked in there too; the cabinets were piled high with a designer-mustard collection and assorted preserves from London's Fortnum & Mason. Does my mother feel worldlier knowing that if the munchies strike, she can make a quince sandwich?

"What would you like me to fix us?" I asked.

"Darling, you relax. I'll cook." Mom poked around in the stuffed refrigerator, and started in on the first meal I'd ever seen her make. I strolled back to the living room and took it all in, this alien but familiar environment, the apartment I grew up in, forever being redecorated.

"Come eat!" Mom called and I joined her under my old dining room's Austrian chandelier. I'm not quite sure what my mother's September 11 meal was meant to be. She'd boiled unsnapped green beans until they were soggy and spooned them on the plate without draining them enough. She steamed strips of expensive beef until they were dead gray. Garnishing it all off was an uncooked baby eggplant cut into fat slices.

"I'm a little rusty."

I swallowed another chunk of the flavorless meat. "It's really okay. It's just nice to eat with you."

It was. The end of the world loomed outside, but it felt good to have her taking care of me. It felt good to have that short but obviously heartfelt e-mail from Dad saying how concerned he was. Most days I feel as if I'm on the rim of a carousel that goes around and around and I'm never fully joining in the thrill. But for a moment, with New York in physical and emotional chaos, I got a taste of what it would be like to have grown up with doting parents. Then the horror of the greater circumstance hit me again, and I vomited in the master bathroom with the built-in spa.

★ ★ ★

I'm still goosey when I reach the buzzer for Bettina's ground-floor office in her swanky brownstone.

I chew up a third of my exorbitantly priced therapy time telling her about my unsettling BBC encounter. I take a breath and Bettina hands me a glass. "Try my lemonade. A very famous chef who's my client gave the recipe to me."

"Very good," I say after a polite sip.

"So, shall we begin our work?"

After a few leading questions about the week that was, I explain that the one man I thought was interested in me was Steve Meyers of the Food Channel, and indeed he called, but I see now his only interest in me is for a *seder* segment. And I'm certain Jared S. is all about the same crap. "That's all I am to them," I say, "a woman with a colorful ancestor and a lot of industry connections. What's most laughable is that Jake wants me to follow through with this asinine seder business, pretend we're a functioning family, and even make up family members if we have to. He claims the business is in dire straits." I look up, eager for sympathy. I'm sure that came out sounding awfully whiny, but I've shielded Vondra and Jake from my self-absorption, and Bettina is being paid good money to listen.

Instead of calming me, Bettina is reproaching me. "Your cousin is absolutely right. You need to help the family if the business is jeopardized. From all you've said these past months, Jake and you are each other's lifelines."

"My family will be exposed as freaks."

"Isn't everyone worried that their family is on the outskirts of respectability? How are you freaks?"

Hasn't she been listening for a year? "Everything about us is freaky. From little to big. Let's have my mom talk about her new bathroom spigots from Germany. That's what she spent her last two conversations with me talking about."

"She's a smart woman, you've said that yourself. I'm sure she has more sense of what a live special needs than you're giving her credit for."

"Or hey, how about I get my confused dad back in town so he can tell us who he's dating. Michael or Michaela?"

"I think this is a larger issue for you that we may need a series of sessions on. If it turns out your father smokes bloke from time to time, does that make him a *freak*?"

"What?" I snort. "Smokes bloke?"

Bettina smirks. "That's an Aussie expression."

"A colorful one," I concede with the smallest of smiles.

"Right, we're talking lightheartedly now. Easier to work with. Give me an example of what hurt you when you were young. Keep it little, love. If you stay with little it will be easier to talk about big."

I have to think. "Try games," I finally say. "Every family played games with their kids, right? Trouble. Operation. Mousetrap. Life. My parents never once played a board game with me."

"Heather, I find that hard to believe."

"Well, Mom did get a big kick out of her version of 'This Little Piggy,' but that wasn't a board game—"

"How did it go?"

The corners of my mouth turn up a bit. "This little piggy went to Bloomie's, this little piggy went to Lord & Taylor, this little piggy went to Bergdorf's, this little piggy went to Saks. But this little piggy went wee wee wee all the way to Mays—Mays was a department store like Kmart that was down on Union Square when I was little."

Bettina smiles with newly bleached teeth. (From my last two fees?) "That's quite funny."

"It is," I accept.

"My parents never played board games with me, we played make-believe games," Bettina says.

"But at least your parents played with you," I say in that aggrieved voice you get when reliving the lesser moments of a life. So much for lighthearted. "My parents forgot I was a child. I never saw one Disney movie, not one! That's kind of freakish, don't you think?" At this point I completely lose it and sob.

"Heather, we've done a lot of personal work, and I'll say it again—I think it's the right time to tackle your bigger family issues. If you never confront them you'll never be free of this sadness you carry around. Why don't you confront them once and for all instead of sticking your head in the sand?"

"You mean in the matzo meal," I joke wearily through my tears.

"If it's a lousy family reunion, so what? It's a family reunion. Some progress will be made just by having everyone sit down at the same table."

I take a breath and pull myself together before I speak. "But assuming we could get everyone there, which is itself a laugh, what if everything blows up in our face on camera? And where do I even start?"

Bettina slams her right hand down on her clipboard. "Call your mother. The natural start."

"I guess I could do that tomorrow morning."

"Where will you be, at your office or the factory?"

"Tomorrow? Work. I need to catch up."

"Don't be surprised if I call you to get you off your bum!"

SiX

The Parent Trap

When I open my office door Vondra is standing by the window and chatting up a French film-festival director on her red cell phone. I have never seen Vondra Adams without well-applied lipstick and sultry eye shadow. She's wearing skintight black jeans and a low-cut black bodysuit that reveals significantly more cleavage than should be possible on a yoga body almost exclusively fed fruits, vegetables and tofu.

"Bonsoir," Vondra says as she clicks off her phone. She sees my eyebrows rise half an inch when I get the full frontal view. "Water padding. You like?"

"Definitely vavoom. But I have a feeling I'm not the one you're advertising for." No use bringing my personal baggage to work with me. I am *determined* to be chipper. "Did I miss much yesterday? Sorry to overload you this week."

"Family obligations. I understand. Anyhow, the only

thing going on businesswise is a fax from our international rep. We sold the Riker's Island film to Finland and Norway. Three thousand dollars between the two of them, nothing to write home about, but enough to pay the rent for a month and a half. And also some kook keeps faxing us about showing our film in his festival, which he says is world-class."

"Why do you say he's a kook?"

"The festival's at his house. The Third Annual Fred Diamond Festival of American Cinema."

I snort. "One of us should go, just for the cocktail-party story."

"Yeah, you first. Oh, we also have a new intern from the City as School starting Monday. His name is Roswell..." She pauses to look at the paperwork and adds, "Birch."

"What's 'City as School'?"

"It's a citywide New York program that allows high-school seniors to gain real-world experience before they leave school. The administrator called me to see if we could place this kid since she had read in a profile of us that I went to Stuyvesant High School, where Roswell goes. He'd expressed an interest in filmmaking."

"High school? Wouldn't someone from NYU or Columbia be better?"

"We needed the extra hands and I thought, how stupid could he be if he passed that Stuyvesant entrance examination?"

"I'll trust you on that one."

"The administrator—her name is Jacinta—is dropping by later to speed up our paperwork. But I have much bigger news on the personal front, so get your damn coat off already and let me tell you."

"Go on." I drape my powder-blue quilted jacket on the IKEA coatrack that the previous tenant left in the office.

"I met a fabulous man. We had one incredible date together and I'm seeing him again tonight."

"Aha, now I get the bra."

"I'm pulling out all stops. I have a feeling that this may be the one."

"What's so special?" I wait for her answer while she signs for a FedEx package. The deliveryman gives Vondra a very broad smile. I may be a lost cause, but I've always known Vondra would hook up with her version of Mr. Right, however anachronistic that sounds. With her body, brains and spark, she can afford to be choosy.

"He's refined, adventurous and unfuckingbelievably handsome," she says after the FedEx guy leaves.

"Sense of humor?"

Vondra thinks. "Well, to be fair, I don't know him that well yet. But did I tell you he has the coolest job? He's a diplomat."

I lift an imaginary teacup, pinkie raised. "How did you meet him?"

"Remember we were looking for that Egyptian woman who studied sexual views of Africans. Bahiti Rateb—the Virginia Masters of Africa?"

"Yeah."

"Well, since it was so quiet here yesterday, I called the Egyptian consulate, and a secretary accidentally put me through to Mahmoud Habib. He said his mother is practically sisters with Bahiti Rateb and to come over and he'd have his assistant pull together background information, and he'd be willing to talk more about his personal acquaintance with her. We talked for three hours, and we continued the conversation—"

"Where, at his house?"

"No, bitch, at the Beekman Hotel at their deco bar, Top of the Tower—"

I blow out air enviously. That's one place I've always wanted to go on a date. (Well, that and Union Square Café, but look where that got me.) "I've heard that place is so romantic."

"Is it ever. I couldn't believe how generous he was with his time. Heather, he's cultured and very open-minded. He spoke to both sides of the Palestinian issue, and didn't flinch when I said my business partner was Jewish. He's buddies with everyone in his countries from the latest Egyptian rock stars to Omar Sharif. And, get this, he worked under Anwar Sadat!"

"Under Sadat? How old is Mahmoud?"

"Not that old. He's a former journalist who started his career very young."

I stare her down like a camp counselor. "How old exactly?"

She clenches her teeth and spits it out. "Fifty-five."

"Ouch. Kids?"

"No, but he was married. He got divorced a few months ago. He was married to an Egyptian model but the distance was getting to them."

"Oh, you're not going to get blindsided," I say like a churlish narc. "A divorce takes a long time to heal from."

Vondra shrugs and smiles. "I'm a big girl, Heather."

"Don't mind me, I'm a jealous bitch."

"You'll *love* him. He's stopping by tomorrow for lunch. What's your favorite country? He knows *all* the diplomats—"

We're interrupted by a perky knock on the door. It's Jacinta, the City as School internship administrator. She's a happy, happy woman with woolly eyebrows and plump cheeks. Jacinta hands Vondra the paperwork.

She admires the framed photo on Vondra's desk of us two dames from Two Dames Productions accepting our first Emmy. "Roswell was thrilled when I told him about your respect in the industry," she adds. "He's ready to learn."

As soon as we sign the paperwork she breathes heavily, and says, "Oh, terrific. If I can be honest with you, it's a big relief. We didn't know where we would place him, and the term started yesterday." She pauses before she continues, "He didn't click with the more traditional intern outlets for film like New Line and Miramax."

"Is there something you're not telling us?" I ask.

"Oh, no," she says after what feels like a pretty long pause. "You girls will love him. He's a little unconventional. A charmer though."

When Jacinta leaves, Vondra, sensing my concern, says, "Don't worry, we can cut him loose if he doesn't work out. Oh, I forgot to tell you, some cranky woman named Batyna called. English, I think."

"Bettina. Australian."

"Well, she was a pain. Wanted to know if you have made your phone calls, whatever that means. Wouldn't leave a number. Who was she, if you don't mind my asking?"

"My therapist."

"You pay for that? I never understand why white gals are so nuts about their therapists. Black gals have *mommas* to talk to."

I come very close to telling Vondra that she doesn't have my momma, a woman who hasn't held more than a fifteen-minute conversation with me since 9/11. We're interrupted by a phone call from—wouldn't it figure, *her* mother—who apparently has some hilarious story to share with her beloved daughter.

Vondra ribs her family a lot. From my observation, that seems to be a thing happy families do. "You mean you've been eating my banana cake, Momma, and now you like hers better?" Ten minutes of laughter and whooping subside with a "Godspeed, Momma, I love you!"

"She's such a riot," Vondra says after she hangs up. "She's waiting for my dad to pick her up from her Weight Watchers meeting, and she was bored. She always calls me when she's bored. An incurable chatterbox."

"Uh-huh," I say.

Vondra opens her bag and hands me a ten-dollar bill. "I'm going to get cigarettes." (Vondra's body is a temple except for her lungs.)

"So, you're paying me penance?"

"No, I ordered us sushi. That's for my share if the guy comes while I'm down in the deli."

"See ya." When the door closes, I finally feel free to ring Bettina back.

"Did you call your mother yet?" Bettina barks at me.

"No, I just got in."

"Well, that should be the first thing on your list. Call me when you've spoken to her."

"But I haven't even told Jake I'm prepared to do the family seder yet."

"So call him now, and then call your mother," she says. "Let's try to get both done this hour. Forward march!"

After I put down the receiver, I count to three and call the factory, and reach a female matzo underling. She must be a recent hire because she dutifully asks, "Heather? Does Mr. Greenblotz know what it's in reference to?"

"So, are we doing this?" my cousin says as a greeting.

"I think I might be able to handle it."

"Now we're talking! You're the best."

"You're going to have to be the main person overseeing it though. I'm not sure I have the stomach for that."

"I can do that if you want."

"That wasn't a choice. By the way, before we discuss this travesty more, who was the girl who picked up the phone?"

"That was Dimple, our sexy little high-school intern who started yesterday."

"Dimple?"

"She swears that's her real name. Dimple Goldstein. I picked her right away from the bunch of students who wanted to work here. From the back she's Judaism's answer to J. Lo."

"Nice to know a big butt is a qualification for learning the matzo trade."

"Always."

"Nice."

"Ssh, you, I have good news. I called your favorite cousin, Greg, to see if I could enlist him for this seder thing. Happy to be asked. Said he was getting sentimental this year. Wants to help our family profile. He asked after you."

"Please. I'm not on his map."

"You got it wrong. Greg thinks you're a rock star, always tells his distributors in Miami when your documentaries are on. He was shocked that you wanted him to come."

Okay, proof positive that I don't give people their due. Greg watches documentaries? The last time I had what passed for a conversation with my Floridian cousin, he told me how he picked up his latest girlfriend by showing off his skill for tying cherry stems with his tongue.

"That's good of him to say, but I never said he should come, *you're* the one pushing—"

"Well, I told him you said you did. He was ecstatic. He was under the impression you want nothing to do with him, that you thought he was a sleazy idiot."

I swallow my guilt. "No, I don't feel that way at all. Tell him I'm thrilled he's coming."

Maybe I have everyone in my family wrong. Maybe Bettina and Jake are right, that this will be easier than I'm making out. Maybe the real trouble is all in my horrible head.

"If Greg's coming, that's real news. I'm going to call my mother now."

"Attagirl. I'm sure she'll be happy to be asked. So your mother's not the warmest person, but do you ever ask to spend time with her? Here's a chance."

"You're right. I'll give you a call with updates." Newly optimistic, I beep Bettina on her emergency number, a number I'm sure half of the fucked-up celebrities in the Tristate area use. She calls back pronto.

"I'm doing it. Wish me well."

"March on, soldier!" she trumpets so loudly that I have to pull the receiver back an inch.

I touch-dial my mother's number but there's no answer, so I have to look up her cell-phone number in my Filofax. She picks up on the fifth ring.

"Mom?"

"Oh, how are you, dear?"

"I'm fine."

"Working hard?"

"Yes." I drum my fingernails on my desk. "So, I have something big to ask you about. I have a problem I need to discuss with you." A pregnant silence ensues. I have hardly asked my mother for anything since I left Brown. Even in college I kept favors to a minimum. Mom has never been the kind to ask if I need anything, and I'm not the kind to volunteer it. I've always just held back and listened to her polite prattle in that quasi-British lilt she's picked up from her many cruises. Sometimes I fear I'm on par with her favorite dry-cleaning clerk, and after she's determined I'm having a good day, there's nothing left for her to say.

"A problem, darling? Since when does my little girl have a problem?" The Queen Mother, blissfully ignorant of a brewing Northern England mining strike.

"I've been at the factory this week."

"What factory?"

"It's March, Mom. The factory. There is something important Jake needs your help with."

"My help?"

"Have you ever watched the Food Channel, the big cable network?"

"You're so funny. I don't have cable, darling, you know that."

I did know that. The week our Rikers' film aired I messengered over a VHS tape to her, even though she didn't ask for it. She left a short message on my voice service—"Congratulations!"—and never mentioned the film again. If I grip the receiver any harder I could remold it.

"Mom, they would like to film the Greenblotz *seder*."

"But there is no Greenblotz seder," she says, like I've zinged her with a trick question.

"Oh, believe me, I know. But Jake wants us to pull one off. We can pull together a nice family gathering. Greg's even flying up from Miami, and Siobhan will help us cook."

"Us?"

"Yes. Usually the women cook on Passover. Maybe we could find some recipes in a Jewish cookbook together. I've never cooked with you. It might be fun."

"Honey, of course you remember that I have travel plans set."

My voice takes on an anxious vibrato. "I'd really love it if

you would join us. Jake and I would be very, very grateful."
I can see that this is getting me nowhere, so I go in for the
kill. "Jake just told me a shocking thing."

"What's that, darling?"

"That business is declining, and he needs all the PR help
he can get."

"Declining?"

"The other companies have been bought out by conglomerates and Jake's afraid they can out-advertise us to our
death."

"Baloney. We can advertise too. Your grandfather adver-
tised in the Jewish circulars. Who is Jake's advertising agent?"

"We stopped printing ads years ago. Grandpa Reuben
didn't want our name lining birdcages. Other than flyers, the
current strategy is word of mouth. It could take months to
get Marcy and Rebecca to agree to restructure. In the mean-
time Manischewitz is jumping in and trying to shore up our
customer base with their new cash flow, and the others can't
be far behind. We don't have anything budgeted, and this is
a big opportunity—"

"Jake's going to have to call Marcy or Rebecca then. He'll
just have to do it, poor soul. I would help you two out, but
I have a long-term reservation on an expedition cruise down
the Amazon. You understand, don't you? I am going to
study native medicine with a shaman. You don't want me to
cancel that, do you?"

"No snorkeling?" I snarl.

"No, but I just paid for the optional extension to the Inca
ruins. I thought I'd get some culture this time—and I have
Portia Seidner's insider shopping addresses for Cuzco. She
told me to avoid the alpaca sweaters at Machu Picchu, but
says there's excellent quality to be found in the city. I'll get
you one if you like."

"Not necessary."

"I'm going to have to speed this up. I'm at Saks and my shopper just brought over some lightweight pants for the jungle I might like—"

"Yeah, bye." I nearly slam down the receiver on the near stranger who gave birth to me. September 11 was a definite anomaly. I lay my head on folded arms, paralyzed with self-pity until I hear a key at the door. I raise my head again.

Vondra opens the door clutching a fragrant paper bag that she sets on her tidy desk. "Hysterical thing just happened."

"What?" I say in a miserable whisper as my R. Crumb screen saver kicks in.

"I'm down in the deli getting my ciggies, and while the counter guy's reaching for them I see one of the tureens says Chicken Soup and the other Split Pea with Jam. And I'm having a stupid spell, so I ask the deli man about the soup. He looks perplexed and says, 'Jam very good.' I have to clear this up, so I say, 'Jam, like strawberry jam?' He stares at me like I'm an idiot. 'No, no, pig jam!' 'Pig jam?' I say, and then we both realize our mix-up at the same time. You know, the way in Spanish *j* and *h* have a similar sound. Anyway, we start laughing and the other customers are looking at us like we're *both* idiots—"

"That's pretty funny," I offer feebly.

KEEP ON TRUCKING! reads my current screen, in psychedelic lettering.

"It gets better. I asked him to explain to me why Jose starts with a *j* and *huevos rancheros* starts with an *h*? And he laughs so hard he gives me the soup for free. By the way, did you notice the deli is all different? Jose says he borrowed a book from the library on feng shui. Can you imagine? What next, the gas station is going to feng shui the minimart?" She pauses and studies my face for a second. "Hey, is there something wrong?"

I burst into tears, the kind that come with gasps for air.

"You're freaking. You gotta take a breath, start from the beginning."

I inhale and exhale, and say, "The beginning is I had a date with one of the guys from the matzo shoot, and I let my guard down and got myself in an awful position."

"Happens to all of us."

"The middle is I am rich."

This one takes Vondra off guard and she looks at me funny. "Money ruins everything," I continue. "It ruined my parents—well, maybe my dad's sexual confusion helped speed that to a close, but money didn't help."

Vondra is silent, wearing a worried expression.

"And I've just realized for the ninety-ninth time my mother doesn't love me."

"That couldn't be true," she says softly.

"If Mom loves me it's in a small sector of her brain." I sniff hard. "You know what a seder is, right?"

"Of course, the Passover meal."

"It's supposed to be the big family get-together." I stop again to breathe. "It's practically written in the Bible that your family has to hang together on Passover. But my family never celebrates it. Maybe they did when I was four or five, but not in years. The biggest feast of the year for Jewish people, and we're the family that caters it all."

"Your family does catering? I got it wrong then, I thought—"

"No, I mean, our products are on every Jewish table in America in the spring. And I mean every table. Vondra, my family is very, very rich."

"You said that already. I thought you were well-off but—"

"Not well-off. Filthy rich. And let me tell you, rich stinks." I take a second to sniffle. "I'd trade it in a second for the love you get from your family."

And then I go to pieces altogether.

I never wanted my friends to see me this way. I'm no weepy poster child for The Poor Little Rich Girl Preservation Society, because I wasn't beaten or raped or orphaned. I was never dragged through a nasty custody battle; my folks waited until I left college before they separated. My parents do care about me, even if it takes a world catastrophe for me to hear it. I have a life most people surveyed would put on the plus column. Not a lot of close friends, but enough. A creative career. No money worries. Vondra leans over and pulls me into her arms.

"Okay, now I'm getting claustrophobic," I say into her elbow when I really do need some air.

She sets me free and says, "You're really that wealthy?"

My forced smile straddles misery and relief at finally releasing the truth.

Vondra hands me a folded tissue from her pocket. "You have mucus running out of your nose."

"Thank you," I say with a wipe.

She holds my hand as if I just said I have weeks to live. "Is there anything else I can do for you right now? Would you like to take a walk in some fresh New York City polluted streets, maybe?"

"Will you come to my seder?" I ask. "I don't have much family—"

Vondra strokes my wrist reassuringly. "Baby. Of course. And as far as I'm concerned we are family. You're like my sister." She smiles. "My filthy rich white sister."

"Can you say that on television?"

Vondra looks puzzled. "That you're filthy rich?"

"No."

"That you're white?"

"No, that we're family."

"What?"

"It's a long story."

"Where am I going? Go ahead and tell it."

So I do. About Jared S. and standoffish Tonia, and the scheming Steve Meyers whose help I need to save the family business. And then about adorable Sukie the Tibetan Jew and most importantly, Jake's proposed masquerade to save the family trademark.

Another deliveryman arrives, this one with our deluxe sushi lunch. She opens the plastic tray and places it between us.

"Come on, take the crab rolls, Heather. You know you want them."

She's right. I live for crab rolls. I force a smile and take a nibble of one. There's yet another knock on the door. Followed by the entrance of a beautiful man impeccably dressed in a black suit and tasteful green tie. It's Mahmoud Habib, who has taxied down from Le Cirque to say hi to Vondra.

"I'm selfish. I couldn't wait until tomorrow to see this gorgeous thing again." He gives Vondra's ready hand a suggestive squeeze.

She leads him over to me by the cuff of his jacket. "This is Heather."

I force a hand out in greeting. "Glad to meet you."

"The famous Heather," he says after a shake.

Mahmoud is marquee material, with dark brown skin set off by green eyes and the long lashes that you hardly ever see outside of Disney animated films. His salt-and-pepper hair is styled neatly and expensively. And my God, that lusty voice. Deep. An Arabic variant on the graying leading man who still can get away with starring opposite the latest ingénue. No wonder he's friends with Omar Sharif. He's a younger version of him.

Vondra is peacock proud. "How did the French ambassador like Le Cirque? Was he as tough a critic as you've heard?"

"He gave the meal twenty-eight out of thirty stars, and the wine twenty-nine out of thirty stars. I said, 'Thirty stars? *Monsieur*, what kind of system is that?' "

I force a lumpy smile as Vondra chuckles into Mahmoud's neck. His appreciative laugh in return is throaty and likable.

After a lively conversation about the day that was at the U.N. Security Council, I cough and say, "I have to get home." Anger and envy is clouding my brain.

Seconds after I shakily unlock my apartment door, Jake rings.

"She said no?" he says incredulously after I spill the gory details.

"Didn't even consider it. She's going to the Amazon to study with a medicine man."

Jake pauses to digest my report. He knows my mother's dilettantish comings and goings well enough to know that's the God's honest truth. "Well, okay, on the brighter side, Greg had a great idea. We should ask Gertie to pose as our grandmother."

"You're going to ask her?"

"Already did. Gertie loved the idea! She must have pinched my cheek ten times over the course of the day. I thought she had plenty of family. Turns out she has outlived everyone. All these years Gertie was alone on Passover!"

"That's good." I mumble. "But I'm really having second thoughts about this again. I can't see pulling it off."

"Heather, I know you can do it for me." Jake is not above whimpering.

"I have my friend Vondra coming," I say hesitatingly. "We just need a few more people now, maybe one or two."

"Maybe we can pass her off as one of those Jews from Ethiopia, the falafels."

"The Falashas."

Jake laughs. "How dumb do you think I am?"

"Regardless, there was a woman in my Anthropology 101 class at Brown who was an Ethiopian Jew. I've forgotten what the better word is, but she told my study group that Falasha is a very disparaging name to the community. Anyhow, can't Vondra just be my business partner? Friends come to seders, don't they? Or is it always families only?"

"You're asking me? The last time I was at a seder Jimmy Carter was in office."

"Help me, Lord."

"Who else? Who else?" Jake mutters to himself on the phone.

"I *guess* I could invite my new friend, Sukie. She's half-Jewish and says she's always wanted to go to a seder."

"What's the other half?" Jake asks.

"Tibetan."

"Falashas. Tibetans. We're in different circles, kiddo. That's for sure. So tell me again about that mailman. I really think we're going to need someone who can actually read Hebrew."

"I'll see if I can mention it to him," I say nebulously. "He may be on vacation." This is madness.

Before I call Bettina, I sneak a look in the makeup mirror in my pencil drawer. My eyes are red and bulging from my constant bouts of crying. I sigh and dial.

"You're taking the easy way out," Bettina says sternly.

"Excuse me?" I am thrown for a loop. Begging my mother isn't trying hard?

"So your mother said no. Invite your father. Track him down in Amsterdam."

My silence answers her.

"Are you going with my methodology or not? Why are you paying me?"

Why indeed? "I don't have an address or phone number for him."

"What about e-mail?"

"He said he'd send me his new e-mail address after he moved to Europe but he never did."

"You can figure it out. Call the American consulate. Maybe he's registered with them."

"People register when they travel in Pakistan. I've heard the only thing an American has to fear in Amsterdam is getting fat on beer or Indonesian food."

"Not true. I spent a month in Amsterdam. I had to register after I had spacecake and got my wallet stolen."

Spacecake? I can't imagine Bettina stoned. She's wacky enough without hunger giggles. What other therapist in New York has a nude painting of herself in the hallway?

"Try the Internet too. There can't be too many Greenblotzes in the U.S., let alone Holland. You're a documentary producer. I don't have to tell you how to find someone."

I want the woman I'm paying to get on my back off my back. "I'll think about it, Bettina."

When Dad abruptly moved to Bali six months after my college graduation, and one month after Mom agreed to a separation, Jake invited me to dinner.

Where was Siobhan, his new Irish girlfriend that went everywhere with him?

Before the waiter could take our order, Jake took a breath and said, "Don't say anything to your mother, but your father is a bisexual." Jake may not be hip, but he has two parents who were killed in gory circumstances, and he is not one to mince words. "I'm the only one in the family he's told. And that's about all he told me, so don't bother asking for details. He has also given me the temporary go-ahead to run things until the summer board meeting. He's giving you his vote."

I desperately wanted to talk to my father about this bold-type news. I had suspected there were men or a man involved with my parents' final breakup. Maybe we could finally clear the air. But Dad was either mortified or shackle free: he was simply not returning messages I'd left with some houseboy with a heavy Balinese accent. Indeed, it was my shaken mother who finally returned my call: "I'm not sure why he left. Your father got strange after you left home."

She had to know what Jake had revealed to me. "Strange?" I prodded, hoping she'd start elaborating on her own before I would have to say "Dad" and "bisexual" in the same sentence.

She burked the unmentionable issue with a laundry list of faults: "There are only so many years you can hear a man say *pit-sa* instead of pizza." And: "The nose pads on his eyeglasses are always broken." This was apparently as annoying to her as his obsession with his natural fibers, which got to the point where he wrote SOL GREENBLOTZ on his buckwheat pillows with a black laundry pen, so the maid would stop making up his (separate) bedroom with Mom's low-allergen polyester-fiber pillows.

"Is that all?" I asked with sheeplike docility, eyes screwed up. "Why the separate bedrooms?" For God's sake, don't make me say the obvious.

"I snore. If you ever talk to the idiot, tell him to get his rock collection out of my closet. I'm going to throw them out soon. They've been sitting there for twenty years."

Alone in my bedroom, still mulling over Bettina's suggestion about tracking Dad down, more memories stir inside my brain.

Dad still has never spoken to me about his marital problems or his typical day abroad. During my PBS research days, I talked out some of my theories about him to an empathetic gay co-worker who had once been married to a nurse and raised two children with her. He told me that Bali, where Dad was living at the time, made perfect sense to him as a hideaway for an American in sexual transition. "Maybe your father is seeking an Eden he can be free in," my co-worker suggested, passing me Cheez Doodles.

"Is Bali a gay Eden?" I said.

"Balinese men walk down the street hand in hand with their male friends, oblivious to Western disgust at the sight." If my old co-worker is right about my father's Eden-seeking, then Dad's recent move to Amsterdam would fit the pattern. I heard recently on NPR that the Netherlands was the first country to recognize same-sex marriages. And Dad moved before Canada followed suit.

Dad forgot to specify whether this Dutch *new luv* he's sharing a house with is male or female. Like I can't guess. I'm sure he'll fly in for a weekend soon with a boy-toy and an impressive bouquet of pink roses and give me a big kiss on the cheek, and ask, "How's my pumpkin?" He'll probably want me to join him for yet another Broadway musical, even though Dad spoiled Broadway musicals for me in 1982 when he treated me to a summer matinee of *Joseph and the Amazing Technicolor Dreamcoat*. Right around the time Joseph was telling his treacherous brothers about his dream of their stacks of wheat bowing down to his stack of wheat, Dad whispered to me that his friend Timmy who had come with us to the Royale Theater was a "very special friend." Then he tacked on that it was extremely important to him that I like Timmy even though he'd leaned right over me and my freshly cast broken arm to say to Dad, "Andrew Lloyd Webber is going to be huge. He's like Metro-Goldwyn-Mayer. He gives the public what they want."

Even at the age of eleven I understood enough to know that other fathers don't talk about their "very special friends" to their little girls. But I never said anything to my mother.

Whenever Dad gets back to New York next, and he's once again raving about the brave new musical he read about that we should really see, I'm not about to remind him of my preference for meaty Pulitzer-worthy dramas. Reminding my parents of anything important to me is opening a Pandora's box and liberating thirty-plus years of venom and anomie.

My day doorman, Verne, buzzes to tell me there's a deliveryman on his way up with flowers. Verne is always sending people up without checking if it's okay, but my annoyance quickly subsides. The bouquet of irises and hyacinths is huge and gorgeously blue.

The card reads: *Forgive me for my shocking lack of tact. Please let me see those Greenblotz blue eyes again.*

From that creep! I lay in bed again like a rabbit hiding in the brush until danger passes. But danger isn't passing. I can save Izzy Greenblotz's dream, but I'll have to sacrifice my self-respect.

I dial Steve's cell-phone number.

"Hel-lo."

I take a breath and speak, "It's Heather."

"Hey. You're talking to me?"

My voice is treacle sweet. "Yes. I want to apologize for kicking you out."

"You do? I figured you have my picture up on the wall as a dartboard. My timing is not so great, huh?"

"Well, no. But let's talk seder first. I think it's a great idea. My family would enjoy doing the broadcast, and frankly it would be good for business."

Steve pauses, perhaps considering how to read my directness. "I spoke to my boss. I told him I'd spoken to you and you were, uh, undecided. He's incredibly gung ho. He wanted me to approach you again, but I didn't know how. This is uncomfortable for me—I wanted to see you on a personal basis again too."

The flowers. The rhetoric. Yecch. But before I can tell this snake to slither out of my life, Steve says, "Do you want to play with the piano or the felt?"

"Excuse me?"

"Sorry, not you. I'm baby-sitting my niece." Several ivory keys are hit loudly and discordantly. "Now Charlotte's using more technique," he says after a laugh. "What a pro. The little girl breaks my heart she's so beautiful."

There's something about men talking to and about small children. Catnip. "How old is she?" I say despite my plan to get what I need from Steve and get off the phone.

"Fourteen months. My sister's ready to kill me because the baby's just got over a urinary tract infection, and I messed up, big-time."

"What did you do?"

"The doctor attached a teeny pee bag to skin under her diaper for a sample. But Charlotte didn't pee when Mommy was home, so I was supposed to remove the bag when it was full and keep it fresh. I thought my sister meant keep it fresh in the freezer, not the fridge."

"Yikes. Be careful not to eat the yellow Popsicle."

"You mean the peesicle."

I laugh loudly—that *was* funny—and Steve's voice brightens even more. "So when can we meet to discuss all this? How about in two hours?"

"Okay," I say, interested again, defeated.

As I sit waiting near the dog run in Tompkins Square Park for Steve, the sight of him launches a battle between my brain and my libido. I don't think anyone this attractive has ever given me the time of day.

He extends a hand and bends his knee in front of his bench. "Forgiveness, milady."

"Let's talk seder first, and then I'll bust your chops."

Steve laughs and rises. He sits extremely close to me on the bench. "Thanks for coming downtown. So do you want to go over what will happen at a live feed?"

"Yes. I've only ever taped video for my films."

Two pugs hump vigorously behind the bars of the dog park. A bear-size black Newfoundland, the dog park's gentle giant, is roused out of his sleep to chase the female pup.

"We'd keep it small and intimate," Steve says after the ensuing melee between the respective dog owners settles down. "There'll be a remote truck parked outside your apartment—"

"We'd do it at my cousin's house in West Orange."

"That's fine. Anyhow, as I was saying, inside the room it will feel less intrusive. I'll get Jared as the DP. You liked Jared, right?"

"Yes," I say.

"The beauty of Jared is that he understands lighting as well as the lens. There's nothing he can't do. Tonia told me he developed this crazy method when he couldn't change the lighting in a room. He floated a teeny battery-powered light over the interviewer's head with helium balloons."

"Isn't that a fire danger?"

"It worked, what can I say? He's insane, but he's creative."

I laugh a little. "I wished everything floated in helium, imagine books on a string. You could really get use out of it."

"I love the way your mind works," Steve says with a large white smile.

Steve's as smooth as Muhammad Ali during his finest hour. He always knows the exact thing to say to keep himself in the ring.

"We'll have Tonia there. She's a great girl."

I study his face. Did he have a fling with Tonia? Steve's a pro. Nothing revealed.

"When this seder is over, how are we going to celebrate?"

"Any suggestions?" I say.

"Have you ever been ballooning?"

"No."

"With all this helium talk, I'm thinking we could pack a champagne lunch and go ballooning."

"That sounds unusual," I say, even though my mind says to run the other way.

"So," he picks up. "Back to the seder. Can you give me the names of who's going to be there, and how they are related to you?"

"Let's start with my father's mother, Grandma Gertie. She's the one who runs our little store."

"She's your grandmother? I thought you said during the tour that she died a while back. Is this your mother's mother?"

I panic. "Did I say grandmother? I meant that she's like a grandmother. She was my father's mother's sister."

After more initial planning, we leave on patched terms. He plants a kiss on my lips before he rushes off to his shoot of East Village coffeehouses.

★ ★ ★

A Google search gets me to Telefoongids, the Dutch White Pages, in a twenty-first-century second, but I have no such luck with Dad's Telefoonnummer. Plenty of Ganesvoort and Groesbeck but no Greenblotz. I try other search engines, looking for any correspondence he might have written in newsgroups, but come up cold.

Then, taking Bettina's suggestion, I call the American consulate general in Amsterdam. As I suspected, Dad isn't registered.

Jake calls. "I got my intern, Dimple, to buy me *Judaism for Dummies*."

"Oh, please. That's going to save us?"

"They're really good, those *Dummies* books. That's how I learned Excel. Remember how condescending you were when you tried to teach me?"

"I wasn't condescending. Everything was a joke to you. You wouldn't buckle down and listen."

"Anyhow, I've got the whole seder memorized. Go ahead—test me."

"I remember there's something bitter we serve, right? Horseradish or beets or something like that."

"Yup. That's the *maror*. To remind us of the pain of our ancestors even as we have a big meal. You can grate it yourself, but with all we have to do, a jar of Silver's horseradish is fine for the *maror*. It's balanced with *haroset*—the sweet stuff. Siobhan found a great recipe for *haroset*—with walnuts, prunes and apricots. She's got the wine for the kiddush and the menu planned already for the main meal. We're having— wait, I wrote it down for you—chopped liver and sliced tomato, hot borscht, smothered chicken, piquant carrots, a mixed-vegetable salad and lemon pie."

"Isn't the pie against the Passover rules?"

"Not if it firms through refrigeration, and not rising."

"I'm impressed."

"All we needed to get our engines going was *Judaism for Dummies*. I ordered you your own copy."

I laugh. "Are you getting a commission from the *Dummies* publisher?"

"That's a good idea. Maybe we even make some immediate money off our airtime with Jewish-product placement."

"It would defeat the purpose of the whole thing. We want to look like we know what the hell we're talking about. Now listen, don't forget to tell Siobhan she's a lifesaver for pulling that menu together."

"Will do. I was going to get it catered but Siobhan wants to learn the meaning of the seder by cooking it."

"The Ghost of Grandpa Reuben must have gotten to your Irish lass in her sleep."

"Boo, *schmooe*, you're not a Jew!" Jakes chants in a very good and slightly scary impersonation of our raspy grandfather.

"Instead of borscht, why don't you have Siobhan serve matzo ball soup? We want to push the matzo meal. I've heard customers tell me during the factory tours that matzo balls never fail if made in batches of twenty-six. Can't imagine why, but maybe that would help."

"I'm writing that down because matzo ball soup is an excellent idea. So it's coming together, huh? You'll do fine. You don't need your dad."

"My therapist thinks I should go to Amsterdam and track him down," I confess. "She thinks it would calm me down to drag him back and have him there."

"Worth a try. I could use your help over there anyhow. Jan Quacken from Albert Vroom Supermarkets recently dropped his entire order. He was our biggest buyer in the Netherlands, and now he's not returning faxes."

"Quacken's really his name? Poor guy."

"Uh, hello, your name is Greenblotz!" We both snort, and Jake adds, "If you want to go, I'll share the cost."

"Jake, I have the money."

"I guess you got your dividend check."

"Yes, thanks."

"If you want those checks to keep coming, we have to go through with this Food Channel thing."

"I'll go for a weekend if you can handle the high season by yourself—"

"If getting your dad here will calm you down, I'm all for it."

"First I have to find him. I've had no luck so far."

When I get off the phone with Jake, I take a break from the dad search and check my e-mail. I have two, one from Vondra who, unsolicited, asked Mahmoud if he has any contacts for me in Amsterdam. He's given her the number of Prince Willem-Alexander and Princess Maxima, whose wedding he attended as the official representative of Egypt. Prince Willem-Alexander as in the crown prince of the Netherlands.

Honey, I know you have a short trip, but Mahmoud thought maybe you can scoot over to The Hague—V

Yeah, like I'm going to follow that one through: "Uh, hello, is this the Crown Prince? You don't know me, but a mutual friend of ours told me to call..."

Vondra's enthrallment with Mahmoud's power is getting on my nerves. It's official. There's also a creepy e-mail from a bachelor in New York who checked out my America Online profile—the one I thought I'd deleted a month ago when I started getting bombarded with creepy e-mail from a bachelor in Alaska.

Dear HeatherG23: I see you live in New York City too and that you enjoy books and good television. I think you'd be a good match for me. I'm 38 + handsome. I collect old Zenith televisions and I'm looking for a steady. ZENITHGUY

I compose the nicest possible *Fuck Off* I can think of, one that would leave this weirdo's ego intact:

Dear ZENITHGUY. I am 87. Thank you for your interest. You sound like a very kind young fellow. It really made my day. HeatherG23.

I start checking on flights to Amsterdam and open my file cabinet to make sure my passport is current. It is; there are six more months before I need to reapply.

My expired passports are also in that drawer, in the Important-Paper File, and I can't resist checking out my teen self, a mousy girl in an argyle sweater and a ponytail. My old yearbooks are there too, and I pull the 1988 yearbook from Dalton and turn to my page. In this picture my hair is shoulder-length and notably flat even without a nineties flatiron. (No bad perm for me—I religiously performed the eighties grooming step of a crème rinse.) My smile is decidedly forced. I'm wearing the same brown argyle sweater in the Dalton picture as in my passport. I wasn't a geek, or particularly unpopular. Just there, under the radar. I had a few close friends who were equally low-key, the kind the popular kids nod to and occasionally invite to a party. My shopping addiction started later, when my parents finally broke up for good. My mother's shopping got out of control around the same time. Sometimes I'd see bags from Madison Avenue boutiques near her bed, untouched for over a month. Back in high school though, most of my shirts and pants and dresses were still different shades of tan. I can fake my well-being better these days. It's amazing what a bright red outfit can do for your image.

We took two trips my senior year of high school, unusual for the Sol Greenblotzes. The first was down to Mom's parents' ritzy house in Miami—I'm still not sure where my mother's parents got their money from. This visit was a big, big deal. The decades-old rift between Mom and her parents began when they sat her down at the age of twelve and told her that there was something she should know. She thought she was about to hear she was adopted, but the truth was even more upsetting: They had never wanted children. She was a mistake. Not expecting she could conceive at forty-six, Mom's mother (my grandma Bertha) carried five months before realizing she was pregnant not menopausal. Mom quickly confided this whole story to me in the rented Cadillac while Dad was in a 7-Eleven paying for gas. "Such cold demeanors!" (Um, like guess who else? I thought.) She'd hardly seen them since college, but they were both old and sickly now, and she wanted to make amends with them before they died. For a good chunk of their lives, Mom's parents were German-Jewish Gurdjieffians, adherents of a philosophy verging on cult. From the beginning of his rise, Gurdjieff, who I have since read up on, had many rich and famous disciples including *Mary Poppins* author P.L. Travers. Way after Gurdjieff's death, his ideas caught on among progressive rockers Robert Fripp, Kate Bush and Peter Gabriel. According to his worshiping biographer, he never tarried over words and believed cold hard facts—like telling your children the most awful truths—were good for the soul.

No wonder Mary Poppins just up and left when she was

done with her charges, Jane and Michael Banks. Her creator was a hard-ass.

"I told her a little more about my upbringing, Sol," Mom said when Dad was back from the 7-Eleven. "About Gurdjieff and the speech they gave me 'for my own good.'"

Dad took over the conversation for the remainder of the car ride to my grandparents' house. "This is who they followed? I think Gurdjieff was evil," he said, checking his road map. "What a master manipulator. I read he had one of his followers build a wall and then tear it down just because he could make him do that."

"Gurdjieff sounds awful," I said to both of them. "Heartless."

"Now you know what awaits you on this visit," Mom said with a sigh.

I'd met my Grandma Bertha only twice before, when I was a week old, and when she and my grandfather came to a political convention in New York around my tenth birthday.

Grandma Bertha pecked my mother on the cheek, but for me and my father she could only muster handshakes. Her face was quite wrinkled, with indentations at her cheeks— she looked like a giant peanut. She also had no saliva, so she continually sipped a Fanta.

Grandpa Irving looked like Confucius with a Semitic nose. His gray beard was so long and ragged that the tip of it singed when he was lighting a smuggled Cuban cigar, creating the awful odor of burnt hair.

There was a stiff conversation between my grandmother and Mom about some imported Israeli cabinets that were falling apart. Grandma Bertha blamed the cheap Israeli glue and in doing so sounded just like Mom about to forcibly return a silk blouse with a snag.

My grandfather said to my father, "I was thinking about the invention of butter today."

"Butter?" Dad said politely.

"Who first invented butter?" Grandpa Irving said.

Dad quickly glanced at Mom. "It must have been a happy accident."

"What accident takes two days, Sol? Put some milk in a bucket. Take a plunger and go up and down for two days. Then you have butter?"

Dad nodded politely. Mom looked at Grandma Bertha like a five-year-old running from the playground with a fresh gravel rash, waiting for her mother to hug her and stroke her and call her Lamb. I was startled to see my mother so raw and needy. I kept waiting for some emotion to leak out of my grandparents. "We missed you, Jocelyn." Or, "It is thrilling to meet up again with our only grandchild."

But Grandma Bertha just sipped more Fanta.

We had planned on staying the entire afternoon, but there was an unrehearsed change of plans. Tight-lipped, Mom stood up and bid a quick goodbye to her parents. Grandma Bertha gave us polite kisses on our foreheads, and Grandpa Irving shook my father's hand, and patted me and Mom on the back before the door closed behind us.

My father had happily agreed to go to what was supposed to be the Kaufman Family Denouement. He thought it would be good for his wife and also a chance for the three of us to later see the Everglades. For more than an hour we drove along in silence in the Caddie until my mother faked a laugh and said, "Glad that's over." We sailed through Alligator Alley, an expressway that cuts through the Everglades reserve. Three pelicans whooshed down the highway for a crustacean lunch. Dad stopped the car by an official Everglades learning center.

A park ranger paced the packed mini-auditorium like a clown taking a walkabout in the Big Top, pausing briefly for his stopact: "The barred owl's two-colored plumage makes it appear like he's got bars of color."

Dad took enthusiastic notes. He had recently attended a lecture in which the travel memoirist and fiction writer Paul Theroux advised, "You can predict the future in your writing. Just write down everything you hear exactly. I don't know why this works, but it just does."

Mom read a mystery she'd bought at the airport; she hid it behind an array of environmental newsletters that Dad had shoved in our hands as we'd walked through the door. I caught my mother's eye; she smiled and moved her head back and forth like an owl's. I couldn't help a snicker.

"Determined as a screwdriver to have a bad time, both of you," Dad said crisply when we were back in the Caddie. "That's the last time I try and seek out something new to do with you. You would think after seeing your parents, Jocelyn, you would have learned how important it is to keep this an active family unit."

Using my grandparents as ammunition was a huge miscalculation. Mom was mute until we returned to New York.

I thought we'd never go away together again. But we did. We had that last hurrah at the end of the very same year, my senior year of high school. First the Russian Tea Room, and then a trip to Australia. Money wasn't an issue for these lavish graduation gifts. Interaction was.

Our optimistic itinerary was three cities north to south. First the gateway to the Barrier Reef, Cairns, then Sydney and then Melbourne. My mother wasn't snorkeling then, and somehow when I was out with my newly graduated friends it got shortened to the latter two. Mom wanted to skip the Great Barrier Reef and head straight for big-city action.

On our second day Down Under, Dad went solo to a matinee at the Sydney Opera House. Mom and I shopped The Rocks, an urban mall in a neighborhood paved with pick and shovel by the first convicts sent over from England.

The next night, after another speech by Dad urging us to be more of a unit, the three of us saw a revival of *South Pacific.* Dad sat next to a swishy theater historian who delighted him during the intermission with tidbits about the original production in 1949. He went on and on about Mary Martin, about how when she played Ensign Nellie Forbush, she washed her hair onstage every night during "I'm Gonna Wash That Man Right Outta My Hair," and about when Martin washed her hair so much that she had to cut it short and wear it tightly curled with poofy sides and bangs. "That was the start of the poodle cut," the historian said. "The hairstyle later mistakenly became a trend attributed to Lucille Ball."

Dad, still on his Paul Theroux kick, wrote everything down in the bulging notebook he had labeled *THE IDEA CATCHER.*

"Here's something dishy to write down," his new friend said as he leaned in and touched Dad on the arm. "Ethel Merman was demoralized by Martin's success and told everyone around her after a *South Pacific* performance how uncouth it was for an actress to shampoo onstage."

"*Ethel Merman* was threatened?" Dad marveled.

Mom was less than impressed, not only with this man's expertise, but also with her husband's never-ending jottings. There was some pretty nasty bickering that night back at our suite in the Regent Hotel.

"You talked to him with a shine in your eye and corked me if I asked you the littlest question."

"Jocelyn, don't be moronic. He was a nice guy, that's all."

"Just because I'm not gaga about opera and theater doesn't make me moronic. Most *normal* people share my views. Give me a drama any day. It's less—embarrassing."

"I don't butt in when you're talking about hemlines with your girlfriends, so if you don't cork me when I'm talking to people who share *my* interests, we'll get on fine."

"Cork you? That's my line! Now you're quoting your moronic wife to your moronic wife."

On the plane to Melbourne, Mom took the open seat in front of us. Dad seemingly forgot I was eighteen not eight, and read me the most unusual Australian-animal names from his guidebook. He especially loved the sound of moon jellyfish and sea walnuts.

From Melbourne we drove in near silence to Philip Island, three hours away and a token gesture of compensation from Mom to Dad for skipping the reef. Dad had read in a guidebook that there was close viewing of koalas to be had, and also a stand set up on the beach for the Penguin Parade, a daily spectacle of thousands of penguins returning to land at dusk.

After five-star hotels, Mom was disappointed by the only accommodation available, a low-key guest house that had a roach or two and framed jigsaw puzzles of tall ships and flowers in our room. But Dad, who was now reading Theroux's *The Great Railway Bazaar* on his downtime, was pleased to receive a kiss of kismet to color our heavily planned-out trip.

"It's fine, Jocelyn. There's nothing wrong with this. We have a beach view and beds. This isn't Paris."

"This is ridiculous," Mom hissed. "I wouldn't have come if I had known it would be like this. You could have asked the travel agent if there was more than a shanty on this hellhole. We're Jews. We ask."

"You were born a snob and you'll die a snob."

The next day got off on an equally bad foot.

Mom and I took an early-morning walk on the beach to catch the sunrise and sand down our calluses. The gift stores weren't open. Mom had left her sun visor in Melbourne and the only replacement she could find at 8:00 a.m. was a novelty octopus hat she borrowed from the owner of our guest house.

As we walked toward a good spot on the sand, Mom sneered at my beloved ripped jeans, and declared she'd "take me shopping back in New York."

I scowled at her and laid out my towel. There was quite an eyeful on the beach: gorgeous half-naked Aussie men everywhere, baking in the sun like adobe bricks. I reached into my Le Sportsac for my baby oil. Who the hell replaced it with sunblock?

"You shouldn't use oil." Mom said from her towel. "You'll thank me in twenty years when you're not a raisin."

"I live in Manhattan. For one day I can get some color."

Mom pushed one of her felt tentacles away from her face. "Everything I say doesn't need a smart answer. Why do you write us off as friends? We just want to help."

That night at the Penguin Parade stands, Mom was hunched against the cold in her rich citified clothes, and had a sinus attack from the wet and impossible night. But when the tiny alpha penguin came ashore to signal to his kin that it was okay to head to the beach, and then twos and threes and fours and fives of penguins waddled to their nests, falling over but picking themselves up again through sheer determination, everyone oohed—even teenage surly me, even Jocelyn Greenblotz. That night mysteriously transformed into the best I ever remember. We ate in a locals' pub, and were joined at dinner by a chatty fisherman who had caught a cow skull in his shrimp net. Back in our one-star room, we still yakked away about the characters we'd seen at the pub until a late hour. Dad decided we should take a midnight swim in the rain. Mom and I agreed.

We raced out in the ocean waves, hand in hand, a happy threesome.

I felt so damn normal.

I forgot about the rumors that my dad liked to do more than just hang out with other men.

I forgot my mother was more aloof than anyone else's I knew.

I swam back, dug my feet in the wet sand at the edge of the water and smiled at the barely visible moon and the light raindrops falling on my head, diamonds.

Seven

The Hall of Ocean Life

Roswell Birch, a lanky, blond, and pimply seventeen-year-old, arrives on Friday morning at the offices of Two Dames Productions looking as if he just dragged himself out of a hard-core mosh pit. I take his German army jacket (which stinks of just-smoked weed) to hang on the coatrack. His office attire is a vintage, or more probably reissued, Clash concert T-shirt, and black jeans so holey as to border on offensive.

After brief niceties, Roswell fills out some paperwork then savors Vondra's ass when she bends over to a bottom drawer to show him the filing system.

Vondra gives him the classic bullshit speech every intern on earth has had to endure: "Filing is an excellent way to get a basic understanding of what we do. That's how I started at PBS. I read everything before it was put away. Once I was an invaluable assistant to my boss, he gave me meatier projects until I was a bona fide producer."

The shrewd kids know they are being vetted and chirp, "Yes, I'm going to work hard."

But Roswell says, "That's fine for a day or two, but I have a film idea I was hoping to develop while I'm on this internship."

"Maybe you should get to know the ropes first," I say from my desk.

"But you're gonna want to do this. It's a documentary about the history of the documentary. I'm going to ask Albert Maysles to narrate. Do you know who Albert Maysles is?"

I highly doubt that the surviving Maysles brother, a god-father of cinema verité, would jump to narrate a film by a seventeen-year-old pothead. "That's an interesting concept," I manage to say.

"Isn't it though?" he says with a self-satisfied nod. "My dad says my grandfather knows him. He helped him get the film about Dylan made."

"Maybe you mean the one about The Rolling Stones. *Don't Look Back* was the Dylan one. D.A. Pennebaker directed that."

"I'm sure Dad said it was Dylan."

I sneak an exasperated look at Vondra. "Do you want to learn mail merge? I'm the high priestess of Word around here. Although Vondra's got me converting to the church of Excel."

During the next hour or so, getting Roswell to merge or file anything right is about as easy as terraforming Mars.

Roswell eats from a large plastic bag full of cherry plums he produced from a bicycle-messenger bag graffitied with his versions of hardcore and punk–band logos. After each plum, he spits the pit into our wastebasket.

I gather what's needed for a just slightly more exciting task: the latest trade magazines, rubber glue and scissors for our clip book. "Cut and paste down any clips that mention our films or our film subjects." I plop it all down on the intern table.

Roswell eyes the lot with disdain. "Uh, Vondra, could I make a quick phone call?"

"I'm Heather. And of course you can if you keep it quick—"

"I'm with ya." He nods vehemently.

It's hard not to listen. The kid is particularly animated with his phone pal.

"Dude, you'd do Ms. Lambert? No way! She's full of surgery. She's like Pruneface in *Batman.*"

Another five minutes later, after a searing look from the real Vondra, Roswell hangs up and asks, "Could I ask you a huge favor, Heather?"

"Maybe."

"Dude, this is so sad. The government thinks my best friend Abdullah's a terrorist. He fits their profile."

"I doubt that if he's in an American high school."

"Trust me. He lives with his aunt. His parents live in Saudi Arabia, but he's such a math god that his parents wanted him to go to Stuyvesant because his cousin went to school there. He graduated in December, 'cause he's such a brain. But now he's in trouble because his visa ran out."

"So what's the favor?"

"You've got to write a letter pretending he's interning for you a few months. He was going to go to the University of Riyadh but now he wants to apply to Duke and Columbia. If he gets in to either school, the student visa should hold him."

"Roswell, I don't know Abdullah." I sigh. I'm really missing last year's intern. Darius was a razor-sharp, enthusiastic NYU film major with Rasta braids pulled straight up with a rubber band, so that his head at first glance looked like a pineapple.

"Dude, he's my friend. He's not a terrorist. He dates Jews at Stuyvesant. Would a terrorist get a blow job from a chick named Dimple Goldstein?"

"Dimple Goldstein?" says Vondra from her desk.

I make a mental note to share this choice gossip with Jake.

"That's her name, dude. Her dad is some comedian with Comedy Central. No shit. Her brother is on the Ultimate Frisbee team with me. Flicker Goldstein."

"Roswell, why don't you ask Vondra to write that letter? She's the Stuyvesant alumna." I laugh to myself as Vondra looks at me from her desk with a crinkled forehead.

"But, dude, you're the Jew here."

"Excuse me?" I gasp.

"I think a letter from a Jew with an Emmy is going to carry more weight."

"I really don't think it's my place to write that letter. I'm sure his principal will help him out."

Roswell shakes his head and says, "I feel so bad for you."

"Why?"

"It's not for me to say."

Call me an idiot, but I had to know what this punky plum chomper had to say about me. "No, it's fine. I really want to hear this."

"Your bitterness. It's your aura."

Yes, I asked for it, but that stung.

Roswell's on a roll now: "You must hate your life, right?"

"Now, why would you say a thing like that?" Vondra asks as she crosses her well-toned arms.

"I love my life, man. I have good friends, and my folks totally love me. I know your type. You're just like my old girlfriend."

"Really? How's that?" I'm quite rattled, but the filmmaker in me yearns for a camera in hand. *This* should be good.

"Her coldness. Her father abandoned her when she was ten. Did your parents desert you or something?"

I summon up a dignified and pious look.

"Heather, don't answer," Vondra says. "That's plenty enough, Roswell."

"I'm well adjusted because my parents are beyond cool. When I was a baby, they rushed me to hospital after I ate a sponge. There was nothing they could do. So they waited there nine hours until I shit it out. That's, like, a legendary story in my family."

"You shit sponge?" I say shakily.

"Could I talk to you in the hall?" Vondra says to me.

"I didn't mean to offend you. I'm just a straight-talking guy. That's what my friends like about me."

"Excuse me," I say.

Roswell removes a browned banana from his messenger bag. "Sure."

Vondra closes the door and motions me closer to the bathroom we share with other businesses on our floor. "Asshole! No one should talk to you like that."

"I did ask him. And he was spot on about my family. Let's let him finish the morning out."

When Roswell takes his bathroom break, Vondra dials Jacinta at the City as School to demand a stop to this.

"Busy," she whispers. "I'll try later."

Vondra calls Jacinta all morning and early afternoon to no avail. She passes me a note on a pink Post-it: *Maybe her line is off the hook.*

At a quarter to three, Roswell springs erect, his shoulders braced as if he was reborn. "So, I'll see you girls on Monday."

Before we can answer, he leaves for the day.

"Unthinkable," Vondra says as the phone rings. She answers and says Uh-huh a lot. When she hangs up, she hits me with troubling news: "Mark Lander just got a feature in Paris. We need a new DP to shoot the next *Grand Ladies* segment."

"That's two days away."

"You're telling me. I'll call Tom to see if he could fill in."

"Tom? God, he's such a perfectionist on a shoot. We'll spend two hours setting up for fifteen minutes."

"Who else could we call?"

"Let me see if I have someone's number on me." I fish out the *Jared S.* business card in the depths of my Kate Spade purse. I stare at it for a moment. Should I do this?

"Who's the someone?"

"A cameraman I met during the Food Channel shoot. A guy named Jared."

"Can he do lights too? After the last shoot we have no budget for a gaffer and we're screwed if the museum is too dark."

"I could just pay for the extra help." Why hold back? She knows now that I'm loaded.

"No. This is a fifty-fifty business. Let's proceed as usual."

"Well, I think he knows lights. If I get him, I'll ask. He seemed capable. My only worry is that he asked a question and told a joke while the producer was interviewing me—"

"Well, tell him *no* questions. We're the producers. It's such a short shoot. I'm sure he'll do. Can you call him now?"

I'm having second thoughts. "On a Friday night?"

"Yes. We need him Sunday morning."

I dial the number on his card. After four rings the answering machine picks up: *This is Jared. I'm not able to come to the phone now, but if this is about work I'll be able to get back to you after Saturday night.*

"Hey, Jared. This is Heather Greenblotz from the matzo

factory, although I'm calling with my documentary cap on now. Are you free for a shoot Sunday morning? Our regular cameraman got a big job in Paris. You can call our office..."

"Machine?" Vondra says in a disappointed voice.

"I don't think he'll get back to us until Saturday. His machine says he's tied up."

"No pager?"

I pout. "No."

"We're up shit's creek if we don't find anyone."

"I can shoot," I say.

"If we want our film on a Heather diagonal."

"My eye isn't that bad."

"Not if you're filming a Van Gogh painting—"

It takes a second to think of that famous picture of Van Gogh's room on a slant. A delayed smile. "Good joke, bitch."

"Thank you very much."

"At least I can shoot a camera," I rally. "You just give orders."

This time Vondra laughs with her hand straight up in a Black Panther fist. With her other hand she flips through her Rolodex for other cameraman possibilities.

"Let's give it to Sunday morning," Vondra says to me by phone on Saturday night. "If we have to cancel we have to cancel."

"Fine."

"How're the seder plans going?"

"Well, so far all I've got is my cousin Jake, of course, and my cousin Greg from Florida, but he's a flake—"

"How about your father?"

"No luck. I might go have to Amsterdam next weekend

and look for him. My therapist thinks I should pretend he's a documentary subject."

"I could have saved you a session. Remember at PBS how you got the Brooklyn-born oboist in the Mexico City Symphony Orchestra on the phone in five minutes?'

"His name was Murray Bernstein. It wasn't that hard to find him."

"You'll track your father down if you get in the docu-zone."

"You think?"

"You'll have to pick up *stroopwafels* for me of course—"

"What's that? A clog?"

"That's the cookie that helped me gain ten pounds during my year abroad."

"Yeah and you were what, a size two then?" I stick my tongue out at her in disgust. "I forgot you went to school in Amsterdam."

"No, in Leiden. Where Rembrandt studied."

"So, tell me, world traveler, how long is the flight to Amsterdam?"

"One hour more than London. Six hours. I love Amsterdam. I was there every weekend when I was in Leiden. Great Indonesian food."

"I've heard that."

"What will really get you going is the shopping. There are cool specialty stores all over. I'm talking microspecialty, like a button store on Wolvenstraat you have to check out. I bought some silver ladybug buttons there I sewed on a summer shirt, and also some reindeer buttons for the Christmas sweater my sister was knitting for my niece."

"Sounds like it's worth a look."

"And oh, there's a store just for toothbrushes."

"Great, if I don't get to my dad, I'll bring home a designer toothbrush."

Vondra signs off from our America Online account and looks up.

"Did I tell you I'm going to invite Mahmoud?"

"Where?" I ask absentmindedly.

"To the seder," Vondra says.

"To the seder?" She's got my full attention now. "Um—"

"Is that a problem? I thought you needed more people."

"Vondra. That's not a great idea."

"Why? You're worried that he's Arabic, am I right? I told you, he's very open-minded. He doesn't hate Jews. He's curious about them."

"Vondra. He's *Egyptian*. You can't have an *Egyptian* at a seder. From what I remember, the whole seder is about how God disses the Egyptians so the Jews can get out of their clutches."

"You're nuts. It's ancient history. I'm sure he'll love it."

For a woman with incredible smarts—she knows the capital of every country and still remembers where the anus of a starfish is from her biology classes—Vondra can on the odd occasion be as naive as a fresh-off-the-bus Midwesterner smiling at a pimp in the Greyhound bus terminal.

I quickly strategize. If Mahmoud were asked, and declined himself, I'd be spared any animosity. I have enough problems without having Vondra angry with me. Mahmoud's a public figure. An Arab public figure to boot: official spokesman for the Egyptian consulate. With all the unrest in the Middle East, the last place he'll want to be seen on TV is at an American *seder*. To the wrong people, an unseemly choice. He could get assassinated by, take your pick, a) some crazy schmuck from al-Qaeda; b) some crazy schmuck from the Jewish Defense League.

I'm confident in my plan. "Okay, so why don't you ask him?"

★ ★ ★

Saturday night I'm alone on my couch watching ten-year-old cable repeats of *America's Funniest Home Videos*. During a commercial break, I drop the contents of my cooked frozen dinner in the cutlery drawer, and extract everything I can out of the drawer, plucking the last penne pasta off a fork tine, and put the salvaged meal back in the microwave and then drop the tray *again*. I am so determined not to be on the losing end of a battle between a Lean Cuisine box and me that I replate my food off the floor with the floor-tile and culinary-drawer grime and crunch and crap mixed into the cream sauce and head back for the living room.

The phone rings. I pull a wet piece of dust out of my mouth, and start without a pause: "No luck, Vondra. Haven't heard from Jared. I called Mark Lander to see if he could send anyone our way before he left for France but his two-year-old was screaming like a banshee because she snuck a gob of wasabi out of his take-out sushi tray."

"It's Jared, Heather."

"Oh, hi!" I lurch forward for the remote to mute the four nominees who have a shot for the grand prize $100,000 funniest video. Too late: "Kitty Pileup!" booms the announcer.

"So tell me about the shoot. I have Sunday free."

"Terrific. I hear you do lighting, too."

"Who told you that?"

"Steve," I say.

"Yes. I was a gaffer for two years before I got into camera work. So, what are we filming?"

"It's an HBO documentary about sex."

"Let me chew on that for a minute," Jared says dryly. "Uh, okay."

"Don't get too excited. The woman who's talking about sex is a grandmother of three."

"That still sounds more exciting than my typical *Secrets of a Super Soufflé* segment."

"Whatever gets you to say yes. I can't believe you're available. Damn, that's great. From your message, I thought you might be away on a shoot this weekend."

"No, but I just had other plans Friday and earlier today."

"Well, the pay is okay considering it's a tiny shoot. We should be there no longer than an hour, and it's two hundred bucks for the segment."

"That's pretty fair."

"We don't have a Betacam, but we do have an XL–2."

"Bingo. That's the one I use on my downtime."

"There's a tiny scratch on the viewfinder but it doesn't affect the picture."

"I'll bring mine so you don't have to bother getting it checked."

"You're my hero, Jared."

"You have enough DV tapes?"

"Plenty."

"Where should I meet you?"

"We'll meet you at the American Museum of Natural History in the Hall of Human Biology and Evolution, 9:30 a.m. The woman we have scheduled coined the term *Elastic Marriage* and there are a couple of threesomes in the caveman dioramas."

"Very clever."

"Vondra's idea."

"How did you finagle the museum into letting you film? Steve wanted to use the Hall of Ocean Life for a fried-fish segment, but they told him no way very emphatically."

"That section just reopened. Maybe they weren't ready."

"He knew one of the women on the design team who was going to let him in for a preview. Dated her, I think."

That figures. "Really?" I ask as neutrally as possible.

"All the same, her boss knocked the idea back."

"What can I say? I'm better on the phone than on the camera." I'm pleased I outgunned Steve in one area. "They're fine with it as long as we have the filming over by mid-morning so it won't interfere with the afternoon rush."

"Can't wait."

The Hall of Human Biology and Evolution is on the ground floor of the American Museum of Natural History, just past the booth where volunteers give visitors the little metal admission buttons to stick on their shirts. Vondra wants to leave me with the equipment and the cavemen while she gets a sip of water from the fountain around the corner.

"Why are your lips purple?" I ask.

"Grape Pixie Stix. Mahmoud and I are giving up smoking, and I need something to get me through the day. They may not be good for your teeth but they're very low in fat."

"You like him enough to quit smoking? That's incredible."

"I like him enough to father my children. I'm on cloud nine."

I shake my head in amusement. "Go get your water."

Jared taps me on the shoulder, and I'm surprised by how happy I am to see him.

"Thanks for stepping in," I say. He'd be so, so cute if he just shaved that beard.

"My pleasure." Jared unzips his black nylon jacket. As he unhinges his hard camera case, Roswell arrives. We haven't had the heart to fire him yet, and we can't get perky Jacinta on the phone to do it for us.

"Hey," our would-be Scorsese says with a big yawn.

"Roswell, this is Jared, our cameraman for the day."

"Hey," Jared says.

Roswell removes a tiny spiral notebook with Japanese Anime artwork on the cover from his military jacket. "That's a cool-looking camera. What is it?"

"Canon XL–2. Nifty little thing, much easier to maneuver than a Beta camera, which is what they use on the networks. But it's broadcast quality."

"How much does that cost?"

"That's the real beauty of it. About $3,500. Thousands of dollars cheaper than a Beta camera. They call this a prosumer model because it straddles the professional and amateur markets."

Roswell writes down some notes in his spiral book. "Where do you buy it from?"

"I picked it up from B & H."

"What's that?"

Jared smiles. "B & H? A New York institution. It should have its own documentary—picture a hundred ultraorthodox Jews in waist-length nineteenth-century black coats selling state-of-the-art electronics."

"Cool. What kind of light is that?" Roswell continues to write down every item of equipment Jared says in his notebook. Maybe he is interested in what we do, after all.

"Heather, do I have time to make a quick phone call?"

Roswell shirking set-up responsibilities? Shocker. Our interviewee, Rina O'Riley, is not here yet. I'm never comfortable being a ballbreaker. "A quick one, Roswell. On and off."

"Gotcha!" Roswell presses a stored number in his cell phone. "Listen, Dad, you have a pen? Great, for my Albert Maysles film, I'm going to need these things at home. You can get them ordered from this kosher camera store—"

"He's seventeen," I explain to Jared. "Our intern."

"Gotcha, dude," Jared says.

After Roswell is finished placing his order with his father, he takes a whiff of the immediate vicinity. "You guys smell that stink?"

"No," I say.

Roswell wrinkles his nose. "It's like the fucking ocean around here."

Jared stiffens, and smells his open jacket. "Is this it? We did a calamari shoot Wednesday. I thought I got the squid smell out."

"Yo, you didn't," Roswell says with another nose wrinkle.

Jared's face is grave. "That awful?"

Now that it's been brought to my attention; it *is* rather pongy in the immediate vicinity. "It's not that bad," I assure him as the stench vines up my nostrils and my fingers fiddle with the button on my blouse. "But maybe you should keep the jacket in the corner if you're going to be self-conscious about it."

"Burn it, dude," Roswell says.

Turning to Roswell, I say, "I see Vondra coming in with Rina O'Riley. Could you go over and see if there's anything Vondra needs you to do?"

When Roswell walks far enough away, I whisper, "He's also passive-aggressive. But we don't have the heart to let him go. He won't graduate if we let him go. No other suckers will sign him up."

Jared nods. As he unpacks his microphones, Vondra escorts Rina O'Riley to our little area. Rina is an attractive woman in her seventies who still clings to the pink headband and girlie Izod Lacoste clothes of a preppie youth. Around her neck is a huge white orthopedic neck brace. Is she keeping that thing on when she goes on camera?

"This is Heather," Vondra says. "She's my business partner and she'll be doing the questioning today."

"Nice to meet you," says Rina. "Gorgeous sweater. Brings out your gorgeous blue eyes."

"Thank you."

"Greenblotz Blue," Jared says, straight-faced.

"Anything special I need to know?"

"Just remember to rephrase my questions. It's easier for editing. If I say, 'What's your name?' you should say, 'My name is Rina' rather than 'Rina.' You've probably done this before."

"Oh yes. I've been selling sex since before Dr. Ruth. I did *David Susskind* at least eight times, and *Dinah!* about a half-dozen times and Johnny twice. "

"Great. We'll have to look into those archival appearances for our documentary. Especially *The Tonight Show*."

"If they have it at NBC, could you dub me a copy? The first time I was on with the animal expert from Mutual of Omaha and I remember Johnny made me hold the world's tiniest mouse."

Roswell is big-eyed. "How small is it?"

"About one inch," Rina informs him. "Its heart beats at some ridiculous beats per minute and they often die of heart attacks. At first we thought it was having a heart attack in Johnny's hand, but then we realized it was taking a mouse poop."

Roswell breaks up laughing but Rina laughs harder, with her stomach as well as her mouth. She's a delight and happily I realize she's going to add to our documentary tremendously, neck brace or not.

"Rina, this is Jared, our cameraman."

"Howdy," Jared says. "Do you mind if I creep up your sweater with the mic?"

"Not at all. I might enjoy it."

"What's with the brace?" I ask Vondra quietly as Jared and Rina make small talk.

"I asked her on the way in," Vondra says. "The right muscles on her neck disintegrated after radiation therapy. She beat the cancer. She says she can take the brace off for the shoot."

Despite the early hour, we find ourselves at the middle of a loud and inquisitive horseshoe-shaped throng of museum guests. "What are you filming?" asks the boldest, a heavily made-up middle-aged peroxide blonde wearing a sweatshirt appliquéd with a pig being lifted up by balloons.

"A segment of a documentary."

"On what?"

"On sexual partners."

"Oh, you should put me in. I've been married to everyone. I never give up on the institution of marriage. I'm the world's number-one optimist."

"Heather, can I get a white-balance read?" Jared interrupts the optimist.

"Roswell!" I call out gratefully. "Come and get the white poster board off the floor." Roswell's chatting to one of the younger members of the crowd, a pretty teen with long curly black hair, urchin eyes and high-in-the-sky breasts that would make a middle-aged woman weep. "Jared has to check the colors on his camera. Can you hold this in front of him?"

The buxom girl looks at Roswell admiringly as he stands with the poster board. "Okay, we're cool," Jared says to Roswell.

"Are you ready, Rina?" I ask.

"As I'll ever be."

"Then let's warm up with your basics, please tell me who you are."

"My name is Rina O'Riley. I guess I could be considered one of the Grand Ladies of Sex. With my husband, Frank O'Riley, I coined the term *Elastic Marriage* back in the 1960s. It was the end of the era when men could socialize after work and their wives slaved over the washing and cleaning like dray horses. Women wanted more, and enlightened men wanted more. We needed a new name for the options available to modern families. We publicly advocated that as long as there are two consenting adults and there is complete communication between them, anything goes. This sounds like common sense now, but in 1960 it was considered *scandalous*."

"Did you get hate mail?"

A diminutive Mexican man enters the wing on what first appears to be a tractor but is in fact a museum floor buffer, one that produces a waxy stink and a noise as loud as a John Sousa march.

"Stop the camera, please," I say to Jared.

Vondra rushes to the scene, has a few words with the driver, and he tractors off.

"Where were we?" I say.

"Hate mail," Jared says from the camera.

"Yes," Rina says. "Did we get hate mail? We had hate mail in which we were called everything under the sun. Heretics. Devil worshipers. We even had death threats, particularly after one television appearance where my husband said that, as anthropologists, we felt exploration was the way nature intended us to be." Rina glances at a caveman and his wife in the museum diorama, and I motion to Jared to focus in on her eyes taking in the scene.

"So everybody should have as many possible partners as they want?"

"Do I feel everyone should have as many partners as they want? I feel it should be a consenting decision. Perhaps the husband wants to be monogamous and the wife wants to explore, that would be fine, as long as they know what is going on."

"Does that happen too often?"

"It doesn't usually happen that way, of course," Rina says after a silent smile. "Usually it's the other way around."

Vondra scribbles me a question to ask. "What about sexually transmitted diseases?" I read off her note.

"I'm not advocating a secretive liaison—"

"I'm sorry, could you repeat the question for editing purposes?"

"Oh dear, I was being so good. Okay—ready?"

"Ready," I say.

"You may ask but what about sexually transmitted diseases? I say, you can't go about an Elastic Marriage in a willy-nilly way. Lying and mistrust breed like kudzu. There would be a lot less victims of AIDS if husbands and wives talked openly and took protective measures together. If you want to explore the perimeters of marriage, do be brainy about it. Elastic Marriage does not mean do as you please. It means do as *we* please."

"Why bother being married at all?"

"Why bother being married at all?" Rina dutifully repeats. "So many reasons. Primarily, because we want to be. In my experience, individuals who love each other want to publicly celebrate their union. For some people, there is safety in marriage—psychological constancy, but also life insurance, benefits. Look how hard it was for same-sex partners to get benefits after the Pentagon and World Trade Center attacks. Heterosexual couples take the rights of marriage for granted."

"Did you have an Elastic Marriage?"

"Did I have an Elastic Marriage? Let's just say that whatever the agreement we had, we also agreed to keep it private. That's what worked for us."

After I wrap up with the remaining questions, Rina excuses herself to the "powder room." Roswell returns to his doting high-breasted fan, and Jared packs up his audio equipment.

"You're a terrific interviewer," Jared says. "She was relaxed around you, even when you pushed her with some of the hard questions."

"Thank you," I say.

"Excellent!" Vondra says.

"Great segment," Jared agrees as he reaches for a runaway roll of black gaffer tape.

"He's adorable!" Vondra mouths when Jared's several feet away.

"I know!" I mouth back.

She tugs at an imaginary beard and makes a frown. I mime a shaving gesture.

"I haven't been to this museum in years—" Jared picks up with me and Vondra.

He's cut off by Roswell who asks, "So can I help anymore, Squid?"

"No, but I have to know—did you get your friend's number?"

"You bet," Roswell says.

Vondra and I laugh as Jared gives him an older-brother high five.

"She's a little weird though. Her favorite color is brown."

"Brown?" Jared says sympathetically as he zips up his knapsack. "Brown is *fecal*."

"But she has nice boobs," Vondra says.

"Amazing boobs," I say.

"So maybe you shouldn't worry if she likes brown," Jared says.

"Tell me," Roswell says to all of us after a testosterone-addled snigger. "What's a good western to rent? My dad said I could get ten movies in a row at Blockbuster for passing French."

"Not my genre," Vondra says.

"Nor mine," I say.

Vondra breaks me away from the guys to discuss Rina.

"Do you mind if I listen to them talk?" I ask.

"You're right, this should be good."

"Start with the spaghetti westerns," Jared advises.

"Why are they called spaghetti westerns?" Roswell asks.

"First of all it has to be Italian. And the leading director of the genre was Sergio Leone. *Fistful of Dollars* is my favorite."

"Oh, that's a spaghetti film? That was a fucking cool film. I saw that at my friend Abdullah's house. I bought a poster of Clint Eastwood after I saw it. My mom accused me of being gay, having a thing for Clint. Then she made me chuck my old Pee-Wee Herman doll just because Pee-Wee masturbated once in public. She's normally cool. Must have been on the rag that week."

I can tell Vondra is as entertained as I am. I smile at her. Is Roswell's uncensored idiocy growing on us?

"I bet you're thinking, you had a Pee-Wee Herman doll? How *queer*. But, dude, I loved that doll. It was my childhood being thrown out, you know?"

I can clearly hear Jared's voice even with his back to me. "No. I was thinking it would be worth a mint now. I never got over the loss of my Hong Kong Phooey lunch box. My mother made me give it to charity."

"Who the hell is Hong Kong Phooey, dude?"

"Only the best Saturday-morning cartoon, dude. By day he is Penrod Pooch, a janitor in a police station. But when a crime comes to his attention, he jumps into a file cabinet, which turns into the Phooeymobile. He becomes Hong Kong Phooey, a superhero dog who thinks he saves the day with these very cool karate chops. It's actually his sidekick cat who saves the day, without Phooey knowing about it."

"Sounds a little lame."

"And a guy with a squeaky voice and a bow tie isn't?"

Roswell chuckles. "Yo, man, you're cool." How about that? A new friend. Vondra beckons Roswell over to help her mark the digital tape. "Excuse me, Squid," Roswell says.

I reach inside my own knapsack for my clipboard and pen to check off everything we need to take back to the office. My pen has run out of ink, and Jared sees me scratch the paper to no avail. He lifts his left jeans cuff and fishes for a pen stuck in the elastic of his sock. He hands it to me as he says, "Do they still have the giant blue whale suspended over that enormous room?"

"Thanks. And yes, in the Hall of Ocean Life. Where you and Steve were denied access. They just renovated the whole hall but kept the whale. I was just there for the Moth, this adults-only storytelling night."

"I heard about that. Steve was raving on about the Moth. It's a monthly thing, right? And it moves from venue to venue?"

"Yep. The one I went to was stories by documentary makers. It was packed because HBO underwrites the non-fiction film one every year for the Margaret Mead festival. They lined up some pretty impressive names to tell stories, people like Michael Moore and Albert Maysles."

"Wow," he says. After a small silence that goes on a beat too long, Jared says, "What's the next Moth theme? I've been missing out."

"Actually, I got an e-mail about it yesterday. It said the next theme is *Family Matters*. Usually they have celebrity guests, but it's an open call this time, like a poetry slam. They're giving people five minutes to tell a good family story."

"Then you should do it. You have a great voice, and such funny family stories—"

"Do you want to look at the whale?" I say quickly.

"Sure," he says quizzically.

"Vondra," I call out, "can you tell Rina I thank her and I'll call her tomorrow?"

She gives me a knowing smile.

The Hall of Ocean Life is possibly the most sexual room in the world. Especially in its renovated form, everything in the room suggests one big submerged orgasm, from the sleek blue lighting to the enormous video screens featuring whales spouting water.

Jared stares above him to the room's focal point, a ninety-four-foot blue whale that inspires awe in everyone from two-year-old kids to jaded science professors.

Jared shakes his head at the sight of it. "Ever think how lucky we are to be alive? You could have been born a blue whale. Imagine having the consciousness of a blue whale. The poor semi-extinct bastards."

"What would I think about?" I ask.

"Plankton?"

I laugh.

"So we never finished our conversation before," Jared says. "When is the Moth *Family Matters* night?"

"Next Sunday at the Nyorican Poets Café on Third Street. Or is it Fourth Street?"

He brushes me on the shoulder. "Hey, do you want to go?"

I read Steve's signals wrong during the matzo shoot—he was about getting ahead in the industry, whatever it took. But how off can I be now? Jared's blushing, I'm sure of it.

"Thanks for asking. I wish I could, but I'm flying to Amsterdam. I won't be back until early Sunday morning."

"Are you going for a film shoot?" he says with enough disappointment to flatter me.

"No, a personal trip. I'm visiting an old family friend who has a house there."

"Well, I guess I'll see you at the seder."

"Yes," I say somewhat dolefully.

"Great shopping in Amsterdam," he says. "My ex-girl-friend was a *big* shopper."

I snort sarcastically in my head. Put her in the ring with the Greenblotz women, let's see how she fares.

"Amsterdam was one big mall to her. Sarah said there's a fun toothbrush store there."

"So I'm told."

"So, which family members are coming to the seder?"

"Oh, the usual hodgepodge." Um, maybe my mailman and an Egyptian diplomat.

"Did Steve tell you that the publicist for the Food Channel has already lined up a profile on your family in the Wednesday Food section *and* the Arts and Leisure section? And that's just New York. Apparently the *Los Angeles Times* is biting too."

"Yeah? Wow." I hope I've mastered my immediate terror. This seder is really happening.

When Jared's cell phone rings with the same default tone half of New York City has, several tourists in the room check their pockets to see if their phone is the one going off. "Excuse me." Jared seeks out an open space in the lobby outside the Hall of Ocean Life.

The *New York Times!* How are we going to pull the wool over the *Times?* I imagine it's harder to do in the post–Jayson Blair era.

"That was Steve," Jared says on his return. "We have another shoot at Aquavit in about half an hour. Steve's not big on advance notice."

"Yes, I know. He called me up and asked me to meet him for dinner for that same night last week."

"To discuss the seder idea he had? I hope that's all he discussed though. Steve's a bit, well, Steve."

I look away. A Japanese couple in matching "I Took a Bite out of the Big Apple" T-shirts is watching us intently. Maybe it's all the water imagery, but they remind me of dolphins swimming close to a ship for amusement.

"You should get to your shoot," I say.

"I'll see you, then," he says softly. "After Amsterdam."

My stomach is tight and my breath is fast. I rush to the nearest bathroom, lock the door and sit on a closed toilet lid. How did I get mired into this mess?

The sneezing woman in the neighboring stall gets a phone call. "I'm glad you're better and I hate to say it, but I'm not shocked you got food poisoning. Nobody orders clams casino at a Chinese restaurant."

She sneezes and flushes, and I raise my knees to my chest in dread.

eight

Amsterdam

Two rows ahead of me on my early-morning KLM flight to Amsterdam is a cliquey group of couples on vacation together, mapping out what coffeehouses they're going to buy their hash from. Couples who travel together are their own countries, and serve as their own government. What's the point of travel if you are going to hang around the same people you did before you got on a plane? Adding to my annoyance is a lousy movie, starring one of the interchangeable recent graduates of *Saturday Night Live*. I'm not sure who he is, and I'm too willfully disinterested to even catch his name. Somehow I thought the Dutch would have better taste in cinema. On the plus side, the in-flight meal is quite decent, and dietary diligence be damned, I eat the two Drosté chocolate truffles tucked into the tray beside the chicken with lemon cream sauce. A bored thrill. Food is high entertainment at forty thousand feet, especially when you've struggled to get a pen out of your knapsack in the overhead compartment only to find someone already filled in the crossword puzzle in the in-flight magazine. That same previous passenger has X'd all the places he or she has been and blocked out most of the airline stops in coastal Europe. Was he some weary old salesman or maybe a catch I missed by one flight, a handsome and lively Sotheby's expert chasing fine examples of scrimshaw?

I stare at the pen, the one I borrowed from Jared in the natural history museum and never gave back. Another one of those cheery promotional pens from the Tumor Society, with Jared Silver printed all over it in different colors and sizes. Silver. Would nice Jewish boy Jared *Silver* like to travel in Europe, or is he a backpack type of guy with his heart set on Patagonia?

But fate has delivered another type of man to me today: Groot, my five-year-old blond seatmate. His hair is sleekly parted on the side like a mini-Hitler, and he has considerable snot hanging out of his tiny Netherlander nose. Groot worships this *Saturday Night Live* comedian, whoever he is. Groot's mother, Barbara, the lady with a matching button nose two seats over from me, keeps trying to wipe her son's nostrils, but her interruptions to his beloved movie causes much flailing of his arms and a noise a young pterodactyl might elicit if prodded away from some engaging but poisonous Jurassic plant by its doting mother. The snot stays.

When the movie is over, Groot immediately buzzes the airline attendant, who is waved away by his mother. As soon as she's halfway down the aisle, the fat-cheeked tyke flashes the light button on and off again seven times. After an earful from Mummy, Groot promises to be good and then glowers in silence. He flips through his easy-reader picture book on spaceships that Barbara produces from her nylon carry-on. All good. Until her son starts to mimic the rotor noise of a helicopter.

Loudly.

"If only I could fax Groot to my husband," Barbara says to me with a grimacing smile.

Barbara earlier told me (in her perfect English) that she's originally from a watery province called Zeeland, but her family now lives in an Amsterdam neighborhood called The Jordaan. I would love to ask if she has any suggestions where to go to find my almost definitely gay dad, but with her live-wire kid and airline-enforced lack of cigarettes, I'm sure this line of questioning would do her in.

When at last Groot succumbs to the sandman, Barbara also closes her eyes for a breather. I sheepishly open my knapsack, slide in *Judaism for Dummies* and slide out *Fodor's Gay Guide to Amsterdam*. Another passing female flight attendant, tall and also dirty blond, is carrying a tray of plastic glasses filled with water. She gives me an inviting look.

On the buffet line at the American Hotel on Leidesplein, a Dutch businessman asks if I've tried this country's superlative Gouda and Edam. "That's why we're the tallest nation," he says to me in the elevator ride down. "Dairy. Do you notice the Chinese are getting taller? All those basketball players? It's dairy. They're slowly turning into the Dutch."

I pile mostly fruit and a sampling of cheese onto my plate. I pick a window seat in the restaurant. The cheese *is* superlative—I may never touch New York supermarket cheese again. I open my guidebook and checkmark the bars that have gay-dad potential.

The most recent photo I have of my father is the one he e-mailed of himself in front of his Balinese villa with a pink sun behind him on the beach. Armed with a color print-out, I am set to scour Amsterdam's drag bars, leather bars and gay dance clubs. I plan to grill homosexual men of every fetish with "Have you seen my daddy?"

At 9:00 p.m. I take a cab to the infamous red-light district, where I'm sure some of the gay bars will be easy to spot. But all I see is half-naked women in neon-illuminated windows.

"You want men?" says the bearded man behind a late-night newsstand stocked with European porno mags. "You're not in the right neighborhood. This is for the boys who like, how you say in English—"

"Pussy," says a hooded customer behind me who purchases a magazine featuring an obese naked cover girl with enormous nipples, round as saucers.

By the wee hours I've poked my head into seven bars. I am convinced that finding my father flirting with a man in an Amsterdam bar is about as likely as my finding the sultan of Brunei on line at the corner store buying a Lotto ticket. I dread going back to Bettina and Jake with a sob story, so I try the last bar on my list, De Amstel Taveerne, touted in the *Fodor's Gay Guide* as the first gay bar in Amsterdam. The Fodor's writer loves the bar's campy Dutch sing-alongs.

I stand outside for a minute watching gay men stream from the door. Most of the newly coupled guys sport the thick mustaches heterosexual men cling to in the American Midwest as proof of their virility. Inside, the crowd is lively as promised. The tail end of Liza Minnelli's "Losing My Mind" booms on the sound system, followed by her gay ex-husband Peter Allen's "Bicoastal" as an ironic chaser. I seat myself in the corner, crestfallen, thirsty and hungry.

A burly drag queen says something quickly to me in Dutch.

"I only speak English," I say, miserable and not feeling particularly chatty.

"You're in luck, honey. Are you a Canuck like me?"

"New Yorker," I say.

He points to a fat drag queen tottering near a bar. "Did you see those heels she's wearing? Doesn't suit her legs at all. If Carlotta doesn't buy a pair of flats, we're going to see an elephant slip. Did you ever see an elephant slip? An unforgettable sight."

"When does an elephant ever slip? Elephants don't slip."

"Not true, darling. I saw a nature documentary last night about elephants. They had one tragic shot of a dead elephant carcass, and the narrator explained that it wasn't poached— it had fallen to its death."

"He must have gone after a particularly tasty frond, and misplaced his footing."

"*Frond*. Great word," the queen says to me. "Are you a writer?"

"A filmmaker. Here from New York."

"I'm Charity Royall, and I'm going to sit down and cheer you up. You look like you need it, and I want to know all about New York. I'm ashamed to say I've never been."

I force a smile. "Charity Royall. Isn't that an Edith Wharton character?"

"A gold star if you can tell me which novel."

I concentrate until it comes: "*Summer*. Required reading for my Women in Eighteenth-Century Literature course. Charity Royall had a sexual awakening."

"You may be a sad little bird, but you're a well-read one."

Before we can continue our not-unpleasant repartee, there are brilliant flashes of light hitting my eyes from an unknown source. It's emanating from a friend of Charity's, who sits down at the table with us as if we've been expecting him. He, (or she, as I guess drag queens prefer to be called), is at least fifty, maybe sixty, but it's hard to tell under the Pan-Cake makeup and heavy Dame Edna glitter dress.

"Natasha, how was the cataract operation?" Charity asks.

"It was nothing," says Natasha in a British accent.

"An operation on your eye is nothing?"

"It was the early stage of the cataract, and I think, right, this needle is entering my skin for four seconds of my life. I could live with that. When it comes to pain, it's mind over matter."

Charity twists her pink-lipsticked lips. "If someone jams a red-hot poker up your arse for four seconds, you're fine with that?"

My hands unclench as I laugh loudly. I didn't expect to laugh at all tonight.

Charity's bony buddy turns to me: "I must compliment you. You look so much like a woman. It's *just* wonderful."

"I *am* a woman."

Charity lets loose a gut-busting guffaw.

Natasha makes a wry face. "Teasing you, love. We get plenty a mixed crowd in this bar. Nothing and no one is new to us. I only tease the ones who look like they can take it. So what's a nice real woman doing at a place like this? Here to check out the barside show?"

"A lot of straight tourists tiptoe inside just to see *us*," adds Charity. "We're as much of a draw as the music."

"Sorry. I'm just looking for my father."

"Wrong establishment." Charity smiles knowingly.

"Maybe not. I think he's gay. I haven't seen him for a while."

"In that case, what's his name?"

"Charity knows *everybody*."

"Can you be discreet?" I ask in a choked voice.

"Of course!" Charity nods vigorously.

"Sol Greenblotz from New York—would you happen to know him?"

"Is he a queen?" Charity asks.

"I'm not sure." I pull out the picture I printed on my computer and they shake their wigged heads no.

"Greenblotz like the matzo?" says Natasha.

"Yes. That's my family. I'm the youngest generation."

"I can't believe it," Natasha says. She smiles broadly at Charity before turning back to me. "My birth name is Jacob Weiner. My father was in the London *schmata* trade before he retired."

"*Oy veis meir!* I'm Larry Moskowitz," Charity says to me. "My father was in furniture export."

We fall about ourselves laughing, until Natasha manages to say, "I've been eating your family matzo since I was knee-high. Has anyone else ever been this excited?"

"Most people—well, most Jews—get excited," I say. I tell them about Oleg, my hyperfriendly Russian mailman who I'd assured Jake was not a choice guest to drag to the fake family seder—even though Oleg practically whirled in joy when he first realized who I am. Oleg was a research scientist in Minsk a decade ago. The day he asked about my last name was the day I had registered mail from my trust fund, and the day after he'd bought his family their first box of matzo. Buying Jewish foods is a big deal for a Russian used to tucking away religion. Now Oleg considers me a star resident of the building along with the two *All My Children* ingenues that share penthouse B. "An autograph from The Matzo Ball Heiress!" he singsongs when I sign for my quarterly checks.

Charity orders us on-tap Budweisers, not the watery kind from America, but the really nice lager from the Czech Republic. Charity and Natasha may dress like women, but they knock beer back like a couple of lumberjacks.

Charity leans over with a woozy smile. "So tell me, Miss Matzo Ball Heiress, why are you really looking for your gay father in Amsterdam?"

"I haven't spoken to him in months, but this is the last place I heard from him. I think he's still living here."

"Would make sense. That's why we're here. Everyone is

so open here. It's a better life. The way the world should be. Open."

"If he wants to live overseas, that's his right. But this year, Dad needs to come home for our family seder. The Greenblotz seder is being broadcast on American TV and he's desperately needed. No one else can read Hebrew."

Glutted with Brazil nuts, Charity gets up heavily in his seat and stands on top of the bar with all of his considerable girth and projects: "Does anyone know Sol Greenblotz from New York?" And then just as loudly in Dutch: *"Kennen jullie Sol Greenblotz?"*

I'm too tired and drunk to get angry.

Natasha *tsks* for me. "Discreet as they come."

A few stares transpire before a ruddy man with jug ears and severe acne calls back loudly in an Australian accent, "Everyone thinks they're a movie star and if you're Tom Cruise then okay, but otherwise sit the *fuck* down."

"Well," Charity says in a huff to anyone in the vicinity who will listen. "That's rich coming from a man with a dried-up head like something you'd find on the bottom of a boat—a barnacle head."

Natasha gives me an amused look.

Charity sighs out loud and smiles at me: "I tried, darling."

"Thanks," I say.

Natasha produces a red compact from her silver clutch bag. As she checks her mascara, she says, "Funny we're talking about fathers. My old man calls today and puts me on hold. Why? Because he wants to look up a bird copulating on his windowsill in his bird book. Lunacy. He lives in Primrose Hill. I told him, 'Father, you don't need the bird book. I tell you what it is. It's a pigeon. It's always a bloody pigeon.'"

When Charity and I laugh loudly, Natasha continues with an almost proud glint in her eye, "Then my mother gets on to say she's won another Tidy Town award. She's eighty and still so neat that she would scrub germs if she could. She folds and color-codes their dirty laundry."

"She sounds obsessive-compulsive," I say. "Maybe she should get help."

"Too late for the world's foremost mopper, love. I barely even sweep, and that fills her with horror." Natasha exhales noisily. "My parents are *real* characters."

This from a six-foot man named Natasha dressed in a purple evening gown and kitten heels.

Another drag queen friend of Charity's minces over to our table. A black "gal" named Simone who is beyond thrilled to chat up a visitor from New York. Simone's fake nails are so long they spiral. She talks as fast as a ticker spitter in a thick French accent, and her fingertips make a faint clacking sound as they inadvertently tap on our table. "I hear Manhattan has *zee* wonderful natural energy. I read *zis* in a holistic magazine. Apparently *zee* souls of *zee* original box turtles and beavers are *zill* hovering."

Back in the Big Apple I would roll my eyes at the ridiculous carryings-on of these ex-pat queens, and their wacky stories and theories, but here near the Amstel River I am free from the shackles of New York cynicism. Believing in protective animal spirits floating over my hardened twenty-first-century city is a very comforting thought.

I expand my confidence: I am looking for my father. I love him. I need him. His homosexuality is not a problem; I'm hip with it. The immediate problem is not having anyone at my seder who speaks Hebrew. But my long-term goal is to get to know my father again as a friend.

"What a wonderful daughter you are," Charity née Larry says woozily with a pat of his fat, furry hand.

I sniffle.

Natasha, née Jacob, takes my other hand and gives it a small squeeze. "Listen, darling. My test for relationships is the same test I use for pure fibers. You burn a tiny bit. If the fiber turns to ash, it's silk. If it isn't, and it goes beady, it wasn't worth pence to begin with."

"Huh?" says Charity. "If her father burns and turns to ash, that's good?"

Natasha shoos Charity out of her space with her free arm. She squeezes my hand harder. "Heather, find your father, and push him to his limit. He'll be angry, but if he cares, he'll take action."

Alcohol has always given me funny dreams. Tonight, sometime after I pass out with my clothes on, I'm a hen. A hen who lays an egg that Hitler bursts out of, laughing manically and saying: "Jew hens to the left." I wake up like a newbie soldier in sweaty sheets, and grope in the bathroom for my hotel glass to fill with water. Nude on the toilet seat, I sweat fear in a wet isolation. Eventually I brave it back to the bed, and pull a notebook out of my suitcase and a pen from the Bible drawer and begin to draw: snails, elephants, a whole zoo of animals until I'm groggy enough to fall back to sleep. Even then I stare at the ceiling for twenty minutes, my tongue sticking out like I'm an overheated dog.

I start to finally drift off to sleep, when the room phone rings.

"What time is it there?" Jake says when I pick it up and answer after a clumsy delay.

"It's 4:00 a.m."

"Oh, I thought it was 4:00 p.m."

"It's okay, I was having nightmares anyhow."

"About what?"

"Chickens and Hitler."

"You know what I dreamed about last night?"

I yawn. "Let me guess, Britney Spears doing the breast-stroke in your swimming pool?"

"Ooh. So close. Christina Aguilera gave me a lap dance."

"Jake, is there a reason you're calling? I'm dead tired."

"Just seeing if you had any luck finding Uncle Sol."

"None." I yawn again. "But I've found out the reason the Dutch are so tall. It's the dairy."

"Then how come the Jews aren't taller? Look how short Grandpa Reuben was. I'd say he ate a vat of sour cream a year."

"He also ate stuffed intestine."

"That will set you back," Jake concurs. "Look, I had an idea about how to find Uncle Sol. I called the bank to see where his ATM withdrawals come from in Amsterdam. We deposit his money in his New York City account, but he has to take the cash out somewhere in Amsterdam."

"Any luck?"

"Well, all they can tell me is that he seems to take it out of the ABM-Amro branch in The Jordache."

"The Jordaan. It's not a jean, it's a neighborhood."

"Listen, Miss Condescending, I'm trying to help you."

"No address?"

"None."

"So what am I supposed to do—wait in that branch for him to show up?"

"Well, if you keep to the area, don't forget about the supermarket there."

I yawn again. "Yes, the Quacken guy."

"You're making me sleepy just listening to you."

"Let me go then."

Jake quacks like a duck before he hangs up.

★ ★ ★

After I find Vondra's *stroopwafels* in the biscuits aisle, I seek out the foreign and specialty food section to ascertain the damage brought on by the change in owners by our biggest Dutch distributor. It's odd to see American staples like Hellmann's mayonnaise and Betty Crocker brownie mix classified as exotics, mixed in with cans of Chinese water chestnuts. I spot a jar of Manishewitz gefilte fish. And Manishewitz matzo meal. Oh boy. Every kosher item inside Albert Vroom Supermarkets is from our biggest competitor.

I ask a shop assistant unloading a case of Swiss-fondue fuel, "Do you know where I can find Jan Quacken?"

The assistant points to a metal door near the massive cheese section.

I knock, and a towering man with military-short hair answers the door.

"Hello, are you Mr. Quacken?"

"Yes."

"Hi, I'm Heather Greenblotz."

"From the matzo?" says Quacken. A harp's string of drool steadies between his lips when he says the letter *o*. It breaks as he continues, "We're going with Manischewitz, cheaper to get from America. Bulk deal."

"I've heard you dropped our line, but this isn't an official business call. I'm on vacation, and I thought I'd drop in to say hello since you are such a valued buyer."

"Were."

"Yes, well, I can say this since I'm on our board—we're willing to match the price and give you an ad spread wherever you want. My cousin who heads our factory heard there's a Jewish paper here—"

"Yes, I'm Jewish. Nieuw Israelietisch Weekblad."

I'm no Jewish scholar, but I've heard of Kahns and Rosens

and Levines. And Portnoys and Rothschilds and Grossmans and Lipschitzes and Schecters. All *in the tribe*. But *Quacken*?

"Was your name shortened from Quackenberg?" A little quip, so sue me.

"No," he says, drooling again, without a trace of a smile. So much for the Religion of Humor. He checks the hour on the promotional-cheese wall clock, and I'm escorted out in record time.

Earth is a hep place these days, home to two men who can kiss each other in a Dutch toothbrush store without fear of comment from the other customers: me and two Australian punk rockers (the kind with credit cards) deciding between Lucy and Charlie Brown brushes or ones shaped like a naked man and woman.

It takes a minute for the tree to fall on my toe. One of those nuzzling gay men is my father, Solomon David Greenblotz. Having spent the evening with Charity and her gang, I was now convinced Dad must also have a radical alter ego who loads on the mascara and sports a beehive wig and falsies. But other than his wavy hair succumbing to gray, Dad is dressed exactly as he would dress in Manhattan. Slobby. Unhip ethnic shirt, probably from Bali. Back home, my mother was constantly on my father's case to update his stuck-in-the-sixties fashion sense. She once told me that when she was at Ithaca College, where rich kids go to party in Cornell's shadow, Ivy League Dad was well liked by her lively crowd, but apparently he was the standout in need of a wardrobe intervention.

The major physical difference I spot off the bat is that he's lost the glasses and also heaps of weight since his last very brief trip to the United States three years ago. (We saw *Rent* together, and had a rushed latte at the Starbucks closest to the theater.)

In time to the backbeat of a dreadful Euro-pop song, I inch closer. Do I have enough iron in my soul?

"Daddy?"

Dad reels in my direction with a look another father might make if you caught him stuffing dollars in some stripper's cleavage in a tittie bar.

Face paling, breath short, he says, "Heather, what are you doing here?"

"Buying a toothbrush."

I'm surprised how natural Dad looks as a skinny man. He's always seemed to me as if he should be as big as he was, that was just his luck of the bone-size draw, but a smaller frame has emerged. His whole torso is thinner, even his skull seems thinner. He should get some clothes that fit though. Now his cotton pants and appalling natural-fiber sweater just hang off his frame like the dingy clothes former tribal hunters wear when they're doled out from a nearby missionary.

On the other hand, the object of my father's affection is painfully groomed. Are those eyebrows plucked? I hate that look on men, gay or straight. Dad's new love is also dressed head to toe in skintight rubbery dark purple leather that, stretched over his slender build and considerable height, makes him look like one of those long, hot dog–shaped balloons that hired clowns twist into flowers and giraffes at a children's party. Dad's lover is sizing me up too, I can tell. With arm on hip, a fey purple knight reaching for a sword in anvil, he stares at me as though I'm covered in some medieval pox. "And this is?" Leather Boy demands.

"My daughter, Heather, from New York."

Dad's lover hesitates, but offers a hand. I shake it politely as I give him an even more thorough once-over in return. This grape is who my father has chosen over his matzo career, Mom, me and fifty-four years of New York City living.

"Heather, this is Pieter Eicken."

Pieter's face is a definite ellipse, and his quick thin brush stroke of a mouth makes it that much more comic.

"Darling, you look terrific," Dad says shakily. "A skinny *malink*. You always looked good, but you know, I think you could model now."

"Hardly," I say after a small smile. "I've been trying to finally check off some of my resolutions." Flattery is all he has to offer me after three years? I should model?

"It's been a while since we've seen each other," Dad says.

"Yeah," I say. "You've lost a lot of weight too. You got contacts?"

"Yes."

The Euro-pop CD is over, and silence fills the toothbrush store.

"Would you like to come over to my place?" Dad finally tacks on.

"I think so."

"Would you like me to leave you some time with your daughter?" Pieter says. I've heard enough clipped English words from him now to pick up that he is Dutch, and not one of Amsterdam's many expatriates.

"That would probably be best," Dad says. My father glances at me and I can see him struggling with a decision. He leans over to give Pieter another peck. "About an hour would be good."

"Very well."

As Dad and I walk to his place in The Jordaan, a block from Prisengracht Canal, we confine our conversation to inoffensive comments like how picturesque the canals are and how bumpy my flight was.

"It's not large," Dad says after endless steps up the centuries-old building toward their loft. "But then nothing in

Amsterdam is. The government used to charge taxes by the inch."

The interior of his place looks like a trendy spread ripped from *Wallpaper* magazine. Chrome and black leather everywhere. Not at all what I expect from the home of the man, who in one of his rare e-mails from Bali, wrote that he was learning to design his own *ikat*, Indonesian textiles. The furnishing in this new home is not too dissimilar from my mother's hypermodern taste Dad and I always made fun of back in New York City. Perhaps it's even a bit edgier. There wasn't an ounce of Dad's style in our Park Avenue residence—and there isn't here, either.

Like Mom, Pieter must also be on top, so to speak, when it comes to decorating. Eeesh. Would my father sexually be a bottom or a top? This disturbing thought catches me by surprise, and I immediately will it out of my mind.

"Do you want a cup of tea or coffee?" he asks.

"Coffee would be great."

"It looks like you've been dieting, but I have a package of *stroopwafels* too, they're Dutch—"

"Cookies, I know. I guess I should try one. My business partner loves them. I have a package of them in my bag from the Albert Vroom Supermarket."

"That's funny. That's the chain that stocks our products."

"Not so coincidental. Jake knew I was coming here and asked me to drop in. All the shelf space has gone to Manischewitz. I tried to make a pitch for our brand. The manager wouldn't hear a word I had to say."

"That's kind of surprising. Who did you talk to? Quacken?"

"You know him?"

"Yes. Sort of. I'll talk to him. He's...how do I put this?"

"Mean? Jewish?"

"No, um—gay. He used to be involved with Pieter. But I

was talking to him for years when I ran the factory. I didn't think he'd go that far. He dropped the whole line?"

"The whole line."

"Incredible."

"Do you think he'll out you to the matzo world?"

"Jan Quacken? Not a chance."

"How can you be so sure?"

"He is happily married and has three kids."

"So, Dad, you know from my math grades that I've never been too good at pattern recognition, but is every Jewish man living in Amsterdam gay?"

Dad laughs. "The ones I know."

"Is Pieter Jewish?"

"No. His parents are very active in their church."

"Does Pieter have a Jewish fetish?"

Dad laughs. "I never thought of that before. I guess he does." As Dad puts the kettle up, I go to get a better look at the framed erotic photos on the wall. I can handle this, I sell myself. Sold too fast. On one half of the first photo I examine is my father's face, eyes shut in what appears to be ecstasy. A black man's erection frames the other side like a tree branch. Dad comes out of the kitchen with a coffeepot and a plate of crisscrossed sugary *stroopwafels*.

"Pieter's photographs. He's quite respected in the Dutch gallery circuit. Nudity is no big deal in Europe." I've heard that preemptive voice before. Dad used it when I came home from school in third grade and the budgie my parents had given me (in lieu of a sibling) had escaped her cage and flown out the window.

Still I try to be nonchalant. "Just checking them out." It gets harder: the next jaw-dropper I spot is an enormous close-up of an asshole over the fireplace. "Is that yours?" I ask for lack of anything more appropriate to say.

"No," Dad says quickly. "That's Pieter's—he used a timer."

"Oh," I say in a teeny voice, mildly relieved.

"Mine's in the kitchen."

"I think I need to sit," I say.

"You've got the right house," Dad says dryly to my extended silence. "This is who I am now."

"It's just that, well, I kind of thought you were a newbie to this. You know, bi-curious, like you see in the personals." Averting my gaze now to the only clothed artwork I see, a sculpture of a Roman warrior with a prominent codpiece, I add, "I thought you have to creep before you walk."

Dad speaks with a solid gaze. "I've been walking for a while, Heather."

This time I say nothing.

Dad sighs and jerks the welcome mat: "What do you want me to say? You spring in like a character in a pop-up book."

"You just abandon New York—"

"I was miserable there. I was living a lie."

"So why couldn't you talk to me about it? To Mom?"

"She's in denial. I adore your mother, believe it or not. At first I fell in love with an image. You had to see your mother strolling around Ithaca with her pretty face and smart dresses. She was curvy and sexy, but never too overtly. She's got a real style and a certain personality—I'm not sure what to call it—"

"A cold personality?"

Dad offers a scrambled smile. "That's not fair. She connects very well to the smart set. She went out with the head of the debate club at Cornell before she met me. Jocelyn knows a lot more than you're giving her credit for."

"Maybe once, but these days could she be any less involved with the world outside of expedition cruising? She never even reads the paper, but she's got plenty to say about the latest sale at Bloomie's."

"You're not too shabby in the shopping arena."

"Yes, but I read more than two books a year. And I know what's going on in the world."

"Listen, I adore her. Go easy on her."

"This is my mother you're talking about? The woman you left for a one-way ticket out of America?"

"Your mother and I have always been more friends than lovers. Opposites attract, and for a while it was working. I kept denying my inner voice because we enjoyed each other so much."

"Does she know you're officially gay now?"

"Before we separated she said I abandoned her emotionally, not just sexually. She won't really listen to what I have to say about my sexual past, or my sexual present for that matter."

"Tell me you at least used a condom with Mom."

"Honey, we haven't slept together since you were born."

"Um, wow." I'm fascinated. But I feel a bit like Chelsea Clinton being dialed in by her father on the long-standing family arrangement. Did I really want to know this?

"Abstinence is not so uncommon on Park Avenue, let me assure you. There are plenty of bankers covering up their true lifestyle. How is your mother, anyway?"

"She's leaving for a trip soon. To the Amazon."

"Good for her."

"This traveling the world as one big shopping mall business started when you left. The shopping I get. It's the snorkeling that throws me."

"Your mother snorkels?" Dad laughs, then adds, "Again, good for her. What do you want her to do? Sit and mope?"

"Oh, by the way, she once said that if I ever spoke to you I should tell you that you never got your rock collection out of the apartment. She said she was going to put it in the trash if you don't take care of it soon."

"God, I hope not. Tell her those rocks are from Franklin, New Jersey. Please tell her *not* to throw them out. They are fluorescent. They glow under black light. I picked them myself from a quarry in New Jersey when I was in high school. Franklinite, tourmaline, natrolite, calcite. Can you hold those bags for me, honey?"

"Dad, they're three duffel bags full of grime and dirt. Mom has a point. Show up and claim them or they deserve to end up in the Dumpster. And she said it so long ago that the rocks may be history already. I forgot to tell you the last time you came to New York."

"I couldn't take them with me to Bali of course, but I held on to them so I could eventually donate them to Cornell. Each bag is worth thousands of dollars. I'll give Jocelyn a call. Same old number?"

"Same."

"Can you believe I can't remember it anymore?"

I reach in my bag and write it down for him.

He smiles dolefully at the digits. "You know, Jocelyn and I always entertained each other. But entertainment is not enough. I needed to leave my world behind to figure that out."

"But you left me behind too."

Silence as he stared at my knees. Has that really never occurred to him?

"Heather, I love you very much, you know that."

I can hardly say my next sentence: "No, I don't know that."

"Well, you're the most important person in my life. But I thought you'd be shocked and appalled if you saw how I live now."

"I'm a documentary maker, Dad. What couldn't I handle?"

"You're not at all shocked?"

I swallow some air, and try to answer honestly. "To some extent I am. But I'll get through it."

"I was just protecting you."

"Were you? Usually the most important person in one's life rates more than one e-mail a year. And not just when a catastrophe occurs. I feel like such a failure without you to talk to." I can't hold back the emotion building inside me. Sobs burst out of me as Dad puts his arm around me. "I'm sad without my daddy to talk to," I get out.

"A failure? You are shockingly successful! I *kvell* with pride over you! You're the big success of our family. You have to know that. I'm the one who has let everyone down."

I'm silent again. What can I say to that?

"Do you know what it's like to have so much expectation ahead of you? My brother was running the factory and I was thrilled with that. But after the accident—" The memory of the car crash and God knows what else is too hard for Dad to continue. Have I ever seen my father cry before? "I wanted our family to work," he manages to say.

My tears end. I find it nearly impossible for two people to cry at the same moment. I grasp his hand. "Well, right now we need our family to work. There's an emergency."

His forehead furrows as he speaks through near sobs. "Is your mother okay? Is Jake okay? Tell me."

"I'm not here by accident. I was looking for you, Dad. I took a plane to find you. The Food Channel is airing our seder." As my words tumble out, I realize I'm close to babbling.

Dad is visibly confused. "What seder?"

"We've been pulling together a fake family. The business isn't competing against all the kosher-food merges. All the other companies are owned by megacorporations now. They have much more muscle."

"You're still not making sense to me." He sniffs away the last of his tears. "What does the Food Channel have to do with this? Who's this fake family?"

"There's a producer who wanted to air our seder live, and then run it as a perennial. I didn't want to do it, but Jake's convinced me that our market share is about to fall. Jake's orchestrating the night. Greg's going to fly up. He's the only one who is real. Siobhan's going to be Shoshanna Green-blotz. Gertie's going to pose as our grandmother. Or is it our grandmother's sister? I need to get this story straight."

Dad shakes his head in disbelief. "Gertie's still alive? That's so good to hear. I was going to ask you about her."

"She's alive and she needs you too. You want to have her lose her job? We *all* need you to pull your weight to lead this thing. You're the only one who reads Hebrew, and you've always had a passion for cultural trivia."

Dad touches his forehead like a Talmud scholar contemplating a moral dilemma.

"I'm not asking you to move back. I just want you to visit. One day to pretend all is hunky-dory, so we can capture it on video and give the business a kick start."

"Representing the matzo factory is asking too much. I've just comes to terms with saying I'm gay. There's a Dutch saying Pieter taught me, 'Don't let the herrings swim over your head.'"

I stand up. I make a mental note to dismiss Bettina as my therapist when I get back to America. This isn't treatment, this is torture. "I think I should go."

"Sit down. You're not going anywhere. You've just traveled three thousand miles to see me and I haven't seen you for—"

"Three years. That's the last time you flew in for a Broadway musical."

He searches my face for compassion. "I want to know what else is going on in your life."

I remain seated, stone silent.

"Are you seeing someone special?" he asks.

"No," I muster. "There's one prospect, but I'm not holding my breath. It's hard for me to trust anyone. I've been dating, but it goes nowhere. Sometimes it feels impossible."

"Pieter said to me that finding me in Bali was about as likely as two bits of dust whirling around the sun and bumping into each other."

I look at him without a smile. What's going on in my head? I feel empty of thoughts, as if I've swallowed a new drug designed to keep me from hurting myself.

"Would you like some soup?" Dad says finally. "Pieter's a wonderful cook."

"Better than Mom?" I joke softly, which gets an insider's laugh from my father. "I wouldn't mind a nosh," I add. "I haven't eaten anything but the Gouda slices at the hotel this morning."

"How do you like the cheese here? Out of this world, huh?"

I smile sadly.

Dad returns to the kitchen and brings me a black Chinese bowl filled to the rim with something thick and wet that smells awful. "*Erwtensoep*, it's a Dutch pea soup. Very popular. It has cubes of pig fat, slices of blood sausage and cracked pig's knuckles in it."

I stare in mild horror at my bowl. Quite the offering for a Passover conversation. "You mind if I pass?"

Dad shrugs his shoulder and says, "Let's get some air."

We walk silently down the street that runs along the Prisengracht Canal. I spot a sign for the Anne Frank House.

"I really wanted to see that," I confess. "I didn't have time to go, since I used up my hours in gay bars."

"Are you lesbian? Did I miss that?"

"Dad, I've been looking for you for the last three days! You forgot to give us a phone number or a new e-mail address. It was more important that I find you than hit any museums."

"You've always been good at research," Dad says.

I offer him a halfhearted smile.

"I've never made it inside the Anne Frank House," Dad says. "When are you going to be back in Amsterdam?"

"I'm not sure if I ever will be." I check my watch. "I better pack soon. My flight leaves early in the morning."

"C'mon, then, let's see it."

Prior to today, the one museum that has made me cry is the Birmingham Civil Rights Institute. I visited there after wrapping my first human-interest documentary gig, an eight-minute PBS travel segment on Alabama for an up-market travel-show pilot that never got picked up.

It was a chatty segment in the Lonely Planet/Rough Guide vein, with an opening shot of all the many passengers on the American Eagle commuter plane headed toward the Bible Belt actually reading from their Bibles. Of course, we shot the largest cast-iron statue in the world, the huge bare-assed pagan Vulcan that was originally erected in 1904 for the St. Louis World's Fair and moved back to Birmingham at the end of the fair. There was a small bit on the hooch whiskey that moonshiners in Desoto Caverns cooked up during Prohibition, and another on Red Velvet, a chocolate cake with red food dye that is a wacky but tasty specialty of the South.

Although the Civil Rights Institute was walking distance to our hotel, it was not on my film agenda. It was my then-new friend Vondra who highly encouraged a visit if I had the extra time. My cameraman went back to sleep after the final shoot but I was still wired. When I wandered into the institute, I was unprepared for the asteroid about to hit my brain. I was the only white visitor that day, and the cashier smiled at me when I paid my admission. The rooms were filled with Southern black high-school students on field trips, and a few elderly black women weeping softly as we entered each room.

As I looked at the heartrending pictures, films and relics of everything from slaves packed in ships to twentieth-century policemen sousing black children, I felt ashamed to be white.

Now, in the Anne Frank House, a second asteroid hits me straight in the noggin. This time I feel ashamed to be cut off like an oxbow lake from my own family and culture. Am I a Jew or a nothing? Our ancestors left Europe before the Nazis catapulted to power. Our family has the gift of life and all we do is ignore each other.

After we've left the final room, Dad sits in a chair near the exit. His face and his clothes are crumpled as he puts his thoughts on two overwhelming experiences in order, my visit and this provoking time capsule from the Holocaust. After considerable silence, Dad stretches his hands like Rip Van Winkle awakening from his hundred-year sleep. Then he says, "I've changed my mind. I'll do it. So when exactly is this seder?"

"April 16."

"Let's swing by the KLM offices. It's not far. We'll book me a ticket. April 14 is Pieter's birthday, but I can come April 15, just in time for my U.S. tax filing."

I slip my hand under his arm and we bundle out to the same ground that Otto Frank did with his children on a safe, innocent morning, a day or week or month perhaps before his growing concerns for his family calcified into terror and loss.

The sun is gone, but the sky still holds some light.

NiNe

Silver Lining

"**Y**ou're serious? Uncle Sol is coming?"

I fill Jake in on my roller-coaster three days in Amsterdam, culminating in Dad's last-minute change of heart. "He's staying with me. I have his phone number in Amsterdam now. You want to call him and go over everything?"

"No, I made a checklist. We have the matzo of course, but I have to figure out where to buy a shankbone."

The to-do list for a TV-perfect seder is staggering. After I hang up I hear a soft noise under my door and investigate. Through my peephole, I can see one of my building's maintenance men headed for the stairs with a stack of papers in arm. He's slipped one of his notes under my door:

Dear Co-op Owner:
Maintenance has logged many complaints of rain and even mounds of snow creeping in through our windows this win-

ter. We are pleased to announce that starting this week the thin panes installed for the original tenants will finally be removed and upgraded to a tough double-glazed pane. The installation will be done by Skyline Windows, who offer quality and speed. They are so trusted in the industry that they installed the windows for the Empire State Building and Lady Liberty's crown. This project will save our co-op considerable money as 30% less heat will have to be utilized...

I read on. The penthouses will be done first. My appointment time is Sunday, 9:00 a.m. Today. In one hour! And according to the note, I must be in the apartment until they finish in the afternoon.

Great. I'm not feeling the jet lag yet, but I will. I need this now? I call the board secretary, divorcée Flossie Reicheinder, who prides herself on colorfully written notices and annual reports. You can tell she wrote this memo up even though it's signed *Westin Drimmer, Board President.*

"This is not going to work for me, Flossie. I'm a Greenblotz. This is matzo season. I need to have this done after Passover."

"You'll have to find a way. Find someone who can substitute for you, honey."

"Don't the workers take off Sunday?"

"They rotate shifts. They're booked all week long. We're lucky to get the chance to use them. They're doing the Chrysler Building next! Imagine that. That's how good they are. We were on standby rate, and a midtown office building canceled. The vote on the board was unanimous to go ahead this way. We're doing the top floors first. No exceptions."

I wrack my brain. Who can house-sit for me? I don't want ten guys in my apartment without me to supervise. My shit is valuable.

★ ★ ★

The next morning a team of Skyline Windows workers arrive and within seconds duct-tape plastic sheets over my furniture. If only these commandos of the sky protected the floors too: from my front door to the living-room window the carpet is covered with the team leader's boot prints. What is that nasty red? I really don't want to know.

Within twenty minutes they've dislodged every window in my apartment. A brutal crosswind gushes through, wreaking havoc on my loose bills. This is when a paperweight collection comes in handy. Papers secured, I scoop up my cordless phone, the Hollywood issue of *Vanity Fair* that just arrived, and retire to the bathroom dressed in a wool hat and Isotoner gloves.

The phone rings midway through a profile on born-into-money Reese Witherspoon. "Hello?" I say with chattering teeth. It's April, but it feels like February today.

"Are you okay? It's Jared."

"I'm in the bathroom—"

"I could call you back when you're finished—"

"No, I'm hiding from the cold and talking will use some muscles."

"You didn't pay your rent?"

"My windows are being upgraded and the bathroom is the only trench hole to be found. Who knew a windowless bathroom would be a blessing? It's frigging Alaska in here."

"You poor thing."

"I'll live," I half laugh through my teeth.

"Speaking of cold, how was Amsterdam?"

"Productive. I just got back." After a new big shiver, I add, "How are you doing?"

"I had a rough weekend. My sister's cocker, Milo, ate all her allergy pills."

"God, is he okay?"

"We rushed him to the vet, who made him eat charcoal. He's fine now."

"He's a lucky dog," I say. My teeth have decided to chatter again.

"I have to get you out of there. If you can stay awake."

"I wish you would. I'm plenty awake with a squadron of men drilling in here."

"Well, Hunter Thompson is appearing at the Union Square Barnes & Noble this afternoon. I just read about it in *Time Out*. He's presigned bookplates if you want to buy his new memoir."

"He's not even signing books?"

"Nope. But this might be a great scene. Maybe Johnny Depp will show up. I heard that the last time Hunter was there Depp was prepping for *Fear and Loathing* and followed him into the store. Interest you at all?"

A yucky memory surfaces. The last time I was at that Barnes & Noble was when I bought my accountant's novel. *Hyman's Hocus-Pocus* turned out to be pretty good, but of course my night with Steve did not. I coolly rise above my shame: "My guess is that Hunter won't even show up. Wouldn't that be his way?"

"Oh he'll show. This is his money for easy living. And you never know, with the way he lives, it might be his last. How many living legends are there?"

"What time is the non-reading? I have to stay until the windows are installed."

"It's at 3:00 p.m."

I think fast. There is nothing going on at the factory until the interview with Channel Four tomorrow morning. I can't move ahead on *The Grand Ladies of Sex* until after the dreaded sedercast. Jared is so sweet, and I need some uptime. "Sure, I'll go."

"Would you like me to scoot over and keep you company now?"

"Trust me, you'll freeze," I say, sidestepping. Sweet now may turn sour later. I'm not inviting Food Channel men up to my apartment anymore. I have a reputation to sort of keep.

For atmospheric purposes—to evoke the sixties?—the Barnes & Noble staff has removed all the folding chairs in the special-event area. The audience camps under the political science shelves, seated on corporate-green carpet.

"I can't believe how many people are waiting for this poser to show up," the sniffling man crouched next to us says.

"I figure in a city of more than eight million there would be at least two hundred and fifty fans," Jared says.

I rearrange my knees. "I told you he wouldn't come."

The manager of book events walks by in wire glasses. He's wearing the dreaded bow tie. He's overheard me. "Oh no, he's coming. He's just running late."

"What's going on?" interrupts a frizzy-haired woman toting a socially responsible recyclable net shopping bag. "I was having a coffee and I saw all these people going upstairs."

"Hunter S. Thompson appearance," the nerdy manager says.

"Is he reading?" she asks.

"No, he's, uh, there are, uh, presigned bookplates."

"Bookplates?" the woman asks.

"Yes. You have to go to the cash register and buy the book. Then you get back in this line. You can speak to him for a second or two, and then one of our staff members will paste down the bookplate."

A woman with a baby sits down near our bit of carpet. She holds her infant out for a baby stretch.

A familiar teen voice crackles from somewhere nearby: "Whoa! Check out how long those baby's legs are. Longer than a Zulu baby."

"Hey, Roswell," calls Jared with a big grin. Roswell heads our way with a short olive-skinned buddy wearing oversize black glasses and a purposely tattered Dole pineapple T-shirt.

"Hey, Squid, this is Abdullah. And this is Jared and my intern boss, Heather."

"Nice to meet you," I say to Abdullah. He's sucking on a coconut Frozfruit, so I continue, "I heard you were having some visa difficulties. I hope they work out."

Roswell sneers.

"I'm okay for a year now. I just got a job at NYPIRG," Abdullah says after another long suck. "I start next week. Ms. Lambert in the guidance office hooked me up. They are making a point of sponsoring Arab students."

"Nywhat?" asks Roswell. "You didn't tell me this."

"New York Public Interest Research Group. Ralph Nader founded it."

Roswell nods his head. "Dude, can you hook me up there for when I graduate? My dad thinks I need a summer job before he'll fund my film. Some crap about a work ethic."

"It's a shit job, so don't get worked up. I'll have to work from two to ten."

"That bites."

"They drop you in a neighborhood and make you fund-raise."

Roswell grimaces. "If you knocked on my door, dude, I'd say, 'Cocksucker, why are you bugging me for?'"

"I wanted to work for a think tank," Abdullah confesses.

"I asked Ms. Lambert to hook me up. She said you have to be older to work for a think tank."

Jared pinches the back of my arm.

"HUNTER!" screams an impatient guy at the front of the room.

"THOMPSON!" screams Roswell.

"Dude, that was so uncool," *tsks* Abdullah to Roswell.

"There he is, guys!" Jared says.

"Where? Yo, Squid. It's weird to see him as an old guy. What a rip-off. No one said Hunter Thompson was old. He's older than my father, dude! He's a fat old man with no hair—he's my chemistry teacher. I can't take this. I can't admire someone that old. Did you check out Hunter's rainbow shirt?"

"That's one fucking ugly shirt," says Abdullah.

"This is like that flick *Weekend at Bernie's,*" Roswell says.

"Never saw it," says Jared.

"My dad has it on DVD. They prop a dead guy up. They're going to be propping Hunter up in that chair."

Standing under mammoth posters of *Gulliver's Travels* and *Moby Dick*, Hunter picks up the mic. With obvious resentment at the obligations of an author, he conducts possibly the shortest Q & A in history. "Anyone else?" he asks three and a half minutes in and miraculously unable to spot even one of the two hundred raised hands. "Okay, let's get going with those bookplates." He's unmoved by the audience's cries of protest. The milksop manager look genuinely frightened as he shrugs his shoulders to the shattered crowd.

Jared and I both pick up a copy of Hunter's book and stand on line. We're toward the end of the impossible queue that snakes around, all the way back to the African-American literature section on the other end of the floor. Slowly our part of the line inches past two gold elevators, flanked by a fire extinguisher and posters of Shakespeare and Maya

Angelou. We round the corner to *The Blues Fakebook* and *Classic Piano Rags*. A conversation about cat litter is ahead of us as the line-serpent slithers past tomes about Klimt, Schiele, Van Gogh, and Miró paintings in the Hermitage Museum.

A hipster nymphet with a plunging neckline on her tight sweater has an extended conversation with Hunter, so we have an extra five minutes by the fashion section.

"Dude, he's going to do her. Look at the way he's fucking her with his eyes," Roswell says as Abdullah peruses *A Brief History of Underwear*.

"What do you think of Hunter in the flesh, guys?" Jared asks.

"Check it out, Squid, he's putting his sunglasses back on. Shit, I wanted to look into his eyes and see if there's insanity."

"Yes," says Abdullah. "I truly believe eyes are the windows of the soul."

The line creeps along until we're almost next. After Hunter takes a photo with two visiting Welshwomen with nose rings and matching lilac long johns, Roswell slips Hunter a package and whispers in his ear.

I have to know. "What was in that?"

"I gave him a red, white and blue whistle Pez dispenser and said, 'If you look inside there's something extra for you.'"

"Ecstasy?" I ask. "A microdot?"

"You're in the ballpark," Roswell says.

"What, you're into celebrity worship?" Jared teases gently.

"Squid, the thing is, Christopher Columbus, Thomas Jefferson, they all have their flaws. He is Hunter S. Thompson. He's flawed too, but he's a real hero. People who are not honest with themselves can never really be a hero. Although Jefferson was diametrically opposed to everything he did in secret, like hold slaves."

"Dude," cuts in Abdullah. "I'm looking at the first few pages of his book. Hunter Thompson was arrested his senior year of high school."

"It must of sucked back then."

"Have sucked."

"Who the fuck are you, Abdullah? Mr. Strunk or Mr. White? As I was saying, jail wouldn't suck now. They get HBO in jail. I'm like, fuck, I want HBO, you get to see Shannon Tweed."

Abdullah laughs.

"Do you even know who she is, dork?"

"Yeah? She's a soft-porn star, right?"

"We have to get going," I say.

Abdullah looks up briefly from Hunter Thompson's new book. "Yo, Roswell, what does *copiously* mean again?"

"Shit, I should know that," said Roswell. "I think it's a Stanley Kaplan word—it comes from Latin, shit."

"Are you hungry?" Jared asks down in the lobby, now that we're minus the Wonder Boys.

"I could eat."

"I'm trying to think what's in walking distance."

"There's Republic, they have great noodles."

"I'm not sure noodles will fill me up. I'm really hungry. How about Second Avenue Deli?"

"I've never been."

"You're kidding! You're a Greenblotz and you've never been to the Second Avenue Deli? We're going."

Before we head south to Tenth Street and Second Avenue, we wander through the Union Square farmers' market, which is dismantling for the day. The weather is better than this morning; it's just warm enough now. Under a generous but quickly fading blue sky, a group of Peruvian musicians playing panpipes have drawn an audience. We listen with the crowd for a bit in an urban trance. Even a Mennonite farmer and his sons, wearing hats straight out of *Witness*, watch from their pie stall. The ethereal music seems at odds with the grit of New York.

"Have you been to the Andes?" I ask. "My mother's going there and then on to the Amazon this week." I bite my lip to shut myself up. I keep forgetting that Jared is with the team filming my "family" seder. I have to be more careful or the horrid truths of Chez Greenblotz will leak out.

"You've never been to Second Avenue Deli and I've never been to the Andes. But I've read the new South American issue of *National Geographic*."

I smile, and inside I'm relieved. He didn't think any more of it.

"So are you firing Roswell?" Jared says as we cross Fourteenth Street.

"I think it's easier to let it be. I don't have the heart! But I just can't understand how he got into Stuyvesant. I thought you have to take a ridiculously hard test to get in."

"You forget. All seventeen-year-old boys are like that."

"You think? Vondra went to Stuyvesant. We once went shopping for shower curtains—she ran into some of her old friends and they ended up arguing about the subspecies of the fried fish being served in the Kmart café."

Jared snorts. "My neighbor's kid got in because he had a tiny dictionary hidden between his legs."

"Your neighbor *told* you that?"

"Her son did. Cheaters can be very proud." A driver in a limo honks.

(It's somebody trying to look important in an hourly rental. Here's another little rich-people secret I picked up from my mother: you can always tell a New York limo is rented by the letter Z in the license plate.)

"Anyhow, I'd be disappointed in you if you fired him. You're his first break. How often do you get an opportunity to mentor someone in this world? You know so much about filmmaking. And you should teach him all of it. *Noblesse oblige*. You are obliged to be noble, I genuinely believe that. What would you say to him if you could really be open, and have a heart-to-heart?"

I think. "That his Maysles project is ridiculous. He doesn't even know to be embarrassed. He should watch and learn, and gain the skill set needed for good filmmaking. Then he should find the fire in the belly and make films he has a passion for."

"Well said."

"Thank you."

"So tell him that in a language he can understand at seventeen."

Am I really being too harsh on the kid? I mull over his take on Roswell as we cross another street. Jared has apparently moved on from my lack of mentoring skills, as he says, "Oh, this is an odd story. Did I tell you there's an all-out alert for my mother's new poodle in Westchester? It went AWOL on Thursday evening."

"That's awful. I thought the allergy-pills story was bad. Are all the dogs in your family cursed?"

"My sister stupidly left out an open bottle of pills on her kitchen table, but I think my mother's dog brought this on herself. Mom says Gigi wasn't having it when her stylist gave her a froufrou cut. My mother was devastated when I gave her pooch three days to live."

"Three days at most. A feral poodle?"

"But get this—she just left a message on my voice mail

that a woman over in Larchmont called to say she thought she saw Gigi with a rabbit in her mouth."

His cell phone rings with sitcom timing. "You found her? Mum, I'm with a friend, I'll call you tonight— No, I heard she's fine. Still has charcoal on her paws, but running around like nothing happened—I love you too." He clicks off. "A happy ending," Jared says to me, and grins when I smile.

I bet Steve can't say I love you that easily to his mother. The ones in love with themselves never can. Jared is the one I'd pursue if given a second chance. Damn. He may not know anything about how much of a whore I was with Steve, but he will. Guys talk.

On Second Avenue and Twelfth Street we pass an old movie theater currently named City Cinemas Village East.

"You ever go in there?" Jared asks.

"No."

"At the turn of the century it was a Yiddish theater. I saw *The Matrix* there and when I looked up, I noticed the ceiling has a giant Jewish star in the middle. It looks like a religious cookie cutout from a giant blue and white Wedgwood plate. So I read up on it. Steven Jay Gould even wrote a piece about the theater just before he died."

"The science writer?"

"Yes, he was as amazed as I was that such a relic could survive. There used to be Yiddish productions up and down Second Avenue. They called it the Jewish Rialto. All the stars of the day played here, Molly Picon, Jacob Adler—and across the street from here was Café Royal where the Jewish actors and artists hung out."

The Yiddish-star names mean nothing to me, but Jared's sunshiny demeanor is just what I need in my insecure state. "I love your enthusiasm, Jared."

"I'm a bit of a trivia buff."

"So is my dad. He investigates every oddment he comes across."

Jared smiles. "Oddment is an oddment of a word."

"I'm a bit of a vocabulary buff."

"Jared!" a nasal voice calls out to him from down the block.

"Oh, man," Jared says. "That's my ex-girlfriend, Sarah the shopaholic."

As a tall woman walks toward us, I see she is lugging a nearly bursting Henri Bendel's bag. (Crap, did I miss a sale?)

"Look at this, a reunion," Sarah says on the corner of Tenth Street and Second Avenue.

Sarah is pretty. Very. Her severe Cleopatra bob of black hair highlights her long but attractive nose and her striking green eyes speckled with brown circles.

"Hi," Jared says in a deflated voice.

When it's obvious he isn't going to introduce us, Sarah coughs and says: "Sarah Bergman. I'm Jared's ex."

"This is Heather," Jared says against his will.

Sarah's outsize smile is disturbing. Even though I'm no competition for her lookswise, I'm sure it's the same smile the evil queen dons as she offers Snow White a poison apple. Sarah slowly moves her eyes toward Jared. You can see the wheels going around in her head. "I'm meeting my fiancé at Second Avenue Deli."

"That's where we were going," Jared says even more miserably.

"Oh, join us. Yes, join us. Uzi would love to meet you."

"Heather and I are having a very private conversation. We may or may not go."

"Don't worry, dolls, of course I'll leave you alone." Sarah tucks part of her bob behind her ear, and not so discreetly checks my shoes out before she tootles off in a huff.

(They're from Charles Jordan, so fuck off, doll.)

"Wow," I say when the coast is clear.

"She's still angry that I ended our relationship." He marks an inch with his fingers and says, "This close to being a stalker."

"We don't have to go there if you're uncomfortable."

"No, I promised you Second Avenue Deli, and so it shall be. She has no idea how annoying she is."

"Maybe she misinterprets annoying for sassy."

"I'm sick of kowtowing to her. She sent me a two-page fax with a list of her friends and acquaintances I'm not supposed to talk to. She's not taking my restaurants away from me, too. We'll just sit as far away as we can—unless you don't want to go—"

"*I* didn't break up with her."

Despite Jared's hunger pains, he is so unnerved that he insists we take a detour to *Love Saves the Day*, a collectibles store three short blocks away. "You really have to check this place out," he enthuses a bit too hard. "It's been around for years. I think it was featured in *Desperately Seeking Susan*."

I give Jared points for anger management.

The small store is packed with hokey seventies and eighties TV memorabilia, including a long line of old lunch boxes.

"There's Roswell's Pee-Wee doll," I say, a few steps in the door. I point to a glass case packed with memorabilia. "And there's your old lunch box—the one you and Roswell were talking about."

"Hong Kong Phooey! Where?"

"On the wall."

"Eagle-Eye Greenblotz." He picks it up with a huge smile. "That's the sidekick cat. Spot, that's the cat's name." He checks the tag. "Eighty-five bucks for a lunch box? I'm in the wrong business. Which lunch box did you have? If you still have it, it could be a nest egg."

"I didn't have any," I say.

"C'mon, who didn't have a lunch box?"

"Me." Because Wilson came in the limo and took me back to a hot meal prepared by our cook, Angela. Dad was going through a no-food-dyes stage for a few years, and he made Angela buy unappealing food, like gray hot dogs with no food coloring. At Dalton, going back to your house to eat was peculiar. The other kids were often as rich as me, or even richer, but most of their parents saw no harm in childhood rites of passage, like food fights in a lunchroom.

"Which one would you have had then?"

"Strawberry Shortcake maybe?"

"I'm getting it for you."

"Jared, don't be silly. That's an expensive gag."

"Don't you be silly. Everybody needs a lunch box. I'm getting my Phooey back too."

"Save your money." I laugh, but there's no arguing the point. As Jared hands the guy by the register his credit card, I flick through vintage copies of *Ranger Rick*, the environmental kids' magazine we used to get in my third-grade classroom. Rick is a concerned private investigator raccoon who wants children to value animals in the world, and my class project (which got written up in the magazine) was our mail adoption of a sick warthog named Clyde who lived somewhere in Africa. Eventually our many Save Clyde bake sales paid for his veterinary bills and his air flight to the Bronx Zoo.

Jared taps me when his transaction is done. Lunch boxes in hand—we certainly look like a couple now—we head to the Second Avenue Deli, an establishment heralded by a large sign in English letters designed to look at first glance Hebraic. In the doorway, and spilling onto the street, there's a raucous line of hungry, chatty New Yorkers, each one worthy of his or her own *Seinfeld* episode.

When our spot on line has moved indoors, I silently admire a small section of an inside wall of an Automat. The Second Avenue Deli owners must have rescued the relic for decorative purposes. As a documentary maker, I've seen countless clips featuring Automats while I was seeking appropriate old footage to flesh out my projects. Customers slipped a nickel or a dime into a food slot, and out came a knockwurst sandwich or a nice piece of sponge cake.

The woman in front of me has gray hair sprayed with enough Aquanet to withstand a freak Manhattan twister. "In the old days," she says as she taps the glass of the display, "you paid a nickel for everything. I used to have to pay to *pish* at the old B. Altman department store, may it rest in peace. My girlfriends had a saying—*Paid my nickel, broke my heart, all I did was have a fart.*"

I smile courteously. I think I remember a department store with metered stalls when I was really, really little. Shopping was the one activity Mom always took me along for, even when she was only a yellow belt.

A fiftyish woman in a powder-blue tracksuit yells, "Over here!" to her fiftyish husband in a matching tracksuit who is pushing his way through the line. "So long to park, Morris? I moved my digital camera to the French mode, and I can't get back now because it's in French—"

"Ellen," her husband flings out in disgust, "I don't want to hear about your camera, I just want to eat."

"How long for a table of fourteen?" screams a lady behind us.

Jared leans in close to me, and shout-whispers, "If there's a louder line in America, I'd be amazed."

"Name?" asks the hostess after an amused glance at our lunch boxes.

"Silver."

As we wait, I scan the room. Sarah is nowhere to be seen, and I can tell Jared is relieved.

"You are on sacred ground, my friend. The Second Avenue Deli is one of the great delis in the world. Steve just produced a special on them for the Food Channel."

"What are the other ones?"

"New York's also got Carnegie of course, where Woody Allen hangs out. In Florida, Rascal House is a big deal, although Wolfie's is king. One of the best things we learned during the show was that there was a *Gemini* flight that launched a congressional investigation because John Young smuggled a Wolfie's corned-beef sandwich aboard for Gus Grissom as a treat to eat instead of the dehydrated space ice cream."

The hostess sits us next to the one open spot, a seat away from a guy around my age whose head is topped with a felt *yarmulke* sporting the Nike "Just Do It" symbol. I chuckle to myself. Jake, on every Jewish mailing list, once received a catalog of novelty *yarmulkes* and showed it off to my cousin Greg and me at a board meeting. The *yarmulkes* could be made with designs like a chocolate-chip cookie, a smiley face and the yin-yang symbols. Very funny. But then Jake earnestly pitched Greenblotz *yarmulkes* as a mail-in giveaway for our customers—one *yarmulke* for ten proofs of purchase. He'd even ordered a sample with our logo over a matzo background. Greg and I laughed him right out of the rented boardroom.

"What do you recommend?" I ask after Jared and I are seated and the aging waitress with impossibly black dyed hair slams the menus down on the table.

Jared puts down the menu and looks at me with upraised eyes. "Is there any question here? You have to get the matzo ball soup. You're tiny. That alone will fill you up."

I feel like the proud lady in the Special K commercial twirling around her newly thinned frame in her red dress. "But that's not enough for you," I say without giving away my glee, "you're a big boy."

"I was thinking more along the lines of a brisket sandwich. *And* a soup—" Before Jared can continue, his face goes slack in horror: off-kilter Sarah emerges from the ladies' room still clinging to her bulging plastic Bendel's shopping bag. She's working her way to the table next to us, the one with the guy with the Nike *yarmulke*.

Instead of taking her seat, she hovers over us with a pasted smile. "Don't you love this place?"

"My first time here," I confess.

"Oh," Sarah says without losing my gaze.

"The *kreplach* are excellent, Jared, don't you think?" Sarah pronounces the end "chh" with an authentic-sounding guttural tone. Years of Hebrew school? "But tonight, the two of us are going to split a tongue sandwich," she continues.

I'm not so intimidated by her striking beauty anymore. Away from the sunlight you can see her enviable multicolored eyes are flanked by premature crow's-feet. And I can see why Jared bristled when she saw us in the street; her icy personality brings her way down the appeal index. And this is her trying to be on good behavior. She motions to her fiancé to get up and say hello to us.

"This is my ex," she says to Uzi.

Uzi fixes the bobby pin securing the *yarmulke* to his hair so that it sits farther back on his head. Most women would call him attractive, but to me his forehead is so high and his teeth so large and bright that I can't help thinking of his uncanny resemblance to Donny Osmond. "Nice to meet you," he says to both of us after an uncomfortable but huge smile.

"Jared's a cameraman for the Food Channel," Sarah says.

"Do you know Emeril?"

"Different network," says Jared. I get the feeling he gets asked that a lot.

"Oh," Uzi says, disappointed. "Well, can you answer a food question for me?"

"I can try."

Uzi clears his throat: "I was thinking about this yesterday over pizza with anchovies. We gut big fish. When we eat little fish, are we eating the guts too?" Amused with himself, he flicks out his long pink tongue as he awaits Jared's answer.

Jared pauses uncomfortably. "I've never thought—"

A humiliated Sarah quickly starts stroking Uzi's shoulder. "You're such a clown. This is Heather. What did you say your last name was?"

"She didn't," Jared says.

"Greenblotz," I say.

Sarah raises her eyebrows.

"Like the matzo?" Uzi says.

"Yes," Jared answers for me.

"Well, isn't that perfect," Sarah says.

"Uzi's a doctor," she adds quickly, before I have a chance to think too much about her cryptic words.

Uzi looks at Sarah with a curious expression on his face.

"Well, that's a bit of a stretch, Sarah."

"What sort of doctor?" Jared asks.

"He has a Ph.D. in trombone. He's a…musicologist."

"A trombone doctor? That I never heard of," says a husky voice. Up periscope. We have an eavesdropper: a sixty-something man seated diagonally from Jared and me with a comical Einstein shock of gray hair and a huge gut bulging out of his blue sweater.

Sarah turns to our uninvited guest with considerable

venom. "If you're going to butt in on our conversation, at least you should know what you're talking about. Uzi got his Ph.D. at Juilliard, so he has every right to call himself a doctor."

Our nosy neighbor waves his hand as an apology to Sarah, but facing us smiles with a definite glint of glee. Then he smiles broadly to the waitress bringing a can of cherry soda and a glass of ice to his table. "With you, sugar, I always get good service. On a scale of one to ten, always a ten."

He turns to Jared and whispers loudly, "With the other one never more than a two."

The elderly waitress, whose name tag says Diane, smiles and taps Uzi on the shoulder. "You ready to order, honey?"

"Excuse me," Uzi says after another blinding flash of his overbleached teeth, as he flies back to his seat. "I'm starving." The waitress plunks down a plate of pickles and a basket of bread on Sarah and Uzi's table. Uzi's lips move in prayer before he lunges for a green pickled tomato. He downs it in two fast gulps and then reaches for a roll. "I'll have the stuffed cabbage as an appetizer. And we're going to split a tongue sandwich and one order of fries."

"There's a surcharge for splitting, honey," waitress Diane says.

"Yes, I know."

Jared points out another customer's lime-green can of soda. "That's deli champagne. Cel-Ray."

"I vaguely recall my grandfather used to drink that."

It's incredible—Sarah is still trying to hear what we're saying and not at all discreetly. She leans back and says with a dose of acid, "Having fun?"

Jared puffs his cheeks out and lets the air out of them before addressing her. "What's in the Bendel's bag? Big sale?"

"God, how you want to know everything!"

"I'm trying to be polite here. What did you score? Ten pairs of sandals?"

"Was that facetious?"

"Not at all."

"Borrowed tools," Sarah says curtly. "I'm taking them back home."

"Tools?" Jared says cuttingly. "Who borrows tools?"

"My sister," Sarah says.

"And how is Shira?"

"Not that you ever liked her, but since you asked, she switched her master's degree to concrete sculpture, so she won't be done for another year. She's working on a lifesize interpretation of Lot's wife."

Jared signals to the waitress that he is ready to order. "Give her my regards."

Our waitress shifts her attention to our table. "What are you having?"

"One brisket sandwich on seeded rye, two matzo ball soups."

"Gotcha. Anything to drink?"

"A Cel-Ray for me. What about you, Heather?"

"Diet Coke, please."

Sarah will not look away. "I didn't know you had such a *stockpile* of tools," Jared says finally.

"Under the kitchen sink," Sarah says, "there's a little *stockpile*. The little *tool* area." She turns to me. "And what do you do?"

"I'm a documentary maker," I say as neutrally as possible.

"What have you documented?"

"Sarah—" Jared says.

"My company was just filming a new HBO movie at the natural history museum."

"That must be fun."

"It's fun, though it's tough work."

"I'd love to leave my office for a little *jaunt* to the American Museum of Natural History."

Jaunt you, I think.

Uzi says, loudly, "Sarah, are you going to eat?"

"In a minute." She looks straight into my eyes. "So what is the number-one place you'd really like to document?"

"I'd like to get the scoop on heaven," I say.

"Oh? Even if Jews don't believe in heaven?" She raises an eyebrow.

"No?" I say.

"You don't know that?" she says incredulously.

Jared rushes into rescue mode. "Heather, what do you think would be waiting for you in heaven if you could go there?"

"A lot of pillows and mattresses," I say. "Lots of chocolate cake, but no repercussions—no feeling sick, no gaining weight."

"Is heaven then instant gratification?" Jared asks.

"No, *no*," I reply. "I guess that would just be the environment. There would be stimuli too. Lots of books."

"Who would be there?" Uzi puts in, looking genuinely interested in the conversation now that his stomach has been tended to.

"Interesting people," I say.

Sarah is bored. She is not getting the reaction she wanted, whatever that is. She grabs a sour pickle off her table, and suggestively takes a bite. "Did you hear Gordon Katz is marrying Mandy?"

"Who's Mandy again?" Jared is visibly impatient.

"Mandy with the big jaw."

"Oh, her. What do you have against her? Her jaw is not that big. I liked her a lot. And last I heard, she was learning how to teach ballet under Baryshnikov's tutelage."

"You can't get cooler than that," I pipe up.

Jared smiles toward me. "Yes. You've gotta kiss the ring."

Uzi laughs despite the risks.

Sarah's head is a bobbing ball of anger. "There's nothing cool about the situation. She's not converting—their children will grow up *nishkin* here, *nishkin* there. They'll light a Hanukkah candle or two and spend their days eating *traif*. And his father is a famous cantor. It gives me the shudders."

"What does *nishkin* mean?" I say to Sarah a bit sadistically.

"Neither here nor there," Jared answers for her quickly.

Sarah looks at me again intently with her magnificent eyes. "Are you really from the matzo family, or just have the same name?"

"My cousin who runs the factory is kosher," I white-lie. I'm not sure why on earth I just volunteered that. Nervousness? To piss this bitch off? I take a small gulp of air and say, "But I'm not."

My Russian-roulette gamble on honesty comes back and shoots me in the face. "With your bloodline? That's terrible."

Jared looks right at his ex as he says to me, "Heather, would you like anyone to go to a traditional version of hell?"

"No," I say. "I'd want them to go to oblivion."

Sarah talks past me to the gefilte fish that got away: "This is who you are dating? You with your speeches about the need to preserve our culture. 'The *yiddishkeit* is dying.' Ring a bell?"

"Sarah, you are way out of line."

They stare at each other, at daggers drawn. This time I keep mum. I've poured enough fuel on the fire, and this fight between ex-lovers is way out of my province.

Our nosy neighbor's cell phone rings to the tune of "Hava

Nagilah," which even I know is the basic issue Jewish song for family get-togethers. "Yeah?—W?—eight letters?— Whodiddy—nah, don't worry about it, you got me in with the internist. He did a good job by the way, stretched my ball bag out like a square, got right to the root of the problem—okay, see you at the *bar mitzvah*." He hangs up and sees me looking at him and says, "Everyone calls me for the puzzle. I should start charging."

"Our culture is our marrow," Sarah continues after more scary head bobs and an equally disturbing staccato laugh. "In ten years the whole language will be dead. Isn't that what you said?"

I have to shut this loon up. "I think you've made a wrong assumption, Sarah. We're not dating. Jared and I are friends. We're working on a documentary together."

Under the table Jared touches my knee in appreciation.

Our waitress arrives with our soup.

Finally Sarah turns away and focuses on her own food. Praise be! Hosanna!

"Did you know this is a bona fide Greenblotz of the matzo clan?" Jared crows to the waitress. "The great-granddaughter of Izzy Greenblotz."

The waitress nods in appreciation. "I knew your grandfather. We still use Greenblotz matzo meal to make the matzo balls."

"That's terrific," I say.

"Jack!" she calls to a man behind the take-out counter stocked with knishes and beef salamis. "We've got royalty here! Greenblotz girl, from the matzo."

"Yeah? Meal on the house!" the man behind the counter announces. "Abe would have done that, don't you think?"

The waitress rips up our bill on her pad.

"Please tell your owner that's so kind of him," I say to the waitress.

Jared explains in a whisper: "That's Abe Lebowohl's brother."

"Who's Abe Lebowohl?"

Jared points to a smiling chubby middle-aged man in a set of photos on the wall over our seat. In one he has his arms around Jerry Seinfeld and, in another one, around Muhammad Ali. "Abe Lebowohl started this place. He was legendary even before he was killed about ten years ago in a drive-by murder."

"Who killed him?"

"Never solved. My pop knew him. Very sweet guy. A real *mensch*. Gave buckets of money and chopped liver to the disadvantaged and Jewish charities."

Our food arrives.

"Can I try the Jewish champagne?"

"The Dr. Brown's Cel-Ray? I'd give you a sip, but it's not for the uninitiated."

"What exactly is it?"

"Soda from celery."

"I can handle it," I say. Until I taste it. It's weird and dry, almost dusty. "I don't mean to be rude, but I'd rather drink crab juice."

Jared laughs. "Like I said, it's an acquired taste."

The soup, however—a delicate chicken stock with little square noodles, parsley and one big perfectly fluffy matzo ball—is sublime. I'm proud it's my family matzo meal in the recipe.

As we eat, Sarah keeps craning her neck back from her conversation with Uzi. I'm half tempted to lean across the table and give Jared a kiss to give Sarah something to look at.

★ ★ ★

Outside, Jared shakes his head and touches me on the shoulder. "A million apologies that you had to go through that. What did you make of Sarah? A little scary?"

"An honest assessment?"

"Please."

"I'd say the only person more disturbing in the universe is the toothless woman who sat next to me last year in the number 6 train, the one who poked me and pointed at a terrified mother and infant across from us and wanted to guess the baby's age by his tooth count."

My comic timing's getting better these days. Jared brays. When his laughter finally levels off, he says, "At least you liked the soup."

"I loved the soup, I'll deconstruct the soup later, but back to Sarah—why did you ever go out with her to begin with?"

"The truth? I met her at a party. She wasn't wearing a warning sign, and I thought she was pretty hot at first."

"She's stunning. I'll give her that. But when you spend five minutes with her—"

"She's—please, don't make me say this—"

I squeeze his wrist. "You're obligated."

"She's double-jointed and—"

"And?" I just don't get that answer.

"In bed she was a pretzel. It was kind of thrilling as a spectator—"

I cough and laugh at the same time. "And as a participant, I hope."

This time we both laugh loudly.

"Now that you know too much about my personal life, I have to whack you."

I catch his eye again. "Did you really say all that to her about Jewish culture dying out? That's some pretty heavy guilt."

"All out of context, but yes."

"So you've never dated a non-Jewish woman?"

"In college I did. A Catholic French exchange student named Cathou. She was a gorgeous blond *shiksa* who had me over to her off-campus apartment for an Easter dinner with a big pink hock of ham and plenty of hot cross buns. I ate it all with a smile because she was sexy as hell and I was sowing my oats."

"But now you just want homely Jews?"

Jared play-punches me. "Now I won't get myself into a relationship with a woman before we've spoken at length about religious and cultural values."

Well, that rules this pagan out. "I guess you're not going out with Tonia then," I say as the air-assist platform on the Second Avenue M15 bus screeches opens and lowers a wheelchair onto the ground.

"Tonia?"

"I don't mean to come off sounding vain, but I thought I picked up a certain amount of anger from her toward me at the factory when your team was filming the Izzy segment. I'm really not used to that, so I noticed it. I thought she was being protective of you or Steve, but I wasn't sure which one of you."

Am I trying to find out more about Steve or Jared? At this point I'm not sure. Steve's inner being is still a mystery to me, which I hate to admit to myself is sexy—even after I've been burned by his arrogance. But Jared's handsome too. He may not be as picture perfect as Steve, but he's way nicer. What does it matter? Jared's probably crossed me off his list anyhow, since I eat *traif*.

"First of all, stop selling yourself short. You're pretty and talented. Live with it."

"Thanks," I say with a big grin.

"And second of all, you're very perceptive. That tension was real, but for Steve. You should hear how he worked Tonia. Told her he was dreaming about her. Why do women always fall for that shit?"

I cringe on behalf of myself and all women.

"He's a very old friend of mine. We went to elementary school together, and he got me the job when I was floundering after film school. I love him like a brother, but I wouldn't say he's the nicest guy, especially to women. Still, he's very funny at times. A huge practical joker."

I'm smarting, not only from hearing Steve's lines about dreaming of me out of Jared's mocking mouth, but also from learning just how close the two of them are.

"Did he ever pull a big joke on *you*?" I manage to say.

"You bet. I was supposed to go to Puerto Rico with lovable Sarah last year and she said she wouldn't leave Manhattan until I bought a new bathing suit, something more in style. Steve had me convinced Speedos were back, and told me Speedos come in two sizes, large and extra large."

"They size them that way?"

Jared smiles and holds up a hand to let him continue. "We had a shoot two blocks away from the Speedo store, and after we wrapped he said he was walking that way, and had me ask the saleslady for the suit with the extra-large pouch."

"You didn't!"

"The saleslady almost died laughing."

"That's almost too cruel to be a joke."

"Cruel's not a bad word for him. Steve is funny and cruel. It's fine if you are a guy. He's well liked by the men at work, but the women he's gone out with hate him."

"Does he brag about his conquests?" I say with my best poker face on.

"Steve? You'd think so, considering how long we've

known each other. But strangely, there's never a peep about anyone. I only hear about it when it's really bad, from his conquests. Like Tonia. And our sweet little receptionist who he apparently—deflowered. I think he'll get a psychic check in the mail though. He's getting laid, but he's lonely without a serious girlfriend, I'm sure of it."

Yuck. The thought of the way Steve got over on me repulses me. I shudder slightly.

"It's getting colder, huh?" Jared asks. "Want to walk a little? It'll keep us warm."

"Where to?"

"Anywhere. I didn't mean to make you stand in the cold so long. I'm still worked up after running into Sarah."

"Twice."

"Yes, twice! If you're not sick of me yet, we could warm up with an espresso. We could go to my place. I just got a great espresso maker as a Food Channel bonus. I'm over on Crosby Street. A bit of a hike but not that far."

Steve may have never mentioned anything to Jared about our evening together—but why go to Jared's place even for an innocent espresso when I'm so clearly not what he is looking for? Bettina has drummed into me that a mature woman identifies the right person before allowing romance to continue. I pause a bit too long while I pull these thoughts together.

"We're just friends. Remember?" he says.

"Yes." I give him a small cautious smile. I'm worked up from the trip, and the mountain of things to do for the seder. Being with Jared is so easy. "A homemade espresso sounds good," I say, startling myself. That was my id speaking.

Jared smiles broadly. After we cross the first light toward SoHo, he says, "I was surprised when you told Sarah you weren't kosher. I thought since the factory is kosher—"

"I'm not. Never have been. In all honesty, my parents aren't kosher either, but please keep this close to the chest. It could hurt business. I guess you're kosher, then."

"Yes," he says quietly.

"I didn't see you bless any food, like Uzi."

"I did. I blessed the bread silently when you weren't looking."

"Does it bother you that I'm not observant?"

"Look, unlike Sarah, I respect everyone's choice. But honestly, I'm looking to settle down now. These things are important to me now that I'm thinking how my children will be raised."

"You go to synagogue?"

"Every Saturday morning. It's a young congregation. My folks only go to synagogue on the High Holidays."

"So how come you don't wear a *yarmulke*?"

"Honestly? I used to, but then I didn't get any film or television jobs. I'd wear a *tallis* if I could, but in the film and TV world, religion freaks people out. I can't imagine the look I'd get from my peers if they could see me at home in the morning putting on my *tefillin*."

"What's a *tallis*?"

"A prayer shawl men put on under their clothes. Usually you can spot the fringes hanging out."

"What's a *tfillet*?"

"*Tefillin.*" Jared looks at me closely. "Didn't you at least go to after-school Hebrew school?"

"No."

"Weren't you *bat mitzvahed*?"

"No." Is he trying to make me weep?

"You really don't know what *tefillin* are?"

Is this Daniel Popper all over again? "No," I say angrily. He grabs my hand. "I'm sorry. It's just so amazing to me that a Greenblotz was brought up without knowing her heritage beyond the matzo box."

"That's just the way it was."

"*Tefillin* are small boxes that contain Torah passages. Observant Jewish men wrap them to their head and arms in the morning because of a passage in Deuteronomy."

"Do you know the passage?" I'm not sure why I just asked this.

Jared looks me straight in my Greenblotz blues and says:

And these words, which I command you this day, shall be in your heart. And you shall teach them diligently to your children, and shall talk of them when you sit in your house, and when you walk by the way, and when you lie down, and when you rise up. And you shall bind them for a sign upon your hand, and they shall be frontlets between your eyes.

Can I locate the emotion I'm feeling? Is it jealousy? Or a bit of disgust? "Are your parents kosher?" I say neutrally.

"Hardly. My mother's parents were, but when she married Dad, she toned it down quite a few notches. We didn't keep a Shabbat, but I guess a bit of the food laws filtered in because we hardly ever ate ham and bacon. On the other hand, we ate a lot of pork at Chinese restaurants—in wonton soup, dumplings, those sorts of things. Our father had a rule when I was growing up—if you don't know what's in it, it's kosher. I'm much stricter."

I zip up my jacket. I like Jared a lot, but I've pretty much written him off as a love interest. "So what happened to change your view?"

"After college I visited Jerusalem, and then signed on to work on Kibbutz Sde Eliyahu."

"I had a friend from elementary school who went to a kibbutz for a year before she went to Oberlin. She told me she worked for her room and board."

"Yes, it's a communal experience."

"What was your task?"

"I milked Holsteins."

"That's not too bad. I guess you could've had to scrub toilets."

"I did that too. But I enjoyed all of it. It was very international and, honestly, half the reason I went was just to get laid by any hot lady in the backpacking international set. But—this is weird to describe unless you've lived in Israel— I was amazed after one month by the connection I felt to history. God, we were living right on the Sea of Galilee! A seismic change took place inside of me—I knew what was important to me."

"Not getting laid?"

"Well, I got some action too, but that was a bonus."

I think as I laugh. Jared's words make me remember the day before I left the Netherlands. "I don't know if this matches your experience, but I had a very strong jolt of heritage guilt at the Anne Frank House in Amsterdam."

"I haven't been, but I can only imagine. And I wouldn't call it guilt, Heather. I'd call it revelation. I don't want to sound remotely like Sarah, but maybe you should consider going kosher. It's not about the food, it's about the history." Jared looks me in the eyes, and touches my hand like a recent Hare Krishna convert.

"That's just not who I am," I say kindly. These days I'm infinitely more appreciative of human touch, even when I'm being proselytized.

ten

Waterloo

Jared takes my coat and drapes it on a wooden chair near the door as we exit from the freight elevator to his third-floor loft.

"What an amazing place," I say.

"I got it for a song," Jared says almost apologetically. "The previous owner bought it during the huge Wall Street run-up in the dot-com years, but when the bottom dropped out of the market he needed to unload it fast."

I nod politely, but *c'mon*. Nobody gets a place like this in Manhattan for less than half a million. The last I checked, the Food Channel wasn't paying law-firm salaries. Is this a gift from his Westchester parents with the poodle?

"So should I get you that coffee?"

"I'm thinking about my jet lag again, and I'll need to sleep when I leave—by any chance do you have any herbal tea?"

"Chamomile okay?"

"Sounds good." After a few seconds, I follow him like Mary's lamb over to the kitchen area of his loft.

"Nope. I only have Earl Grey," he calls out loudly.

"As long as it's weaker than espresso, I'll take it," I say from directly behind him.

"Oh, hello."

"Sorry. I never squelch a chance to check out other people's kitchens. I'm the world's biggest *Trading Spaces* addict. Nice floor by the way."

"My mother's idea. She says it's easier to clean because it's one piece. She'd put any *Trading Spaces* addict to shame. Her idea of a vacation is a trip to Home Depot."

"One piece? It looks like hand-laid tile."

"Score one for Miriam Silver. You should hear her go on about it. 'Dirt doesn't get through the cracks because it's not tiling. Stop calling it linoleum, Jared, it's the latest rage, completely different, it's *Congo*-leum.'"

"From the Congo?" I crack.

Jared smirks as he opens his natural-wood cupboard to get the tea. As he turns his back, I snoop out the bottom left corner of the magazine on the counter. You can tell a lot about a man by what he reads. When he was living on Park Avenue, Dad not only kept a subscription to every theater magazine in the universe, but also to an absurd number of men's muscle magazines, even though his own tummy popped out like a six-month pregnant woman's. And if it was pretentious as the *New York Review of Books* or a McSweeney's anthology, Daniel Popper had it on his coffee table.

The corner of the magazine reads: *Kosher Gourmet*.

Jared has dog-eared a page with a recipe for a kosher Indonesian seaweed dessert. As he spoons out the tea, I peek in the open cupboard doors. The shelves are packed with kosher foods, like a teriyaki sauce called Soy Vey. I note with a mix of surprise and pride that his olive spread, Garden's Best, is a Greenblotz product.

I pick up the jar and show it to him. "This is from our company."

"Where's your logo?"

"My cousin Jake's been sneaking our products into the traditional-foods shelf space by using another brand name. Even in the kosher section we use different brand names to get more shelf space. Greenblotz is also Bubby's Best. The gefilte fish companies cannibalize each other too. You may prefer Mother's but it's from the same company as Rokeach."

"I've got the goods on you guys now. Good thing I'm not with *20/20* or *60 Minutes.*"

You think that's the goods on my family? Hardly. I'll give you the goods, Jared Silver—you have five hours?

I take a better look around his expansive, well-furnished digs. The guys I've been out with since college graduation have mostly lived in glorified pigeonholes, all they could afford in the New York rental market. I've felt guilty about having them over to my various expensive apartments—especially my current penthouse—so I almost always had sex at their places. When I was twenty-five I spent four months dating a starving artist who never stepped foot in my place. It had a nice side effect though: he kept going on about how mysterious I was, and mystique is important to a starving artist. As far as my penthouse on the Upper East Side goes, I could have gotten a smaller and less showy place, I guess, but it opened up at the exact moment I was looking. The view across the East River to Queens and the Bronx is remarkable. If you are going to be spending a lot of time with yourself, you might as well have a great view.

Jared's place is big and clean. "I can't get over how neat you are. Were you in the military?"

"I can change your mind in an instant. Open the fridge."

"Yes, Sarge." He's right; it's pretty darn gross. One bowl without a lid contains particularly malodorous, scary stuff. I hold my nose as I examine it closer. "What the hell is in that?"

"Week-old tuna slop. Macaroni, mayo and two cans of tuna. I'm a good cook but I need a woman to cook for. Otherwise, my inner Felix Unger turns into Oscar Madison."

"How can you have tuna in with mayo? Isn't that mixing meat and dairy?"

Jared pauses like Aldous Huxley explaining the *Doors of Perception* to a curious teen about to lick acid. "Meat is meat. Tuna is *parave*, it's neutral. There's all sorts of neutral foods. Eggs are also neutral."

"You should apply for *The Bachelor*. The nice-Jewish-boy edition. He has a job! He's nice to his mother! But of course you'd have to lose the beard. Men with beards are never on those shows. They turn off most women."

Gibberish often dribbles out of my mouth when I'm sleep deprived. But Jared looks surprised and slightly hurt. "What do *you* think of my beard?"

"That was far too glib, I'm sorry."

"No, I really want to know."

"Some woman love beards. Look at George Michael."

"He's gay."

"I'm sure I can think of a straight star with a beard, give me a minute."

"You don't think it suits me, correct?"

"You're very attractive, but it makes you look a little—"

"A little—"

I wince. "Rabbinical."

"Eeesh."

"It's not awful. Awful is the man who wears a barrette, pigtails or a beard braid."

"Who braids their beard? Have I missed this?"

"It must be a Generation Z thing. I see young skate-boarders with them on the street."

"They probably have so little beard growth, they want to call attention to whatever they've got." Jared pours hot water from the screaming kettle into two small black Japanese teapots. "I didn't always have it. My facial hair was Sarah's idea."

"Maybe you should shave it."

"You think?" Jared says.

"Maybe. It's up to you."

"Only if you help me."

"Shave your beard? I wouldn't know how."

He disappears into the bathroom for a minute and returns with clippers and a can of Barbisol shaving cream. "How jet-lagged are you right now? Because I'll do it myself if you're about to doze."

"You're actually serious?"

"I need to get the last vestiges of Sarah out of my life. Might as well be right now. Before I shave, you have to clip my beard a bit shorter so a razor won't kill my skin."

I take the clippers determinedly. This is bizarre, and strangely intimate but fun. "To the end of Sarah's reign!" Snipped hair falls to the floor as Jared pretends to sway like a rabbi praying. The word *daven* pops up from somewhere in my secular brain. That's what he's doing.

What's left of his dark beard still camouflages his cheeks and chin, although what I can see I like.

I pour and sip my tea as Jared turns on one of two faucets in the kitchen sink and splashes his face. "I'm not an expert on male facial hair, but wouldn't a hot shower be better?"

"I thought I'd share the shaving experience the G-rated way. You can shower with me if you like."

I laugh. "Not likely tonight, but my legs are getting so wobbly that I might fall asleep on your carpet."

"As long as there's hope for a rain check, that's fine with me."

I bat my eyelashes theatrically. Did Jared really mean that, or was he just being funny? "Hey, why do you have two sinks by the way?" I say.

"Had them put in. Makes my life easier when I make meat and milk dishes. I never mix the two different types of food with two sinks. And it's a luxury for cooking in general. I'm what you call a kosher foodie." He raises the shaving-cream can. "I'm going to shave this weird gray streak under my chin first."

"Is there a mirror you can use?"

"There's one in the bathroom. I'll finish this off and then we can assess the damage."

During the five minutes he's gone I wander back over to the living-room divide of the loft, which is dominated by a huge painting over his couch, one of those instantly recognizable Australian Aboriginal canvases with ocher and yellow dots. I was only a teen when I was in Australia but I remember window-shopping in a Melbourne tribal gallery with my mother—the Aboriginal paintings this big cost a fortune to ship over to the States. Even my mother wasn't going to pay though the nose. How did Jared afford it? And didn't that producer from the BBC say Jared went to film school in London? I know British schools charge Americans a mint. His parents have to be loaded.

I flip through Jared's CD collection. I'm half expecting to find Time Life's Greatest Cantorial Tunes, but except for the large Klezmer collection—I've heard of The Kletzmatics, but are there really bands called The Flying Bulgar Klezmer Band and The Klez Dispensers?—Jared's musical taste is similar to mine. (I spot John Coltrane. King Crimson. Prince. Lots of eighties ska. Cocteau Twins. The requisite Beatles and Stones albums. Jeff Buckley.) I'm relieved: Daniel Popper, before I pulled the plug on our not even three-week run, took a look at *my* music collection and I was branded *mainstream hip*. Daniel had the cheek to label himself *alternative alternative*, and his finer tastes were presented to me in a self-burned CD that was meant to up my in-the-know quotient. The CD came with his own liner notes tucked in the jewel case. It started with Radiohead and just got more annoying from there; artists like Aphex Twin, Slint, Boards of Canada, Godspeed You Black Emperor, Can, Tortoise and, "Of course, Lee 'Scratch' Perry, so you can develop a rootsy fondness for dub reggae."

I hate to admit it to myself, but I really liked Scratch.

I chill out with my favorite mainstream hip album by Everything But the Girl. Jared enters the room, completely shaven with a face that is so dishy I blink. I feel like a single publicist hesitant to book an unknown sexy author on too many television shows. *No, please, I'll keep you locked up for myself.* Great, great lips. Move over, Mick Jagger.

"You like?"

"Okay, you were never meant to have a beard. You have a cleft chin! You know how many men have plastic surgery to get a cleft chin?"

Jared looks very pleased indeed.

"What else can I do to purge the lingering traces of Sarah, Rabbi Silver?"

He hands me an aloe aftershave lotion from upscale Kiehl's Pharmacy on Third Avenue, where I buy my overpriced shampoo originally developed for a silky horse mane. He squeezes a dollop of lotion into my hand and I rub it into his reddened cheeks and chin.

"At the risk of repeating myself, I just can't understand why you would cover this face up."

We may have entered this room platonically, but the mood is getting very sexual, very fast. Jared kisses my neck. He's headed to my ears, my number-one erogenous zone.

"Jared—are you sure—I told you I'm not kosher—"

He breathes hard as he says softly, "We can change that. I can take you to a service. I have the hippest rabbi around." He is so close to me that the word *rabbi* booms into my eardrum.

"I'm not sure. Jewish cultural appreciation is one thing. Giving up my food choice and Saturday mornings is another. I hate to say it, but I just can't believe in those things."

Jared sits with an angry expression on his face. "C'mon. Don't put me in a box. It's not that hard to eat kosher. Most foods in supermarkets, except for the pork chops, are kosher now. You just have to look on the box for the little K or the U in a circle. The companies mark regular foods to secure the kosher marker. I eat Oreos, and all the breakfast cereals you probably like, and I even drink Tang from time to time."

"Tang is kosher? The astronaut drink?" The thought of that micro-fact makes me snort like I do when Jake imitates my vile cousins Marcy and Rebecca.

"Yes." He tries to look mad but he laughs anyway. "That one threw me at first too. I thought there might be gelatin in there, which might mean assorted hoof and hide, hoof is verboten—I hate that word, don't you?"

"Hoof?"

"No, verboten."

I have to rein in this banter fast, before I've crossed the line of cocktease. (Yes, I'm in his home, and I've just kissed him, but my clothes are still *on*.) I gently grab his wrist and hold it. "What I am going to tell you is the horrible truth. I really like you. But if you value tradition in your life as much as you say you do, then I'm definitely not the person you want to be with."

"Heather, please don't say that. Give me a listen first. People say it's hard for women in this town to find what they want. Well, that cuts both ways. I've been going out with women for years, and not one of them has ever engaged me as much as you."

"That's very flattering. But if you knew me better, you'd know the last thing I need is more heartbreak."

"What heartbreak? Your life seems pretty great to me. Awards. Travel—"

"No. My life is a lie. My family is a joke. I lied to Sarah when I said my cousin was kosher. Hardly. *None* of us are kosher. This whole seder is a joke. And my cousin Jake and I are the wobbly axis of sanity in my family. I can't even begin to think what's going to happen at the seder."

"The majority of American Jews have stopped keeping kosher. And how bad can your family situation be?"

"Hmm. Here's an appetizer. My long-lost gay father is flying in from Amsterdam with his leather lover to lead our seder. He's the closest we have to a real Jew."

"Oh," Jared says after a second glance to see if I'm shitting him. "That's why you went to Amsterdam?"

"Yes, oh. And yes, that's why. At least he's coming. Before that we were scrambling for anyone who'd been at a seder after they were ten years old. I know I shouldn't be dumping all of this on you, but you should see the rest of our guest list. My mailman. An Arab diplomat—"

"You better tell me more about this, uh—"

"Waterloo?"

★ ★ ★

Jared struggles with the little nail knick on his Swiss Army Knife, but finally gets the corkscrew out for the kosher Chardonnay. Surprisingly, it's not bad. He puts a different CD on. Nina Simone. The same one I used to seduce Steve.

"Do you mind if you change that?"

"You don't like Nina Simone?"

"I love her. I just have some funny associations that are too distracting."

"You can pick something if you like, or just forget about the music."

"No, I think music might calm me." I reach for the neutrality of John Coltrane's *My Favorite Things*.

"So your father is gay," Jared says as Coltrane's sax begins to spell out the melody. "These are new times, right? That information doesn't affect my feelings for you in the least. But it seems to be messing with your feelings."

"Dad's homosexuality doesn't bother me."

"Are you sure? You don't sound so convincing."

"What's disturbing me is the focus the media is giving us. If his homosexuality comes out it will ruin us with our more traditional customers. Dad's agreed to come as long as Pieter can come as well. 'That's who I am now, Heather,'" I say in Dad's low register. "He said he'll introduce him as a friend."

"So his boyfriend will be there incognito."

"Flamboyant boyfriend. One look at him and America will know."

"My mother still maintains Rock Hudson was straight— even after she watched *True Hollywood Story*. I think you're making a mountain out of a molehill."

"Do you think I should tell Steve what's going on?"

"Why, so he could provide some coaching?"

"No one in my family can follow a seder, and with all these trumped-up guests—"

He thinks hard. "When does your dad get in?"

"Tomorrow. Late morning. He and Pieter are staying at my apartment."

"We'll have a dress rehearsal before Steve and Tonia arrive. Can you get all your guests to come earlier for that?"

"I'll try."

"You better start trying now."

"Steve said you would work, but don't you have your own family seder?"

"I'm going to be right there with you, bubby. You need me. I'm going to take charge without Steve knowing it. I can shut off the camera, after all, if anything goes wrong."

"You don't have any problem pulling one over on America?"

"You mean as a good Jew?" He smiles playfully.

"Yes."

"No, because you'll be introducing Judaism to many families. And if it gets me the girl—"

"I'm not converting."

"You don't have to convert. Your mother's Jewish, so you're Jewish."

"I mean I'm not going kosher."

"We'll see," Jared laughs. "Go make your calls."

My drowsiness is hard to fight anymore, so I start by phoning Jake.

Jake's voice drops in and out from his low-battery cell phone. "A rehearsal is a great idea. I'll get Gertie on the line. You want Greg to pick up that Tibetan girl? I'm assuming she's from Manhattan, so she doesn't have a car."

"I guess. She's bubbly like he likes them. It makes me a bit worried for her."

"She's safe. He's bringing a new girlfriend."

"A new one? What happened to the last one?"

"Really want to hear it?"

"Go ahead."

"Said she was beautiful in every way except her thighs were two large balloons. He couldn't get past them. If a woman is not a hundred percent fit, he doesn't want her near him."

"Greg needs to be hit sometimes."

"He's come a considerable distance, so I didn't go on about it."

"What's the new girl's name?"

"Uh, Amy."

"Does Amy read Hebrew?"

"This is where it gets entertaining. Her last name is Hitler, apparently her family is German and they were here before World War II—"

"Wait a fucking second! Greg is bringing a woman named Hitler to our seder?"

Jared is on the floor laughing when I hang up with Jake.

I scrunch up the napkin my wineglass was resting on and throw it at him. "Yeah, very funny. He's got to be fucking with me. How could anyone in America still have the name Hitler? I find that about as likely as running into Siamese twins."

"If it's true, it's hilarious."

"It would be funny if it wasn't another mark America will have against my family."

"I'll do a national Verizon search and see how many there are." Jared goes over to his computer and hits the little apple key to jog his iMac out of standby mode. "Diana Hitler," he says a minute later in delight. "George Hitler. Millie Hitler. It's very possible. There's a whole bunch of them."

I sway my head in disbelief as I lift the receiver to call Sukie at her store. The answering machine is on, and her perky voice trumpets a spring sale at Upsy Daisy. I leave a message for her to call me ASAP.

Greg's girlfriend's last name hits me again as soon I hang up. I burst out laughing.

"What?" Jared says with a grin.

"Hitler. Her name is *Hitler*." I look at the clock. It's 9:00 p.m. on a Sunday. No wonder there's no answer at Upsy Daisy. I remember Sukie gave me her home number too.

"Ohmi-*gawd*, I was thinking of you, Heather. I'm just so glad you called. I'd like, so love to come."

While I'm on the phone getting Sukie's details of where Greg should pick her up, Jared checks his e-mail. He types a bit and opens Microsoft Paint. He draws a circular smiley face, fills the big circle with yellow and fills the eyes with red.

"How's it going?" Jared asks when I hang up. He clicks his artwork closed and cops another feel of his bare chin.

"Almost done. So far, so good," I say. "Done playing with your Colorforms?"

"All done." He laughs.

Jared shows me a few photos of his family on the bookshelf, and one of his teenage self with windblown hair. "I couldn't even grow a beard then."

We have now spent over ten hours together and I am exhausted but not bored. With more kosher Chardonnay in our bloodstream we leave the seder behind and find we still have more to talk about.

He's very interested in the fact that my mother sips coffee out of a straw so her teeth won't turn yellow.

He's as disgusted as I am over the way most of America's chickens are confined to little crates.

"You're so sparkly," Jared decides after our next exchange about how anytime I see a new product in the supermarket—like single-serve coffee bags meant to rival tea bags, or even ice cream cone–shaped cereal—I have to buy it.

Me, with the sour aura—sparkly? Now *that* is a laugh.

"You're so refreshing from the rest of the women in Manhattan. I don't think I can handle one more conversation about clothing sales and how much weight so-and-so has lost."

What he doesn't know won't hurt him. I stretch out in Jared's funky armchair. I should be going home to my new double-glazed windows, but I'm so tired that the act of getting up and walking frightens me. "What time is it?" I say reluctantly. "My phone's in my bag."

"It's 11:00 p.m."

"Early morning, Amsterdam time."

"You're welcome to stay over."

"Just because I shaved your beard doesn't mean I'm sleeping with you," I say with a yawn.

"Did I say you should? I have a sofa bed for my friends."

"Do you have anything I could sleep in?"

Jared stands up with a smile on his face and a minute later returns with an oversize *Iron Chef* T-shirt. "From the competition. If memory serves," he says, "this shirt has never been worn." I change in the bathroom as Jared opens the sofa bed and fits it with burgundy sheets and a pillowcase. I'm secretly impressed—they're from the better linen shelves—they're probably 300 count.

Jared sits on the edge of the bed with me. "Should I give you a hug or a kiss good-night?"

"Both."

He gives me a quick peck and a stagey hug.

"Can I ask you a slightly nutty question?"

"Of course," he says.

"If you were gay what would you be into?"

"Into?"

"Leather? Drag queens? Effeminate men? I'm just trying to understand what appeals to my father. What makes him cross the line?"

Jared thinks and smiles. "I'm with Eddie Murphy. I'd like her to look as much like a woman if possible." He adds dryly, "Breasts if possible."

I trace circles in his palms.

"What do we have here?" he whispers. "A hand fetishist?"

I smirk.

"What is it? Hitler again?"

"Did you ever see *The Piano*?"

"There isn't a man over thirty whose girlfriend didn't drag them to that film."

"Well, I liked it."

"Because you're a woman."

"Yes, I am." I smile. "You know that scene where the husband, what's his name, the Aussie guy from *Jurassic Park*—"

"Sam Neill—"

"Yeah. He's enraged that his wife is in love with Harvey Keitel's character, and he wants to have sex with her. She gives him a mercy fuck, but she's on top. She controls her husband through her hands. A woman had to have shot that. Women have sex with their hands. A sex scene directed by a man is all grunting and moaning."

"So now you *are* sleeping with me?" Jared whispers. "I'll take a mercy fuck." He tries to kiss me again, and I purposely miss his lips.

"Ay yae yae, Jared Silver. Why can't you love lobster and staying in bed Saturday mornings? Lobster rocks."

"I'm not giving lobster short shrift. I've only been seriously kosher since Israel."

"Wasn't that right after college? How can you remember what it tastes like?"

"You don't forget lobster. I also really miss scallops."

"Scallops too? But they're so good. Is it so offensive to God to eat one scallop?"

"No shellfish. No scallop parmesan, no sautéed scallops. I think veal scallopini is off limits because it sounds so much like scallops."

I laugh at that last bit. "How do you keep track of everything? You must need a guidebook."

"You know, I actually bothered to read Exodus once. It's very specific. I bet you didn't know that you are allowed to eat bugs, but only certain types of bugs, with their knees bent a certain way. I think only grasshoppers and red locusts."

I smile dolefully. "You said it before—these are new times. I don't want biblical restrictions on my life—or my bugs."

He leans over and kisses me on the neck. "Thoroughly Modern Heather, let's just get past your seder. I'm not being piggish here, but you would be way more comfortable in my bed. I wasn't going to tell you, but my cousin from California pretty much ruined the sofa-bed mattress. He's even taller than I am and sixty pounds heavier."

"Whatever mattress you show me, I'm there. But soon please, I'm about to collapse."

I follow him to his bedroom divide. I'm too lethargic to check out his decor. I spot a pillow. My friend the pillow. Give me, give me. Jared removes his shirt and leaves his white BVD jocks on. Good, I hate pretentious boxers, they remind me of Daniel. The jocks are just tight enough for me to be sleepily impressed with a nice kosher package between his legs. What am I thinking? Not getting involved. A mature woman.

He pulls back the comforter and notices my pained face. "Does this make you uncomfortable?"

"Just tempted as all hell."

"Remember, we don't believe in hell." Jared gets up and slips on a pair of black Old Navy sweatpants. As he lies down next to me, the agreeably musky scent of his chest and arms further jumble my emotions.

eLeveN

A Second Opinion

In the untidy heap of events last night, Jared forgot to set the alarm. He nudges me awake. He has to run out to meet Steve at the office to go over the Passover shoot.

"We don't have time to shower." He chucks me a wet washcloth for a birdbath.

I wipe my underarms as I leave a message for Vondra that I'll be in a bit late. She's so used to my double duty at Passover that I'm sure she won't mind.

"I can lend you my deodorant," Jared continues. "Not that you need it. But you'll be set for three days."

I take a sniff of his Mitchum roll-on and decline. "I'm going straight home anyway."

"Ready to go?" he says.

"Let's hit it."

We share a cab with a driver who has blacked over his name under the back-seat photo ID. Not only is that a risky move, it's illegal. I sneak a look at his skin-tone and facial hair. He must have an Arabic name and is worried about bad tips and accusatory words in an angry world. The cab rolls up outside the main office for the Food Channel on Sixth Avenue and Forty-fifth Street. Jared gives me a very sweet kiss on the lips and says, "I'll see you at the rehearsal."

"Yes," I say. "I hate to sound neurotic, but please don't tell Steve about my family's dark secrets. Or about us. I want to appear professional."

"Please, not a peep, I promise. Anyhow, I had a great time."

"Me too," I say a little self-consciously—I notice in the rearview mirror that the driver is listening.

"Can you avoid Forty-seventh Street?" I ask through the open space in the Plexiglas divide. "I always get stuck on that street."

"New boyfriend?" the driver asks at the first traffic light.

"Maybe," I say.

"May I ask what your hesitation is?"

Should I ask this? "Do you keep *halal* in your home?"

"You think I'm Arab?"

I catch his eyes in the mirror. "Yes. Isn't that why you've covered up your name?"

He smiles like someone who has been yelled at by an Iraqi-hating sailor during Fleet Week. "Very observant. I love America, you know. It's given me an opportunity I never had before. I'm scared of some passengers though. They beat up my cousin."

"I'm sure you are a fine man, and that you love America."

"So why do you care if I keep *halal?*"

"Because I'm Jewish, but I don't keep kosher. I really like that man, but I think to marry this man I would have to drastically change my lifestyle. I like my current lifestyle just fine, but I don't like having to say goodbye to someone who makes me happy."

"You should follow your heart," the driver says. "Only now I follow my heart and bought my medallion license. I'm my own business now. No more boss. For the first time I am happy."

My suggestion for the quicker side-street route backfires when we're stopped cold in traffic by men unloading a moving truck. According to its back-panel logo, which we get to know very well in the gridlock, the truck is part of the trusted fleet of *The Official Movers of the Ladies Pro-Golf Association.*

Back at my house I set off to finish the round of seder-rehearsal invitations I began the previous night. Following Jake's request, I call my branch of the U.S. Post Office. "You want to talk to your postman?" says the amused mailwoman who answers the phone. I wait as she gets Oleg on the line, Oleg who is just about to leave for his route.

He is amazed. "The Matzo Ball Heiress? On the phone with me?"

"Yes. I know it's a bit unusual for anyone to call you at the post office—"

"You are my very first call I have had here in twelve years."

"Yes, well, I was wondering if you ever watch the Food Channel?"

"Yes," he says with a confused laugh. "Did you see how they make salami in Italy? Unbelievable. That's why you called?"

"Well, that's the channel that wants to broadcast my family seder. And since you have a true appreciation of what it means to be able to hold one, I'd love to have you join my family."

"Really? *My family*? We've only been celebrating for maybe ten years, since we left Russia."

"It's because you relish it that it would be such an honor to have you join us."

He muses and says, "You are in luck. We are having a big seder the second night only. My cousins can't get away until that night. My kids would love it."

"Oleg—you may have to leave your kids at home. The network wants us to show a big family, so we're kind of faking it that way. You'd have to pretend to be my newly emigrated Russian cousin. I'm not sure if your kids could fit in with the story."

"Maybe it's my English, but I'm not sure I understand. You can explain this all to me when I get to your building. I'll be there in a half hour. Can you come down to the lobby?"

"Of course."

Vondra. I have to call Vondra. Surely Mahmoud laughed her out of the room when she brought up the seder. I just need to be sure.

"Mahmoud is thrilled to be going!"

My God. I let it be and ask them both to come to rehearsal. If he's offended by the Death to Ancient Egyptians rhetoric, at least we'll find out in the dry run.

The phone rings again. "Hello," I say brightly. How the hell did I get in this good mood?

"You sound chipper," Steve says.

"Hi," I say after a delayed start.

"I just finished a meeting about you and yours. The techies are still talking it out, so I'm checking in, making sure you're comfortable. Is your family ready for the seder?"

"They will be."

"Terrific. I was just calling to see if I could ask you another small favor regarding the broadcast."

"Uh-huh."

"We didn't get as much budget on this as I wanted. My boss wants me to use the interns at the Food Channel, but this year most of them are Jewish and don't want to give up going to their own seders. Jared of all people said yes, though, right away. Frankly, I'm shocked. I don't think he's ever missed his family seder."

"Uh-huh. So what's the favor?"

"Well, Jared was telling me he met your intern at the Museum of Natural History, and I was wondering if he's available. Is he Jewish?"

"Roswell? I don't think so."

"Great. Do you think we could borrow him? He already knows Jared. We need someone to help with the cords."

Jared's words of faith in Roswell spring to mind. "He's not the most reliable person, but you're right, he likes Jared. He might come through. And I'll ask my cousin Jake if his intern could come too."

"A matzo factory has an intern?"

"Why not? In fact, our intern and my cousin's intern know each other. They're both Stuyvesant High School students, and part of the City as School internship program."

"Great. So that was fortuitous that you could use Jared on your shoot, huh? He's a nice guy."

Do I detect a note of jealousy? "Jared is a lovely human being."

"Yes, who wouldn't like Jared, he's so—likable."

I have to come somewhat clean, as least as far as my romantic interest lies. What if the two of them talked? "Steve, since this is coming up now, I have something to tell you. I don't know about you and me. I think I'm more compatible with Jared. Not that we're in a relationship. I mean we haven't gotten physically involved, but we seem to be going in that direction."

Steve pauses a while, perhaps more stung than I ever thought he could be. "I knew he liked you, but he said nothing to me about this."

"I hope this doesn't affect the broadcast. The balloon ride is very tempting, but, well, I guess we won't be doing that now. But I'm really looking forward to the special." I feel good now that I got it all out. This is Heather Melissa Greenblotz at the steering wheel, *chickie.*

Steve is silent again. I smile to myself. Hit me with your best shot, Mr. Teflon.

He does. "Jared's ultrakosher, did you know that? Are you kosher?"

"Do you think I am?" Yes, what does Steve think I am? Doesn't he remember the oysters we had at the Union Square Café? What goes on in his self-centered brain?

"I wouldn't ask if I thought you were. You don't give off that vibe."

"Really? And what vibe do I give off?"

"I can't figure you out. You wanted to go on a romantic balloon ride with me, and now you're flat out not interested. I think you are a young woman who is still rather mad at me."

"Maybe I'm still smarting from that night at my apartment. But we need to do this seder, so let's just forget about it."

"Heather, maybe I haven't apologized the right way."

"You sent flowers, it's okay."

"Flowers aren't the same as genuine regret, right?"

"Right," I peep.

"I do feel awful about the way our first date fell apart. If I weren't doing this special, I'd still have asked you out. I'll be a hundred percent honest this time. Maybe I wouldn't have pushed so hard to meet the same day if I didn't need an urgent answer for my boss, but I would have asked you out for that weekend. I'm sure of it. I was and am very smitten with you."

"I'm flattered."

"Really?"

"Yes, really," I say. "So why do you think I'm not kosher?"

"Are you?"

"We're being a hundred percent honest here?"

"Yes."

"I'll tell you the truth if you promise not to say anything on air."

"Of course."

"No. I'm not at all. Remember those oysters we had on our date? I ate mine faster than you ate yours."

"Oysters aren't kosher?"

"They're shellfish, so no. But, uh, Jake is kosher and the factory is kept kosher, so we have to act like I'm kosher for the special."

"That's fine. No skin off my back. I have to tell you, chickie, I'm kind of relieved you're not kosher. I really think it's ridiculous in this age. I think these special holidays are great, but I draw the line at rules that mess up everyday living. Jared and I have had some heated discussions about this."

"He didn't mention that."

"Don't get me wrong. He's a modern guy in every respect. I called him a hypocrite because he keeps kosher but won't wear a *yarmulke*. Then I told him to own up to the mess organized religion has gotten us into. Maybe in India where the untouchables are born with no hope it's needed to get them through an otherwise unbelievable life. But here in America? Stop me if I'm ranting here, by the way—"

"Maybe you are a bit too keyed up for ten in the morning. I haven't had any coffee yet."

"Okay." Steve laughs.

"Much food for thought."

"My biggest fight with Jared was when I said I pity the women who have to keep a kosher home. Why add that to their day? Traditions are good for once in a while. But why would any free-thinking woman go backward? What would be so bad if some major rabbi in the mainstream with common sense came along and said, no, we won't make women do this anymore?"

"I'm sure the reform rabbis don't ask their female constituents to keep kosher."

"Then what's holding back the orthodox Jews?"

"Fear of losing our heritage? Look, Steve, exactly what religion are you anyway? I didn't understand your answer in, uh, my bed."

Steve chuckles. "My mother is Jewish, raised atheist. My father was raised as a Jehovah's Witness until he was older and saw the light, so to speak, that it was fucking him up. So we were a neither-nor religion. When I was younger, I thought they both got it wrong. I craved religion, big-time. People who've been raised without it usually do. I became a religion major and that's when my real education began. For as long as there's been religion, fear and panic have ruled the world. Perhaps with science, now that we can find out that everyone on the planet is virtually indistinguishable except for the level of melatonin, we can finally move ahead."

I'm not as Angry with a capital A as Steve is. But if I'm honest with myself, he's breaking through to me, and that fantasy of life with Jared that's forming in the back of my mind starts to lose its momentum and feel ridiculous again.

Keeping kosher and going to synagogue is just not who I am. Who would think it would be slick Steve Meyers who could snuff my enthusiasm for more dates with Jared?

twelve

Because Family Is Everything

This is the first time I've ever been alone with Roswell. We're in the hired car on our way to Jake's house in West Orange. It's D day. The rehearsal and then the broadcast. I'd really like to talk to someone about how nervous I am. After Jared's suggestion the other day that I actively mentor Roswell, I'm almost ready to give the kid a fair shake, even though he's dressed for the shoot in a hooded black shiny jacket that, although I imagine is punishingly hip, makes Mr. Cool look like something you would swat if he was 1/1000 the size.

"Dude," my intern bug says to our driver from Tel Aviv Car Service. "Is that a CD player?"

"Yes, sir."

"Can I give you something to play?"

"Is it punk, Roswell? He might not want to hear it."

"No, it's Johnny Cash. My dad just gave it to me."

"I love Johnny Cash," says the driver with a Polish accent. "Does it have 'Ring of Fire' on it?"

Roswell studies the back of the CD. "Yes."

"The best," our driver says.

"You seem very close to your father," I say to Roswell as the CD starts to play.

"Yeah, we go on a trip together every year. Just the two of us, and my mom takes my sister somewhere else."

"Where have you gone with him?"

"We've been to Cape Canaveral, the Space Needle, and last year we went to New Mexico and visited Roswell."

"Is that where you got your name?"

He makes a "that's obvious" face. "Uh, *yeah*. My parents went there as a joke in the eighties for an alien-abduction film festival. I was conceived there."

"Does having an alien-abduction name bother you?"

"No, because it's way cool. It's much cooler than my sister's name."

"What's her name, Chernobyl?"

"Ch-what?"

"Forget it."

"Her name is Karen. How dull is that?"

"How old is she?"

"Ten. She was an accident, but I'm not allowed to tell her that."

I smile. "Did I tell you that my father is coming to this seder?"

"Why wouldn't he?"

"He lives overseas. I haven't seen him for a while, so this is a big deal."

"Okay."

"Can I fill you in on a secret?"

"Shoot."

"This is a family dinner, but it's more of a production than reality. I need an assistant who can be very, uh, cool about it."

"You're sitting next to him."

"Whatever I say cannot be repeated to anyone from the Food Channel, or to anyone who didn't participate in the seder when it's all over."

"Not even my man Abdullah? We don't keep secrets from each other."

"Not even Abdullah. This is classified information, Roswell."

"I hear what you're saying."

I give him a thumbs-up and quickly fill him in on the details of my family charade, minus my dad's homosexuality. Even though most urbane New York City teens are bred from birth to think homosexuality is a non-issue, I'm just not sure about Roswell. He's a one-off.

Roswell opens a square of very strongly scented watermelon bubble gum, places it in his mouth and says in between chews, "This is so cool, that you're doing this production with all these fake people. It's like working on a feature film."

We cross over the New Jersey base of the George Washington Bridge. "So how's your documentary faring?"

"Dude. It's not. Albert Maysles isn't returning my calls."

"Why don't you try something else?"

"You don't think it's a good idea?"

"Honestly? No. I think it is a bit over your head."

He huffs.

"Look, I'm being honest."

He catches my eye. "So, say you're right, which I'm not saying. How do you think I should start my first film?"

"I think you should start with a short. Do something you know well, like a piece about high-school graduation—"

"Boring," he says after a pop of gum.

"How about New York–teen hangouts? Skateboarders, maybe?"

Another bubble and pop. "Yawn. That sounds like the Disney Channel."

"Well, something you know well is the way to go. What do you know more about than anyone else? Have a think about it."

Jake opens the door dressed in a slightly ill-fitting suit and a tie with a matzo motif. Siobhan has somehow managed to pick out a certain style of clothing—solid colors, long sleeves and no sexy cuts—that together with her new hairstyle transforms her into a ringer for an ultraorthodox woman.

"What's different about you besides your clothes?" I ask. "It's weird. I just can't pick it out."

"Jake bought me a wig that's the same color as my hair for me to wear on air."

I gasp and nervously laugh a bit. "It's crazy but it really does the trick."

I introduce Jake and Siobhan to Roswell as he runs his finger along the huge flat TV screen that must have set Jake back many thousands of dollars.

"This is killer," Roswell declares.

"Thanks," says Jake.

"Could Dimple come?" I whisper nervously as I look around. Jake and Siobhan have already set up the table in the living room with a translated phonetic Hebrew *Haggadah* on every plate. Only the cutlery is missing.

"No. Her mom wouldn't let her out of their seder. So it's lucky you brought your intern."

"I'm not thrilled about using Roswell," I whisper again. "Big-time slacker. But I've filled him in on our situation."

"So you're going to be a Jew tonight," I overhear Roswell say to Siobhan. "That's cool."

"Yes," Siobhan says with a Mona Lisa smile. Is she mad or amused?

"So why do you need a wig if it's the same color of your hair?"

"Very orthodox women shave their hair so that only their husbands can see their true head. They wear a wig for outside society." It's hilarious. Siobhan knows more about this stuff than I do. "Let's put your coats in the bedroom." She motions for us to follow her.

Roswell blinks. "You shaved your hair for this party?"

"No, I still have my real hair under there. But the wig has a certain orthodox Jewish styling that lends me authenticity."

"My idea, of course," Jake interjects.

"You are truly insane," I say.

"But it works," he says, grinning.

I offer a weak nervous smile. "It does indeed."

"Yo, Siobhan, where's the bathroom?" Roswell asks as she lays our coats on the four-poster bed in the master bedroom.

"Use the one in this room," she says. After Roswell closes the bathroom door, she gives me a reassuring embrace. "You look scared," she whispers. "We're going to pull this off. Jake and I have made Passover flash cards so all the guests can memorize one fact they can let drop on camera." She hands me mine: *Did you know that Moses stuttered?*

Roswell emerges and wipes his wet hands on his jeans. "So what do want me to do first?"

I take charge. "Siobhan may need some help in the kitchen before the TV crew gets here."

"Yes, I could use a hand with the salad," Siobhan says.

"You have cukes?"

"Cukes?" Siobhan looks at me for the American translation.

"Cucumbers," I say.

Roswell nods. "A salad needs tons of cucumbers, because lettuce is so freaking fiddly."

"We have plenty of cukes—and sunflower seeds too," Siobhan says.

"Excellent. I'll throw them in."

"I'll finish the place settings," I say, and we all head for the kitchen.

When I'm back in the kitchen for the knives, Roswell is gnawing the sunflower seeds like a field mouse and telling Siobhan about his ranking among the major players on the Stuyvesant High School Ultimate Frisbee team.

Siobhan chops a tomato into quarters. "We didn't have this Ultimate sport in Cork."

"*Ultimate,*" he mocks Siobhan's Irish brogue. "It sounds so funny when you say that in Irish."

Siobhan smiles.

So does Roswell. "Well, we have the Frisbees, and you have the beer," he says. "I guess that's what makes Ireland such a great country."

"Yes," she says with another genuinely warm smile. Now I'm really pissed at Grandpa Reuben again. Siobhan, a great listener even in the face of teenage braggadocio and stupidity, would be an incredible mother. After the seder I'm going to read Jake the riot act about not marrying her.

Jared arrives with our beloved ancient shopkeeper Gertie in tow.

After that bubble-popping conversation with Steve, I'm not sure how I should greet Jared. I settle on a friendly squash of his hand, while I give Gertie a kiss on the cheek. "How was your car ride into New Jersey, Gertie?"

"We talked. Such a nice boy. Maybe you like him?"

Jared nods at me as if to say, *Listen to your elders.* Jake gives Gertie a hug and finds her a seat. I hear another vehicle pull up. I peek out behind Siobhan's white Irish-linen curtains, ones her mother sent over a few Christmases back. A black Lincoln Town Car is parked outside of Jake and Siobhan's door. Walking toward the front door is Mahmoud, dressed in another upmarket suit, and Vondra, in a black dress and tasteful pearls. In the last few weeks, her style has metamorphosed from funky sexpot to international sophisticate. Looking at her draped off Mahmoud's arm, I could imagine her chatting nicely with heads of state over a Waldorf salad on the menu at the actual Waldorf Astoria.

When they are inside, Vondra waves to Jared. While Mahmoud talks to Jared, Vondra surreptitiously turns to me and points to her chin. She approves of Jared's new beardless face. I smile, and after a pause in Jared and Mahmoud's conversation, I introduce the new couple to the others who are there so far.

"I'm honored to be invited at your seder," Mahmoud says to me.

Before I move Mahmoud along to Jake and Siobhan, chatting in the kitchen, I say: "I'm thrilled you can come. I'm surprised, though, that you're not worried about being seen on the air."

"One cannot live in fear. There would be no quality to your life."

"Still, it's very brave of you in this environment of mistrust."

"Anyhow, the seder is a remarkable opportunity to express the difference between the Jewish people and the Israeli government—"

"No it is not," I say, rapidly alarmed.

"Mahmoud has decided to wear the traditional Egyptian

head covering, an *akad*," Vondra interjects. "We have it in his car. We wanted to check that out with you first, of course."

"This is not the time!" I cry out with reinforced anger. With everything else on my seder plate, I have to worry about Mahmoud's political agenda?

Mahmoud laughs loudly. "Calm, calm. I'm just winding you up. Blame this joke on Vondra. She said you would—"

"Freak!" Vondra finishes his sentence.

"I will get you *bad*, bitch," I nervously laugh as I push her. She almost totters over in her tasteful black pumps.

I shakily introduce Mahmoud to Roswell. Vondra looks stunned and pulls me in to the corner. "Okay, is this a joke on me? What's Roswell doing here?"

"Steve from the Food Channel asked me to bring him along. Roswell is working for them today. All their interns are Jewish and couldn't come. I filled him in on everything so he doesn't blow it."

"You trust him on a live feed?"

I hear a car pull up outside. "I have to. We needed help even before the crew got here. Jared thinks he's smarter than we're giving him credit for. That he just needs growth opportunities."

"Hey, it's your family. Your call."

I make a pray-for-me face.

The doorbell rings.

My father has taken my advice, and for that matter, Pieter's. He has put aside the natural-fiber brown suit he showed me in my apartment when he and Pieter arrived from the airport. Dad's gone shopping, with Pieter probably, and selected a very nice navy suit that looks as if it came from one of Mom's favorite stores like Bergdorf's or Barneys. Dad points to the lapel of his suit, seeking my endorsement, and I give him an appreciative smile. I wish

Pieter would have thought through his own outfit a bit more. Maybe he checked out New York weather on his computer in Amsterdam. It was freakishly cold a few days ago, but today it's seasonal. Yet Pieter's dressed up in some funky European arctic-winter gear completely inappropriate for April in the New Jersey suburbs.

"Who's the Eskimo?" Roswell whispers to me.

"A friend of my dad's." Pieter's coat comes off and his look just gets worse: he's wearing a purple-mesh muscle shirt.

"Here's the man of the hour!" Jake calls and gives his uncle Sol a big slap on the back.

"You must be Pieter," Siobhan says while Jake sneaks a second look of horror at Pieter's muscle shirt. "We're putting the coats in the bedroom."

"The *abba*," Gertie says loudly to Jared.

Jared nods.

"What did she say to you?" I whisper to Jared.

"*Abba* is Hebrew. She said, 'The father.'"

"Sorry I'm so late," Dad says to Jake. "I asked the driver to check his map but he wanted to be a cowboy."

"It's not a problem. We have well over an hour until the rest of the crew show up. This is rehearsal."

"We're going to have to clear the driveway for the remote-broadcast truck," Jared says.

"Oh, I arranged for that. Siobhan is going to drive the cars over to our neighbor's house."

"I am?" says Siobhan, back from the bedroom with Pieter at her side.

"Or I am," Jake says with a chastened grin.

My father does a double take at Siobhan's hair, but gives her a big hug and kiss.

Now he sweeps his favorite employee off her feet. "I missed you so much, my dear dear Gertie." Gertie's so fragile and thin that I'm afraid Dad might break her. But she's not concerned. She beams a big newly dentured grin.

I reintroduce Dad to Vondra, whom he's met once before when I was still at PBS.

Then there's the meet-and-greet line of Mahmoud, Roswell and Jared.

"Dad, this is Vondra's new boyfriend."

"Sol Greenblotz," Dad says with a hearty shake.

"Mahmoud Habib," I say to Dad.

Dad whistles through his teeth. "Mahmoud Habib? Aren't you the United Nations spokesman for the Egyptian government?"

"How do you know that?" Vondra marvels.

"I'm a CNN junkie. You've certainly been around the global block, Mr. Habib."

"I've been in a few places, yes."

Vondra touches Mahmoud's gold cuff link in stomach-churning reverence. "Like every country on earth."

Even Mahmoud looks embarrassed by Vondra's unbridled adulation. "Well," he says, "it's safe to say that this will be my first seder."

My father is very engaged in this conversation, and about to ask trivia. I may not have seen much of him the past ten years, but I know that pensive expression on his face. "Tell me, Mr. Habib—"

"Mahmoud please, Sol."

"Okay, Mahmoud—is there an Egyptian version of why the Jews left Egypt?"

"Yes, of course," Mahmoud says.

"Honey—" Vondra says nervously.

"No, don't worry, Vondra, I'd love to hear what Mahmoud has to say," Dad assures. "There's a long-standing Passover tradition of asking questions."

"Yes," says Jake who is standing next to me. "Asking questions allows others to fulfill the *mitzvah* of telling the story of our exodus from Egypt."

"Where did you pull that out of?" I say very quietly to Jake.

"*Judaism for Dummies*," he whispers. He tugs me away from the history lesson by my elbow. "Where's your mailman? If we're going to do a rehearsal, he better get here soon."

"Oleg declined to come at the last minute. His wife didn't want to break up the family on Passover."

"Shit. I guess we have your dad for the Hebrew. We're okay."

"That's what I figured."

I inch back to the conversation. I'm just as curious as Dad to hear what Mahmoud has to say, as long as this is off the air.

"Go ahead," Dad beckons Mahmoud. "I'm fascinated to hear the Egyptian take."

"Our version is that the Jews, while in Egypt, made lots of converts to their god. So the Egyptian gods were getting fewer and fewer followers. The Egyptian priests weren't thrilled, and demanded the Jews get thrown out of the country. Fewer people were offering sacrifice to the Egyptian gods and the priests feared this would bring the wrath of their gods, not to mention the loss of their power and status."

"Incredibly fascinating," Dad says. "So you think you tossed us out on our ear?"

Mahmoud shrugs. "Then in later years we got along again. Of course, this era is more than a little rougher than back when I was just starting my career—that was during the buoyant days of the Israeli-Egyptian peace accord."

"I was just reading a book about the history of the Arab-Jewish animosity. We're more alike than you may think. In the biblical tradition, the Jewish and Arab people are all descendants of Shem—"

Mahmoud nods. "Yes, Noah's son."

"Yes, and the mother tongue of Arabic and Hebrew was Aramaic, spoken by both of our peoples until the Middle Ages, I believe."

"This is true."

Dad squints his left eye. This action always precedes his keynote trivia-fact presentation. "One of our great rabbis, Maimonides, wrote *Guide for the Perplexed,* his greatest work, in Aramaic."

I laugh to myself. I was right.

Mahmoud smiles. "Did you know he was also the physician to the king of Egypt?"

Dad's eyes widen. "That I didn't know." *(Where's THE IDEA CATCHER when you need it?)*

"Of course, with the rise of Islam, Arabic supplanted Aramaic."

"Of course," Roswell says in a mocking uppity accent.

Jared silences Roswell with a finger to his mouth.

My father extends a hand to Mahmoud and says, "So then we welcome you at the table as a long-lost cousin. It is quite an honor to have you with us."

Mahmoud shakes Dad's hand with vigor. "Yes, if only the peace negotiators could get the Israelis and Arabs to see we should live as family, not foes. Sadat saw that, but look where it got him."

Dad sighs sadly. "Rabin too."

Mahmoud sighs. My father sighs.

As Dad shakes Jared's hand, Mahmoud asks Pieter, "So what is your name?"

My father turns around and answers before his new life-partner can speak. "Mr. Habib, this is my dear friend, Pieter

Eicken. He's traveled in from Amsterdam so he can join us in the seder."

"Vondra told me," Mahmoud whispers somewhat audibly.

"Told you what?" Roswell says.

"Oh," says Dad gratefully to Mahmoud, not answering Roswell.

"What do you do there?" Mahmoud asks politely.

Pieter looks nervously at Dad as he says, "I'm a photographer."

"He's very famous in Europe," Dad says.

"What sort of photographs do you take?"

This time I answer for him. "Body parts."

"I'm not sure I understand," Mahmoud says.

"Very erotic body parts," Pieter says. "The male form—"

"Oh I see," says our Arab diplomat, smiling most diplomatically.

There's a loud triple-horn beep outside the door.

"That would be my brother, Greg," Jake says.

Greg's tan is so dark it looks dangerous, like the news of his skin cancer could follow him in the door at any minute.

"We have arrived," Greg chirps. He drags through the living room an equally tan blond woman. Shs removes her pink coat and reveals a lime-green blouse filled out with tit-job cleavage that instantly gets matching across-the-room ogles from Jared and Roswell.

First-seder Sukie shyly trails behind in her trademark pigtails and a vintage Diane von Furstenberg flower-print wrap dress. I give her a happy nod hello, as my hands are full with plates of matzo to set on the table.

When I set them down, Greg gives me a kiss and a hug. "Loved the prison movie."

"Thanks."

"Just wish there was some prison-chick sex, that would have really made it."

"Yeah," I say, rolling my eyes. Greg knocks me in the shoulder with a fist and says, "No, really, it was moving. Very."

"Thank you for coming, Greg."

"Was there any question? Is Uncle Sol really here?" Greg swirls his neck around for confirmation.

"Here I am!" Dad gives Greg a bear hug. "You look well. That's some tan you got going there."

"They say sunshine is bad for you, but I say they're crazy. Don't I look damn healthy?"

"Who do we have here?" Dad says to Amy Hitler. Like myself, Dad never has too much to say to Greg.

"I'm Amy," Greg's date says in a squeaky voice.

Dad extends a hand. "Sol Greenblotz."

"Uncle Sol Greenblotz," Greg clarifies.

"Amy Hitler," his girlfriend says.

Dad glances over at me to see if this is a joke. I shake my head with gritted teeth. Unfortunately, Amy Hitler is another unavoidable ingredient in our nightmare soup. "Is she going to say that last name during the broadcast?" Dad says to the room at once. Suddenly his homosexuality is not such a big problem.

Amy bites her lip. "You think it's a problem?"

Dad nods vehemently. Jake and I nod too.

Greg pulls his girlfriend away toward Jake and Siobhan's couch. "Let's come up with something else we can call you."

"What is *your* name?" Dad says nervously to Sukie.

"Sukie."

"She owns the shop next to the matzo factory."

"The butcher shop?"

"That's another generation ago," I say. "She owns a boutique called Upsy Daisy."

Jake huffs. "Everything's a boutique now."

"Sukie is half-Jewish, half-Bön," I add.

"That's a Tibetan religion, right?" Dad asks.

"How did you know that, Mr. Greenblotz?" Sukie says excitedly.

"Just Sol, please."

"Sol knows everything," Pieter says from a rented folding chair.

"What's your last name?" Dad asks. "I don't know any Bön names."

"Cohen," I say. "Her father's Jewish."

A sigh of relief from Dad. "Oh. Good. Cohen is a very important name in Judaism. You're the priest class. You can trace your roots to Aaron, Moses' brother. He was a *Kohen,* a Jewish priest."

"You should play that up on the broadcast," Jared says as he finishes screwing a new, higher-wattage lightbulb into a lamp in the corner.

"I'm descended from Moses' brother?" Sukie says. "That's crazy. I so didn't know that."

"We have an announcement," Amy Hitler says moments later, her pink coat in Greg's hands. "We were going to save this announcement for after the dinner."

"The seder, Amy," Greg says. "Not the *dinner.*"

"Yes. The seder. Greg and I are getting married later this year. So Greg thinks tonight I can go by Greenblotz during the show."

Greg raises his eyebrows in frustration. "The seder, Amy, not the show."

"Mazel tov!" my father says with a wink toward me.

"Mazel tov," Jared echoes from the next lamp in the living room.

"Amy Hitler-Greenblotz," Siobhan whispers in my ear.

"And your grandfather was worried about *Moran*. Wait until the press gets ahold of *this*."

Jared is done setting up, and claps his hands. "Okay, everybody. Congratulations again, Amy and Greg. But now it's time to have our dry run. As Heather probably told you I will be the cameraman for the Food Channel tonight."

"How many other Food Channel people are there going to be here?" Siobhan asks. "I'll make plates of food for them."

"I'm the only cameraman. The producer, Steve, who you'll meet shortly, envisions an intimate look on the air. Besides Steve there'll be a soundwoman, Tonia, and a remote-feed guy who'll be parked outside in a truck. I'm not sure who they've lined up for that job."

"Jared's the only member of the crew who is in on the secrets of the family," I say.

"How many secrets?" Pieter asks.

"All of them, I think," Jared says with a knowing nod. "Please don't mention that you've been rehearsing here when Steve arrives. We don't want to blow our cover."

"Is there going to be a high level of deceit tonight?" Mahmoud asks. "I'm a diplomat. I have to watch what I say and do."

"We're not lying," I say. "We're just not highlighting all the facts."

"We don't want to offend anyone," Jared says. "So we might not mention that you are from Egypt on the air."

"Who am I then?" Mahmoud asks somewhat indignantly.

"Israeli?" I offer, straight-faced.

Mahmoud looks as if he might vomit.

Vondra glares at me with horror. "Absolutely not. You can't ask him to say that."

I point at her with a smile. "Sucker. Psych."

"You bitch," she whispers.

"Why do you call your friend a bitch?" Mahmoud says with a reproachful crinkle of his nose.

"She calls me bitch too, didn't you hear her before? That's how we joke with each other." Is Vondra concerned that she has offended her date? I'm secretly glad to see some of her more relaxed personality leak out from her new genteel facade. This girl can curse in high style. She could star in her own Blaxploitation film—*Vondra Adams is Black and Back*. That's a plus in my book.

"I promise you, Vondra," I say. "We just won't introduce him. He'll just be at the table eating a meal."

"Like extras in a Fellini movie," Roswell offers.

"It's okay to a have a few nonfamily members at the table, Heather," Jared says.

"Say whatever makes you most comfortable," Mahmoud says softly. Is he having second thoughts about the seder or Vondra?

"I'm from Cincinnati, not from New York," Amy Hitler says. "Do I have to cover that up?"

"I would," Roswell says.

I shoot Roswell a frown. "No you don't, Amy. It's just your name we're a little worried about. But now that you're *married*, that's not even a concern, right?"

Jared claps his hands again. "Time is ticking, so let's move on. I understand that many of you in the room have either never been to a seder before, or can't remember back to when you have. How many people here can actually read Hebrew?"

Dad raises his hand.

"Yes, Heather told me that. You, sir, will be the head of the seder. Please sit here." Jared points to a chair at the far end of the room. "How well do you know the service?"

"Very well. I have a good memory."

"He's the family genius," Greg says. "Aunt Jocelyn told me you have a 150 IQ."

"Don't crown me the family genius," Dad says. "Heather's IQ is a point higher."

"It is?" I perk up. With my trig grades before I took that remedial class for arty kids?

"Doesn't surprise me in the least," Jared says with a broad smile.

"You got tested in second grade. Your verbal and reading comprehension skills were off the charts. Your mother or I never told you that?"

"No," I say piercingly.

"I guess we wanted Dalton to keep the pressure I had off of you. I think they wanted to skip you a grade."

I will wait until my next session with Bettina to digest this news. I think discussing your incredible giftedness is best left out of the public arena.

"Who has been to a seder but can't remember the details?"

I raise my apparently genius hand along with Jake and Greg.

Jared seats Jake on one side of Dad and me on the other. He seats Greg on the other side of Jake.

"I think Siobhan should sit between Jake and Greg," I say.

Thank you, Siobhan mouths to me.

Jared surveys the room again. "Mahmoud, I hope you don't mind, but you look important. So why don't you and Vondra sit next to Heather?"

"Are you trying to hide me or not?"

"I'm not sure—I might move you around again."

"Can I sit next to Greg?" Amy Hitler asks.

"Sure."

"What about Gertie?"

"Where *is* Gertie?" Greg cries. "I never even said hello to her!"

Gertie is slumped in the corner of Jake and Siobhan's couch, snoring loudly.

I wake her up. *"Vus?"* she says in a sleepy distressed voice. *"Vus* is going on?"

"You're at our seder, Gertie." I guide her next to an open seat next to Sukie. "We're rehearsing."

Greg taps Gertie on the shoulder and gives her a buss on her wrinkled forehead.

"Don't you think I should sit next to Sol?" Pieter says adamantly.

Between me and Dad? I look at my father with pleading eyes. We discussed this! What happened to family friend?

Dad seeks out Pieter's eyes. "Pieter, I think Sukie will feel all alone."

"Don't you think Uncle Sol should sit next to his daughter?" Greg says sharply in Pieter's direction.

Pieter angrily taps the tablecloth like a vexed chimp sick of dancing to an accordion. His eyes dart wildly as he says, "Doesn't everyone know we are together?"

"Yes," I say.

"Yes," Jared says.

"Yes," Jake says.

"Yes," Siobhan says.

"Yes," Greg says.

"Yes," Amy Hitler says.

"I didn't know, but I'm cool with it," says Roswell.

I give Roswell a big smile and mouth, "Thanks."

"That's wonderful," Sukie says.

"They are friends?" Gertie says.

"We're a couple, Gertie," Dad says in a heavy but proud voice.

After an extended silence settles, Jared clears his throat and hands everyone a cheat sheet of Passover information. "Okay, people, let's get this rehearsal going. Steve will be here in less than an hour."

"My nephew out in San Francisco, he's in a couple, too." Gertie says. "Listen to me, *bubelleh*, I'm an old lady. *Vat* makes you happy is *vat* is good."

"Okay then," Pieter says after a sigh. It's out in the open ether, and Pieter obviously feels comfortable enough to give my dad a public kiss on the lips.

Greg grimaces, but Gertie beckons me to her with an arthritic finger. "I knew he was a *fegele* years ago," she whispers.

"But remember, Pieter," Jared says, "we are not mentioning that you are a couple on the air. This special, if I correctly understand why Sol's family is participating, is to raise matzo sales—not gay awareness. The rest of American Jewry may not be as accepting as the Greenblotz family."

"I just want you both to know that I have no problem with homosexuality," Greg says.

"Me neither," Amy Hitler says. "People think we're very backward in Ohio, but truth is, most of us have nothing against homosexuals, we just don't see why they have to go around ramming it down everyone's throats."

Greg pulls at his fiancée's hand. "Not the best choice of words, honey."

THIRTEEN

Next Year in Jerusalem

For almost an hour, Team Greenblotz practices reading from the *Haggadah* at the long rented table covered in white linen. We memorize Passover trivia and go over the items Dad will point to on the seder plate. Only the loud sound of a truck pulling up outside Jake and Siobhan's house breaks our concentration.

"Steve and the crew are here," Jared announces. He races around the room to collect any damning evidence of his meddling; he quickly stuffs the seder fact sheets and Siobhan's flash cards into his knapsack.

"You forgot one of the flash cards," Sukie says as she turns it over to read: "In the Sephardic Jewish culture, families sometimes hit each other with spring onions at the seder table."

"Why?" I ask.

"I'm not sure," Siobhan admits. "I was just copying sentences."

"Where's Roswell?" Jake asks. "Steve's going to need him."

Come to think of it, we haven't seen Roswell since we picked up the *Haggadahs* for Jared to go over with us. I shrug. "I told him he didn't have to rehearse since he was going to be working off air with Steve, and he took off."

"Maybe he's downstairs in the study," Jake says. "I told him we have a vintage 1980s pinball machine down there and his eyes lit up."

There's a knock, and before I can bother to look for my insubordinate intern Greg has opened the door and let Steve in. I know Steve will be on air during the special to introduce my family, but damn him for looking dazzling again. Behind Steve comes blond Tonia, whom I haven't seen since the matzo shoot. We throw each other lackluster smiles, and she gets right down to work unsnapping her sound cases. Tonia looks new-century chic in the film and television world's working girl's latest *shoot* uniform: a girls' department tee, black and tight around the chest, and tight black jeans with frayed cuffs. Greg may be engaged to Miss Hitler but he eyes Tonia like a fresh piece of meat.

His fiancée's nostrils flare.

"Jared should be here any minute," Steve says.

"Nope," Jared booms from the back of the room. "Already here. Had a good run with traffic. I arrived fifteen minutes ago."

"Oh, okay." Steve glances at me and then Jared with considerable suspicion. "Maybe you took a different route, because we had a traffic nightmare."

"Maybe. Anyhow, I set the lights up already. I clipped the keylight onto the tree, but the room has good lighting to begin with. There's a dimmer switch."

Steve glimpses around the room with a puzzled look on

his face. "And the whole family's already seated, look at that. Everyone raring to go?"

I stand to greet him with a nervous handshake. "We are." Although Steve covertly tickles the inside of my palm before he lets go of it, I keep a neutral face.

"Well, who are all the Greenblotzes we have in this room? In case you haven't figured it out, I'm Steve Meyers and I will be introducing you all on air. I truly appreciate that you are letting us share your beloved family holiday."

Was that Siobhan who coughed in amusement, or Jake? "I'll start the introductions with my cousin Jake," I say. "He's the one I was substituting for the day you did the factory interview."

"You're the man who runs the show?" Steve says to Jake.

"Yes," Jake says. My father gets a funny look on his face. "With my uncle Sol heading our overseas operation," Jake adds hastily.

"He's here today?" Steve asks. "Your dad?"

"Yes," I say, leading Steve by his elbow over to Dad. "Steve Meyers, this is my father, Sol Greenblotz, who's, um, been heading our operations overseas, based out of Amsterdam."

"There are that many Jews in Amsterdam?" Steve asks after a friendly smile.

"There's a healthy population," Dad says just as congenially. "And it's a good European base—it's easy to get anywhere from there."

"It's very nice to meet you, sir. You have an amazing daughter. Beautiful and smart as a whip."

What a mouthful of malarkey. Just get your damn career-boosting show on the air.

"From the day Heather was born, she was a blessing," Dad says with a hint of a contrived old-world accent, Tevye talking up his daughters in *Fiddler on the Roof.*

"With her talent," Steve says, "she's going to win an Oscar to put next to those Emmys."

"From your mouth to God's ears," he says.

Jake sneaks an amused look at me. Farther down the table, Pieter looks as if he is seconds from bursting into laughter.

Steve starts to ask a question, but before he can even get a word out, Dad jumps in with "My wife and I are separated, but we are still friends. I'm afraid she's visiting her family seder this year."

Steve shoots him a peculiar, knowing look and I pick up the pace of the introductions. "And this is my cousin Greg Greenblotz from Miami, Florida—"

"I'm his fiancée," Amy Hitler says.

The plan was to say you're married, you Aryan bubblehead!

"She's my wife," Greg says nervously. He tries to fix the damage: "We had a municipal ceremony last week but we haven't announced it to the public. So Amy is a Greenblotz, but she'd prefer to just go by Greg's fiancée on air, no last name, please, on air, for um, security purposes. She had a stalker once."

Steve looks confused. After that garble, I'm confused too. "Greg's fiancée or wife, what was your maiden name?" Steve asks.

My father coughs loudly but Amy answers Steve anyway. "Hitlerstein."

"Pardon?" Steve says.

"Hisstein," Greg says quickly. "Amy Hisstein. Amy has a bit of a speech impediment."

Steve laughs loudly. "Good God. For a second there I thought she said Hitler."

While Steve talks to cutie Sukie in his *The Boy Can't Help It* flirt mode, I hear Greg chide Amy. "What are you doing?"

"In Ohio, most Jews have 'stein' on the end of their names—stop looking at me like that, I'm not stupid, Greg."

"Who's saying you're stupid?"

"*You are*. Yesterday, you explained nachos to me. I know what nachos are. We have nachos in Ohio, Greg."

"And let's see..." I quickly move on to the remaining introductions when Steve has finished chatting up visibly besotted Sukie. "And here we have Vondra Adams."

Steve extends a hand. "Heather's film partner?"

"Yes," I say. I'm surprised he knew who she was right off. Steve listened to anything I had to say?

My ex-fling smiles at Vondra like a veteran press agent. "You should hear how your pal Heather talks you up. She told me how brilliant you were, but she didn't mention how stunning you are." Don't add to my nausea, Steve. Why do I even care that you're flirting with all the women in the room? Is this retribution for my stated attraction to Jared?

Just like Sukie, Vondra is seduced. She locks eyes with Steve. "Yeah?" It's the first time I've seen Vondra let Mahmoud slip from her mind since she met him. For a second—even though, according to Vondra, "Mahmoud is one of the most important people in the world"—I feel kind of sorry for this first-class diplomat. You can see by the way Vondra smiles at Steve, it's not just me. This atheist has *testosterone*.

Vondra regains her senses and introduces a slightly irritated Mahmoud.

"Isn't Mahmoud an Arabic name?" Steve says. "I thought you might be an Israeli cousin."

I interject. "Mahmoud is a diplomat with the United Nations. But we have to be careful not to highlight him. He is definitely not from Israel."

"It's okay," Mahmoud says.

"No, honey," Vondra says. "I've been thinking about it.

Heather is right. It will be incongruous to see you on air. People will talk. I don't want you shot."

Great time for insight, Vondra.

"I'm getting nervous too, but I think I should go through with it."

"Why should you be nervous?" Steve asks. "You're not Palestinian, are you?"

"I'm Egyptian."

Steve spins around to me with his mouth open. Egypt? he mouths. He hurries me to the corner. "You didn't tell him about the Egyptian passages in the *Haggadah*?"

"She's my best friend and she *insisted*," I hiss to him in a whisper.

Steve thinks on his feet and turns back to Mahmoud. "Sir, I'm going to call my boss. If he clears it, I guess we could make your Egyptian heritage an exciting element. He and I will figure out how to introduce you."

As Steve calls his superior at the Food Channel on his cell phone, I look around downstairs for Roswell, but I still can't find him. When Steve is off the phone, he says, "My boss is gung ho. We are going to mention that Mahmoud's participation here is a nod to hope in the Middle East. Nothing else."

"No, I've made up my mind. Introduce me as who I am. Mahmoud Habib, spokesman for the Egyptian U.N. mission. Sadat was brave. I'm no coward."

Steve nods his head excitedly. "This will work."

I still have to introduce Pieter to Steve. I claim he's a business friend of my father's from Amsterdam.

"In Jewish tradition," my father throws in after my introduction of his lover. "It is a *mitzvah*, a good deed, to invite those who are traveling or without a seder. For one night, everyone is *mishpucha*—family."

"So listen up, gang, I have a little gift for all of you. Tonia, have you seen the bag from the promotional department?"

Tonia grabs a large and stuffed plastic bag with the Food Channel logo off the floor. "I have it here."

Steve hands each of us a "Spanish Foods Week" castanet and all of the men a Food Channel *yarmulke*. "Put the *yarmulkes* on, of course, but do me a favor and keep the castanets out of camera view when we're on the air."

Mahmoud fingers the *yarmulke*, and with his eyes shut he puts it on. My father and I applaud. "You're a courageous man, Mahmoud," Dad says.

Steve pipes up, "I'll have an even bigger surprise for you when I come back."

As soon as Steve and Tonia are out of the house and in the remote truck, we all start to talk at once, but Jared claps a castanet loudly and addresses the room. "A few hiccups, but you all did well. I can tell Steve is raring to go."

"What did he mean by a bigger surprise?" Jake says.

"I'm not sure," Jared says.

When Steve returns, he brings with him the man assigned to send the live feed back to the Food Channel offices from the remote truck. Is this our surprise? Kev is fat, bald and desperately seeking the bathroom.

"Around the corner," Jake says.

Kev lumbers across the living room. Midway through, he leaves an empty, grease-saturated box of Chicken Mc-Nuggets on Siobhan and Jake's vintage mosaic table. He bounds out of the bathroom after a loud flush, then disappears back outside to his parking spot.

"So by the way, who and where is my intern?" Steve smiles.

Good question. Where the hell is he?

Roswell sneaks up behind me and taps me on the shoulder. "Where were you?" I say sharply.

"Just outside. Hey, you can eat McNuggets on Passover? Cool."

"Absolutely not," my nearby father answers for me. "Let's get rid of that McDonald's box. The camera might pan the room."

"What McDonald's box?" Jared says in a panic.

Dad points. "A gift from your remote guy."

"Kev is such an idiot," Jared says in a loud huff to Steve. "If we showed the Greenblotzes with *traif* on their tabletop, there'd be an uproar."

"I tried to get Freddy for the feed, but he was on vacation."

"We have plenty of food for the crew if he's hungry," Siobhan says. "You can take him a plate of smothered chicken, and we have a number of sides—"

"I'll tell him," Steve says. "*After* the broadcast."

"My father says McNuggets are way better in low-rent areas where the turnover is heavier," Roswell says. "The ones near our house suck. The batter is orange, dude. That panics him."

"You must be my intern," Steve says sharply, glancing over at me for confirmation.

"Steve Meyers," I say, "this is Roswell Birch." Steve shakes his hand. Roswell's pupils are big round circles. I distinctly smell pot on his clothes. As soon as I am through with whatever Steve needs to set up, I am going to kill the little motherfucker. A live national broadcast and he's outside smoking a joint? Maybe I should ask him to sit the seder out in Kev's truck.

There is another knock on the door, and Steve smiles. "Is everyone ready for the big surprise?"

"We're ready," Jake assures.

Steve opens the door and in walks my mother, entering regally and dressed to the nines.

"Jocelyn," my father says with a shocked but clearly delighted expression.

Mom looks as good as I've ever seen her. Maybe she does believe in plastic surgery, because her face looks much smoother than the last time I saw her. Has she started Botox treatments? Her shape on the other hand, has always been terrific—I got Dad's propensity to paunch. This new peach silk dress she's wearing is lovely on her. She's even had her hair blown out and flat-ironed.

Dad stands up to give her a warm hug. If he hadn't just come out to me as a gay man in the land of cheese, I'd say he was aroused.

Pieter coughs loudly. I'm assuming Pop Genius is smart enough to keep mum about Pieter's special role in his life until after the broadcast.

"So what do you have to say to your mother?" Steve asks me with a proud grin.

"I thought you were going to the Amazon," I say softly.

"An English friend of yours called. She was very emphatic. She convinced me how important this was to you, that you were devastated by my decision to skip the seder. I didn't realize."

English? Oh, *Australian*. Bettina called her? How dare she cross that line!

Steve throws in, "Your friend called me too. At the Food Channel. She wanted me to bring your mother along in our car. She is a persuasive woman."

Bettina called both of them? I'm paying her for this? My family is not a collection of windup toys to have fun with.

Roswell shifts the coil of wires Tonia asked him to hold from one hand to the other. "Heather, does your mother know that your father's gay lover is here, dude?" He looks directly at Pieter as the words *gay lover* leave his lips.

Apparently Bettina left that little fact out when she got ahold of Jocelyn Greenblotz. My mother looks at my father as though he just threw a masterfully compact snowball straight for her gut.

I lean forward in my chair, my elbows on my knee to prop my head. This can't be happening. My eyes peek through my fingers.

Steve's face is stung red with anger. "I thought you said Pieter's a family friend. I knew your parents were *separated,* but what's going on?" he finally manages to say. "Can someone fill me in, for God's sake?"

Roswell looks over to me. "Was that one of the things you wanted me to BS about?" He seems too stoned to care that he just opened a can of worms.

"Maybe I should go," my mother says in the littlest voice I've ever heard.

Although she won't come out and say it, she must have accepted that Dad is gay. There must be a bunch of emotions in play in her mind. But I'm paralyzed with my own inability to deal. Fortunately, Dad is not. He rises and touches his ex-wife on the shoulder. "Please, Jocelyn, stay. We'll talk everything through later. If not for me, for Heather." He tries to embrace her but it's as if he's embracing a pole on the street.

"No, I think I should go," she says shakily, without even a finger leaving her hip.

"How much time until broadcast?" Steve says by walkie-talkie to Kev back in the truck.

"Twenty-six minutes," Kev answers.

"Perhaps I can be of some help here," Mahmoud says to Steve.

"And how the hell are you going to help?" Steve cries. His cool head for business is disintegrating fast. He looks as if he might have a breakdown.

"I'm trained in negotiation."

"You have a better idea?" Jared snaps at Steve. "Let him talk to Heather's parents so we can go on air."

Steve throws up his hands. "Is there a spare room?"

"Sure," Jake says. "Uncle Sol, use the study with the pinball machine, it's right down the stairs on your left."

"Pieter, you come too," Dad beckons. "The three of us need to talk this out."

"The three of us don't need to talk anything out," Mom says. "I really think I should go. I can wait in Steve's car. I'll just call Wilson and have him pick me up and take me home."

"Wilson is still working for you?" Dad asks curiously.

"You always had a thing for him, didn't you?" Mom says softly. "Were you screwing him while you left me to rot?"

Oh boy. Good luck, Mahmoud.

"Please, Jocelyn." Dad says. "Let's talk this out."

"As I said—" Mahmoud rises "—I can help you do that."

"Who *are* you?" Mom snaps.

"Mrs. Greenblotz, Mahmoud's my boyfriend and a very big diplomat," Vondra says. "He's been to Camp David several times. He helped run the negotiations between Begin and Sadat." Vondra and my mother met once when I toured her around the new offices. By my mother's despondent face, I can see she has no memory of Vondra, and that more than a few Xanax will be popped tonight, or even sooner.

"Can I help?" Roswell asks.

"No!" Jared and I say simultaneously.

Mahmoud takes my mother by the hand down the stairs into the study. Pieter takes an audible breath, stands and follows behind.

"You look pale," Jared says to me in a whisper.

"I could kill Roswell."

"It'll be fine."

I fight back tears and gesture downstairs to Jake's study. "There's going to be an eruption in that room. My mother's an obvious time bomb."

Vondra takes one look at my face, walks over and grabs my hand. "You have one of the top diplomats in the world in there." She's back in adulation mode. I hope she's right.

Siobhan and Jake join us on the couch.

I sigh miserably. Jake cracks a dubious smile and sighs too. He reaches over to the table spread and grabs a piece of matzo and dips it in the apple-walnut *haroset.* Jake manages a chuckle as he says, "This stuff tastes great. Now I remember the *haroset* from when I was really little. I never wanted to eat it because I thought it sounded like what our neighbor had, cirrhosis of the liver."

"My brother called it *corrosives,*" Jared says, and Jake laughs.

I motion to Jake's broken-off bit of matzo. "I don't think you're supposed to eat that yet."

"Come on, Heather," Jake says. "This is an act. Don't turn into one of those kosher freaks on me."

Jared gets up quietly and heads back to Steve for direction. I feel bad about any offense he may have taken, but I didn't fill Jake in on anything about our almost-budding romance—so how would he know Jared keeps kosher?

I quiet Jake by waving my hand from side to side. Steve is talking to Tonia about audio, so I lower my voice and say, "Steve knows I'm not kosher, but he thinks you are."

"Who's getting mic-ed?" Tonia wants to know.

"My father when he gets out of the room. And me and Jake."

"Can you slip this in your shirt?" Tonia asks.

Jake's cell phone rings. "I forgot to shut it off."

"Yes, everyone should shut theirs off," Steve says in a crushed voice. "Pagers and beepers too."

"Who is it, honey?" Siobhan asks.

"The number's not coming up on my caller ID."

"Get it later," Siobhan says.

"This time of the year, it might be important business. And it'll get my mind off what's going on with Uncle Sol and Aunt Jocelyn." He flips open the mouthpiece. "Hello?" Jake says.

Even from where I'm sitting, I can hear a woman screaming at him.

"Calm down. Calm down—no, we don't need your permission. I didn't tell you because you wouldn't have participated. No, I don't want to talk to Mortie. Listen, there's nothing you can do about it. It's not costing our company one red cent. The Food Channel is paying for everything. This is going to help us, Marcy, not hurt us. I'm sorry you're just hearing about it now. Jesus Christ, we're about to have a seder. Will you just calm down?—Do *not* curse at me like that— So sue us, Marcy."

"Who is suing?" Steve barks at me. "Is the Food Channel at risk? I need to know we can pull this off. Why didn't you tell me your family is a bunch of freaks?"

"Lay off of her, Steve," Jared says. "You're worked up. Pull yourself together. It's going to be fine. I got here early. We rehearsed it."

"*You* rehearsed it? It's bad enough you ask questions on shoots. Now you want to be a fucking director? Who the hell told you to get here early?"

"We're an item," Jared says. "Live with it."

The new commotion stirs Gertie from her second nap of the hour. "Who's an item?"

"Heather and I. We've made a very real connection."

"We are?" I say.

"Aren't we?" Jared says with earnest eyes. "After our night together, I really thought—"

Steve turns directly to me. "*I thought you hadn't gotten sex-*

ual with him. And furthermore, you said organized religion is for jokers."

"I never said that! You did!"

"You don't really care who you crawl into bed with, do you? Me or Jared, whoever gets you off."

Vondra puts her hands on her hips and is in Steve's face like a true friend. "Being an asshole doesn't seem to bother you in the least, but it bothers me a lot."

"You've been seeing Steve, too?" Jared says quietly in my direction. He looks slightly ill. "Why didn't you tell me?"

"My God, Steve, there's minutes to air." Tonia scowls. "Leave the slut alone and get your own overactive cock in check. Your career is on the line. You told me yourself everyone's watching to see if you can host your own series. Well, now it's time to get your shit together."

I slump into my chair. If only there were arsenic on the seder plate. Who would I kill first?

The doorbell rings.

"Who's ringing the fucking doorbell?" Steve barks. "If it's Kev, I'll kill the *schmuck*. I told him not to move. We have to broadcast something even if it's the damn flea circus in the truck."

"Maybe it's Elijah," Siobhan says.

"Who the fuck is Elijah?" Steve screams. "Did Heather go to bed with him too?"

"No," says Siobhan. "Elijah is a prophet who at Passover we leave the door open—"

"I know who fucking Elijah is!" Steve shrieks even louder at her.

Jake shakes his head at this New Jersey edition of hell. "Not now, Siobhan."

"Siobhan?" Steve throws his arms up in disgust. "I thought you said her name was Shoshanna!"

"Am I going to have to bust your face in?" Vondra yells at Steve, with a streetwise finger in his face. "You're supposed to be helping things here."

The knock on the door gets louder.

Amy Hitler rises to open it. It's Bettina. Her curly hair is in a tidy bun and she's wearing a revealing devil-red pantsuit that suits her tall frame.

"How's it going, Heather? I wanted to be here for your triumphant hour."

"Going? It's not going, Bettina, it's gone."

"You! You're the woman who called me," Steve says. "Which crazy family member are you? Or are you the wife of a Klansman? Because that would be perfect. And do you think you could at least show up on time for a national broadcast?"

Vondra's about to yell again, but something inside me snaps. "Shut the hell up, Steve. This is my therapist. And I need her help or I'm going to leave you here with a live mess that will get your self-important prick fired."

"It's about time," Vondra says as she applauds.

Roswell is in the door frame, either scared or amazed by my outburst. Bettina rests her butt on a love seat well out of the camera's range.

The study door opens. I'm expecting Mahmoud, my parents and Pieter to emerge bloodied and bandaged. Instead, they're looking weirdly peaceful. They sit down at the table and my father calmly says, "What's all that noise about? We're ready to start."

"How much time?" train-wreck Steve calls out toward Tonia.

"Four minutes." Tonia may have just called me a slut, but when it comes to sound she is a true pro under immense pressure. She quickly re-mics my father and does a sound check. She even fixes the mics on the table hidden in flower arrangements, the ones strategically placed to ensure that anyone not wired up can be heard.

"Roswell, hold up the white board for a white balance," Jared yells.

"He's stoned. Don't let him do anything," I say.

"He can hold up a piece of paper," Jared says adamantly. "We just need to get my camera at the right color level."

Roswell listens to his buddy Squid, and grabs the white board.

"Three, two, one," Tonia calls.

This is it.

"Good evening. I'm Steve Meyers from the Food Channel. Why is this night different from all other nights? Because tonight you will experience a television first. Tonight you are going to get a chance to celebrate Passover live with a Jewish family. Not just any family. In the Jewish-food industry there are many players, but only one brand reigns supreme. Greenblotz. A privately held brand best known for their matzo, Greenblotz manufactures over seventy kosher-food products."

Steve walks behind my father. Jared focuses in on Dad's face.

"Every seder has a leader," Steve picks up. "This one is no exception. Tonight's seder will be led by Solomon Greenblotz, grandson of Israel Greenblotz, or *Izzy* Greenblotz, as the family lovingly calls him. The current generation calls their forebear the Henry Ford of Matzo with good reason. His invention of mass-production matzo machinery in 1916 allowed for sales well beyond his neighborhood streets. There are more sales of Greenblotz Matzo then of any other matzo brand on our planet. Seated around the table are Izzy's descendants, and also some family guests who will join in on the celebration. We'll meet all of them as the night goes on."

My hand is shaking.

"Solomon Greenblotz, thank you for letting us join your family tonight."

"We're thrilled to share such a joyous occasion with America. My grandfather had a slogan on every box that we still use to this day on every product. *Buy Greenblotz—Because Family Is Everything*. And I believe that strongly, as does my wife of thirty-three years, Jocelyn Greenblotz."

"What a devoted family you have, Mrs. Greenblotz."

"Thank you," Mom says in a tiny voice. "We are delighted to have America join us at our annual seder. It means a lot to us to have so many parts of the family under the same roof. Sol and I spend much of the year apart as he must constantly travel to tend to our international customers. Domestically, my nephew Jake has taken the helm, and today we are at his delightful home in New Jersey."

Am I crazy, or is my mother imitating Jacqueline Kennedy during the Live-from-the-White-House specials?

"It's also the home of Jake's beautiful wife, Shoshanna, originally from Tel Aviv," my father adds.

"Shalom," Siobhan says with a passable Israeli accent. Her wig looks Mars red under the glare of the lights.

Steve motions with his neck for Jared to zoom in on the living room adjoining our dining room. He tilts toward the brick fireplace topped with lit candles. "As your mother-in-law just said, this is a delightful home. We're minutes from New York City, and yet I feel as if I'm in someone's country hideaway."

"Thank you," Siobhan says demurely.

Dad continues down the table, introducing the rest of our motley crew. When he gets to Vondra, Steve interrupts him.

"Is there something special you also have to share about Vondra's guest to her right?"

"Yes indeed. We have asked Vondra's friend Mahmoud, a spokesman for the Egyptian consulate, to participate in our seder as a gesture to peace in the Middle East. Those of you who have participated in a seder know that a lot is said during the night of the ancient animosity between the Egyptian Pharaohs and the Jews. We don't have to reenact that animosity tonight. Mahmoud is a brave man, and a kind man, and let me tell America the Greenblotz family believes we have to start peace somewhere. If it is at a dinner table, then so be it."

"*Salaam*," Mahmoud says directly to the camera. "And *Shalom*."

"Incredible," Steve says on air. "I want to remind our viewers this is the Food Channel, not CNN."

"I'm honored to have my aunt Gertie here," Dad continues. "She is a reminder of how important our older generations were to our family. She is the sister of my gentle deceased father, Reuben Greenblotz."

Gertie nods happily. She's enjoying this charade.

What did I tell Steve again? That she was my father's mother's sister. To hell with it all. Why will he care now? We've jumped in the pool already.

When the camera is off her and on to Sukie, Gertie leans over to me and whispers, "I vas Reuben's mistress."

"Finally," Dad says, "we have Sukie Cohen, a bright young woman who owns a new store next to our matzo factory on the Lower East Side of Manhattan." Channeling Tom Brokaw, Dad goes on to explain that this is Sukie's first seder and that it is an honor to have a Cohen at any Jewish ceremony.

Sukie smiles proudly, and Jared focuses his camera on her. "I am, like, so honored to be here."

"One more," my mother calls out.

Dad pauses. Did he really forget, or was he just stalling? "Yes, rounding out the table we have Pieter Eicken, a very good friend of mine from Amsterdam, passing through New York. It is a *mitzvah,* a blessing, in Jewish tradition to invite those away from home to the Passover seder."

"Wonderful," says Steve, looking relieved. "Shall we begin?"

"We shall," Dad says with a nod. "We start the service with a blessing to sanctify the holiday. For this prayer, we will drink the first of four cups of wine. I'll first explain to the Food Channel audience that during the seder four glasses of wine are poured to represent the four stages of the exodus: freedom, deliverance, redemption and release. After the meal we will pour a symbolic fifth cup of wine for the prophet Elijah, and at that moment we will open our door to let him in."

Jared pans over to the still-closed front door.

At Dad's instruction we raise our cups and recite the prayer.

"Good," Dad says. "Now I will now read from a *Haggadah,* which literally means, 'The Telling.' It is best described as the book of instructions Jews have used to carry out this ritual celebration for thousands of years. I will first use the *Haggadah* to explain the seder plate. Although I am reading the English version, you may notice I am reading from the top of the right page. That is because we follow the traditional Hebrew *Haggadah* as a guide. Hebrew is read right to left, not left to right. Occasionally you will hear a bit of Hebrew here or there, but I will be sure to translate for you."

He picks up the *Haggadah.* "Before us we have three matzos, commemorating the bread which our forefathers were compelled to eat during their hasty departure from Egypt.

We use the three matzos to represent the three religious groupings of the Jewish people—Kohen—" here, Dad smiles at Sukie, who blushes and giggles "—Levi and Yisroayl. These matzos are placed together to indicate the unity of the Jewish people. In unity, we find our strength and power to survive."

Through my peripheral vision I can tell Jared has zoomed into my face on the word *survive*. I nod my head with conviction.

"Another item on the seder plate," Dad continues, "is *haroset*, a mixture of apples, walnuts and wine that represents the mortar the Jewish slaves used to assemble the Pharaoh's brick. Next there is parsley dipped in saltwater—it symbolizes springtime and the tears of the Jewish slaves. And there's a roasted egg on the plate..."

Dad pauses as he sees what I see from my seat: an empty spot on the seder plate where an oven-browned egg once was.

Roswell's hand springs into view and slides a peeled egg with a small bite taken out of it.

I gasp off camera—don't tell me Roswell fed his afterweed munchies with the seder egg! But Jared has shrewdly focused on a framed Von Gogh exhibition poster on the wall instead of the egg. Even so, Dad doesn't miss a beat. "The egg is another traditional symbol of spring," he says coolly. "And also of fertility."

Dad takes a sip of lemon water before continuing. "Then there is the shankbone, symbolic of the sacrificial-lamb offering of days gone by, and bitter herbs to represent the bitter affliction of slavery." Off camera, Siobhan sticks her tongue out at Jake. Siobhan had wanted to grind a fresh root instead of using the prefab Silver's horseradish bottle. The way Jake nixed that time-wasting activity had made me laugh: "For a girl who speaks fluent Gaelic, you're getting carried away with Jewish authenticity."

"Next," Dad continues, "we wash our hands. This is a spiritual cleansing." At rehearsal, Jared instructed Siobhan and I what to do during this section, so we both jump up and circle the table with our assigned tasks. Siobhan has a small water jug to pour water over the hands of everyone seated, and I'm there to catch the water in a basin, and hand everyone a towel to dry their hands.

We're all hot and sweaty under the lights, but Pieter uses the basin as an opportunity to wash his perspiration off his face. This time it's Jared who gasps at the sacrilege as he points away at the wall again.

"We now pass out more *karpas*, which you will remember from the seder plate is a springtime symbol." Dad says the proper prayer in Hebrew, and Jake translates it into English. "Over the years," my father adds, "the Greenblotz family has found parsley is a good vegetable to use for *karpas* because when you shake the water, it looks like tears."

After we have dipped our parsley into the saltwater, Dad takes the reins again. "Now we place three matzos on the table, Greenblotz Matzos of course, and bless them. The middle matzo is broken in half as a dessert matzo for the youngest to find. More about that later."

Another sip of water. "Now," Dad says, "we come to the big *magilla* as far as the seder is concerned. This part of our seder is the telling of the Exodus narrative. We start with the Four Questions. Traditionally the youngest person at the table asks questions, and we go around the table to answer."

Jared had surveyed the room during our rehearsal to figure out who should ask the questions. Although Roswell is quite a few years younger than Sukie, he is off air tonight. So this is twenty-six-year-old Sukie's big moment in the sun.

She reads the questions in phonetic Hebrew before reading the English translation from her *Hagaddah*: "Why is this night different from all other nights of the year?" she begins.

Dad smiles broadly when she's finished her questions and says, "Wonderful, Sukie. We shall now, together as a group, answer the four basic questions concerning Passover, which you have asked."

Counterclockwise, we each read a passage marked *participant* in the *Haggadah*.

Soon, it is my turn again. I speak as clearly as possible: "'There were but seventy people who arrived in Egypt, but, in time, their number increased. Soon they also grew in strength and became a mighty people. The Egyptians came to fear them for, they reasoned, in time of war they might join with enemy nations and become a threatening force. They, therefore, decided to subdue them with forced labor, and to reduce their numbers by casting male children into the river. Taskmasters were placed over the Hebrews, who whipped and tortured them, compelling them to make bricks and build great cities for the Pharaohs.'"

I skim ahead and gasp to myself. Will Mahmoud really have to read what's next?

"You want me to read this?" Mahmoud asks with a pained smile.

"Yes," Dad says, and there is a group laugh on camera.

Mahmoud coughs loudly and reads in his beautiful voice: "'The task was inhuman and too great to bear. The Jewish people cried out to God, and he heard them cry. He called to Moses, charging him to appear before the Pharaoh and demand that the people be released. Pharaoh was obstinate and would not heed the word of God.'"

I wince as Mahmoud continues on about how Moses predicted the plagues God would rain on the Egyptians if the

Jews weren't released. I miss a bit, but when I tune in again, Mahmoud is saying, "'When the tenth plague was visited upon them, the death of the firstborn sons of Egyptians, a great cry went up throughout Egypt, and Pharaoh finally ordered Moses to take his people out of the land.'" Mahmoud coughs again, and we all laugh again, a bit more uncomfortably.

I may be sated with Steve, but I have to give him kudos for his hosting. He knows this is a perfect spot to interrupt the ceremony with a bit of humorous but poignant commentary. "If the spokesman for the Egyptian consulate can respectfully read that passage, I think there's hope for the Middle East yet."

"Amen," my father says.

Vondra touches Mahmoud's shoulder as we dab red drops of ultrasweet Schapiro's kosher Passover wine on our paper napkins (as Jared coached us to do) and read the ten plagues together first in phonetic Hebrew, then in the translation:

Blood. Frogs. Gnats. Flies. Murrain. Boils. Hail. Locusts. Darkness. Slaying of the firstborn.

There are more prayers for Dad to read, but soon it's time to eat our meal, and time for Steve to make another on-air appearance.

He sticks a microphone in front of my face. "Pop quiz. What's murrain?"

I force a laugh. "No clue." Was that an olive branch or on-air provocation?

"A cattle disease," Bettina says from off-camera. I'd forgotten she was there.

Steve picks up my vibe and smartly moves far down the table to Gertie. Ever the faithful employee, Gertie tells the world how proud she is of her "nephew" Sol.

"Every year, such a beautiful seder," Gertie says. She smiles in my direction after Steve has moved on to Greg and Amy, and Sukie.

"This is an emotional evening for me," Sukie says. "I've reconnected to the half of my ancestry I knew nothing about." Sukie has tears in her eyes, but even red-eyed, she is cute as a button.

"Closer," Steve mouths to Jared. "Money shot."

Jared zooms in.

Amy nudges Greg. "Where's my close-up?" she whispers. *Jesus. I hope no one heard that in their living rooms.*

Amy calls out Steve's name, which forces him to come over with an artificial smile. "I think America should know what a beautiful, loving family the Greenblotzes are," Amy says, as sweet as German chocolate cake.

Greg nods his head to her in approval, but Steve motions Jared to move on quickly to Pieter in purple mesh.

"And our visitor from Amsterdam," Steve says to Pieter. "Any thoughts?"

"Don't buy any of what Amy said. The Greenblotz family is crazy as a fruit loaf."

Everyone at the table laughs loudly.

"But despite that," Pieter adds, "I'm having a *fabulous* time."

"The matzo ball soup is wonderful, Shoshanna," Mahmoud says.

"That's Greenblotz Matzo Meal in the matzo balls," Jake trumpets.

Considering how mortified I was at the start of the broadcast, I'm amazed how quickly and smoothly we got through this night. Could it really be time to drink the final cup of wine?

I look at my watch. Eighty minutes exactly. Dad's pacing was perfect. There's just enough time for a follow-up prayer and a traditional after-meal song, which we sing together phonetically, following along in our *Haggadahs*.

Finally, my father reads the very last prayer: "'As we have been privileged to observe the seder tonight, may all of us be privileged to celebrate it, together, again next year. May it be God's will to preserve us in life and good health. *L'shna haba-a bi-Y'rushalayim!* Next year in Jerusalem!'"

"Next year in Jerusalem," the seder table echoes.

"I'm Steve Meyers, and you've been watching a special presentation of the Food Channel."

We smile like contestants who have performed but have not yet been judged on a talent show until Kev says, via walkie-talkie from the remote truck, "Steve, we're off the air."

Steve and Jared may hate me now, but they would both have to admit that the Greenblotz *mishpucha* did their company proud. I can't look either of them in the eye.

Steve sits down in an empty chair. He rests his face in his palms. Jared puts down his camera on the floor and claps.

Jake smiles big, stands, shakes Jared's hand, and walks over to embrace my mother. "Thank you, Aunt Jocelyn."

"For what, Jake?" Mom says.

"For everything. Thank you, everyone."

"I should be saying the thank-yous," Steve says awkwardly after he removes his face from his hands. "That was excellent."

Mahmoud gives Vondra a kiss on the cheek. I survey the rest of the room: calmed and happy faces. Except for Roswell's: the joint has put him to sleep on the couch.

Bettina is gone. Before I can ponder her absence further, Jared sneaks up behind me and kisses me on the neck.

FOURTEEN

Elastic Marriage

"**Y**our father and I are getting back together."

I believe the word here is *dumbfounded*. Did I hear correctly? "What about Pieter?" I sputter when my voice works again.

Mom takes another forkful of her tuna and arugula salad. We were lucky to get a lunchtime seat in Café SFA, the tucked-away but very crowded restaurant on the eighth floor of Saks Fifth Avenue.

"He's moving in too."

"What? Are you out of your minds?"

"You and I haven't discussed my marriage with your father in depth, I know that, Heather. But after how we all teamed up on the seder, don't you think we should continue to open up to each other a bit more?"

"How did you go from a night's cooperation to a full reconciliation? In one week?"

"The U.N. is out of session this week—so Mahmoud has been counseling us in his office. He's better than all of our therapists combined."

I'm mute. I pick up a fork and stare at its tines. What can I say to this insanity?

"Heather, listen to me good. I love him. He's—gay, but I want to be with him."

"I don't get it. If he doesn't want women, why would you want to torture yourself like that?"

"He's the smartest man I've ever known. I used to read literature when he was around. He used to clip book reviews for me, to challenge me. Now I read *dreck* to pass the time. That's my life now. Mysteries and *TV Guide*."

"Mom, you love mysteries. Don't let Dad tell you what to read."

"I'm not going to stop reading them. I just want your father around to push me to read more." She stops to smile a bit kookily, and says, "I'll tell you a secret. I'm under a growing suspicion that he was looking for a male version of me. Pieter is like a kid in a candy shop when it comes to New York shopping—and he may be a trendy photographer, but he brought three junky Dutch mysteries in his suitcase. His taste and mine are not so far apart."

I move the saltshaker closer to the pepper shaker. "Not to get ugly, Mom, but, um, are they going to be sexual in your apartment?"

"They'll have plenty of privacy for that sort of thing. You can't hear a thing from the guest bedroom."

I whistle softly. "This is too much."

"If Dad holds me and makes me laugh, shouldn't that be enough?"

"What about your needs?"

"What, sex? Not for me. And what am I getting now?"

"What about Angela and Wilson? Aren't you two worried about the backstairs gossip leaking to the press?"

"They've always been discreet. Your father paid them well, and I kept up the big checks. They know we're not kosher, and that alone could have ruined the business. So what's a little queenie Dutchie to them?"

"Tell me, what's Pieter to you?"

"At Mahmoud's suggestion, your father went to see a movie yesterday so Pieter and I could have a private coffee in my apartment. He's a bit flamboyant—"

"A bit? He dresses in purple from head to toe."

"I'm surprised that you're so hostile to this. You, the big activist in our family."

"I'm not hostile," I say with great hostility. Why does this disturb me so much? Even I'm not sure.

Two ladies who lunch sneak a look at our table to see who is going at it in such a classy place.

"Sol looked wonderful at the seder, don't you think?"

"It was a nice suit," I say quietly.

"Pieter's doing. Next he's going to talk to your father about that smelly horse blanket your father still wears for a sweater. Pieter and I are plotting a fashion intervention."

The humor of this situation is sinking in. "Dad scuttling around your designer house in his batik-wear and moccasins won't do?"

Mom smiles. "I think with two of us on the case, he may very well change. We're going to tag-team him. Drag him to see a stylist kicking and screaming."

"Why can't you or Pieter just go with him to a couple of suitable stores?"

"Honey, everyone has a stylist these days."

Our waitress plunks down our grilled-chicken Caesars.

Mom checks her lipstick with a glance at the wall mirror and asks, "So, what's new with you?"

"Other than my mother and gay father getting back together? Nothing new, except people keep stopping me on the street. You can't believe the ratings the seder got."

"I've been stopped too. I know. Tell me, what's going on with Jared? I'm glad you two were talking after the seder."

"We talked, but trust me, nothing's happening there. Jared has moved past what Steve said about me, or a least he says he has. But we couldn't get past the kosher issue."

"Maybe he's more bothered than he's letting on about your date with Steve. I have to tell you, I don't blame you. Steve behaved despicably, but that man is so dishy—"

"Please, not you too, Mom! Trust me, he's an arrogant world unto his own."

"That's a shame about Jared. He's a nice man, and very handsome too. I love the cleft chin."

I don't want to think about Jared. It just makes me sad. "Mom, I want to get back to what's going on with you and Dad."

"There's not much more to say. They're moving in tomorrow and we're going to give it a shot."

"So how open will you be? Are you going to announce to the Jewish press that Dad is gay?"

"Are you kidding? I'm dumb but I'm not stupid. What can I say? I'm lonely—miserable—without him. Am I that nuts?" She looks at me with an exposed face: a woman, a mother, a wife with palpable fear. Her voice quivers as she continues, "Do you know how your mother gets to sleep at night?"

"How?" I'm finding it impossible to look directly at her eyes when she's spilling her guts to me. After years of wanting just this kind of emotion from her, I'm not ready for it.

I push a piece of oily lettuce to the side so that the SFA logo appears on the plate.

"I've bought out the entire New Age CD section at Tower Records. Waterfalls. That's how I get to sleep. Otherwise I dread my dreams. I'm always stuck in a pit or I'm falling down a cliff." She kneads her hands together as she continues, "Once, just once, I was naked and I soared over my high school and I soared over my college and I soared over my apartment building. I didn't care I was naked because I was flying and everyone else wasn't. I flew over the world and I landed on the ground in a green airstrip. There was your father to greet me, naked, and welcoming."

I have to look at her, even though the tears are welling up inside me. I do. A voice inside me commands me to grab her hand before she bawls. "You're not dumb if it works for you, Mom—"

When she can breathe steadily again, she smiles as best as she can. "I should have known what I was getting into at that Cornell-Ithaca social where we met. He was reading *Auntie Mame* when I sat down and said hello."

I laugh as my first tear drips down my nose.

And she laughs that I laugh.

I'm in the bath when I remember that the last Grand Lady of Sex we filmed, Rina O'Riley, is leaving NYC for the summer in a few days. I desperately need to get her all-important release form that schmucko Roswell left in the bathroom of the Museum of Natural History. Rina also has to do an ADR for us, which means the additional recording of a few words that were drowned out by background noise. Like every good cameraman, Jared took plenty of pick-up shots. With the addition of an ADR, our editor can make the film seamless with a spare visual of the cavemen while only Rina's rerecorded voice is heard. Mixed in with the words that are actually coming out of her mouth in the museum, the effect will be seamless. And like most documentarians, except the annoying purists, I don't think using ADRs is cheating. Rina won't be dubbing in new thoughts, she's just repeating words she's already said.

"Sure," she says cheerily, even though it's 11:00 p.m. "Tomorrow morning would be fine."

I check the equipment in my living room. "Two. Two. One. Two." I play it back, and it sounds okay, I guess. I hate recording ADRs without a proper sound person, but who am I going to get at this hour? I'm certainly not going to ask Tonia after she called me a slut at the seder.

I am fascinated by Rina's apartment, a testament to a life well lived. All around the living room are anthropological artifacts and unusual souvenirs from her many travels. The far wall houses a terrific tribal-mask collection. In one photograph on prominent display in her living room, there's an attractive professorial type with his arms around a much younger Rina.

I point to the photo after I've finished my recording. "Is that your husband?"

"Yes," Rina says quietly. "Frank died almost fifteen years ago." She coughs a bit sadly and adds, "By the way, I saw your family on television last week. I'm not Jewish, but I found the whole ceremony fascinating. You seem very close to your family. That's wonderful."

I'm on safe ground, and I desperately need to vent. Of all the people on earth, Rina O'Riley, the woman who co-coined *Elastic Marriage*, is sure to understand an unusual family structure. "Yeah, well, it wasn't exactly honest."

"How's that?"

"Nobody was talking to each other. That nice old lady is

an employee who works in our shop, not a relative. My parents hadn't seen each other for ten years until thirty minutes before the seder. My father flew in from Amsterdam with Pieter, his new gay lover."

Rina seems unfazed.

"It's ironic that we filmed a segment with you about Elastic Marriage just before the seder, because as of today, my parents are going to be living with Pieter in just that, an Elastic Marriage, although the world can't know about the happy arrangement."

She smiles kindly. "You seem unnerved about this turn of events."

"I am."

"When I was your age there was a popular expression, 'The marriage is on its second bottle of Tabasco.' That meant the marriage has lasted, through better or worse. Marriage is about negotiation and compromise. Whatever gets two people through."

"But can I confide in you a little more, Rina?"

"Of course you can."

"My mother doesn't care about sex. She just wants my father there for the companionship. Now she can also tap his lover for a second opinion on her shopping sprees."

Rina laughs. "A need for companionship is a very common scenario. And this is a pansexual moment in history. I know many gay-straight marriages that work."

"You do?"

"This is my business. Trust me."

Rina has helped me isolate the reason behind my discomfort—my anxiety that we could be the only family in the world with such a fucked-up structure. To hear that there are other households like this that work—that *does* sink in. I already feel less animosity toward my parents' reconciliation. I sigh. "It is their life, not mine. I guess they have to try what works for them."

"Love is a hard puzzle to crack."

"Yes," I smile sadly.

"Ah," she says, "having some troubles solving your own love puzzle?"

She's good. "Yeah. I actually found a puzzle worth solving, but I didn't like the way it turned out."

"I'm not following you," Rina says.

"Remember the cameraman you met at the museum? Jared Silver. He's handsome, kind, funny, smart. In fact, he has every quality I'm looking for in a partner, except for his religious beliefs."

"He isn't Jewish? Isn't Silver a Jewish name?"

"Yes. I finally found the Nice Jewish Guy of my dreams, except he's *too* Jewish for me. He's kosher and I'm not. He sees no problem with so many aspects of organized religion that bother me." I sigh again. "It's a dead end."

"Darling, sometimes you have to get creative. It's *very* hard to find love in this world."

Rina bids me goodbye with a handshake and a motherly peck.

Downstairs in her lobby, my cell phone rings.

"Hello?"

"It's Bettina."

"Finally. God, where were you?"

"I've been busy."

"I wanted to talk to you about what happened at the seder. What happened to you? I've been calling you for almost a week, Bettina."

"It went very well, don't you think?"

"You crossed some big boundaries. It's one thing if you push me to make a phone call from your office. But I think it's completely inappropriate to have lassoed my mother into coming without letting me know. If we hadn't had Mahmoud there, we could have had a disastrous event on our hands."

"I had faith in you."

I'm not sure how to respond to that. My first instinct is to say, "You did?"

"Heather, this is what people hire me for, what can I say? Perhaps it's time we part from each other."

"Wait a second! I'm not firing you! I just want to talk this out. I need to talk to you about my conversations with Jared, about what Rina O—"

"Jared is the cameraman?"

"Yes. We talked after the seder. We have a great connection and a deadly disagreement about religion. I just don't see how it can work, but I feel nauseous about giving him up."

"This is where I leave you, love."

My stomach tightens. "What do you mean, leave me?"

"The best thing I can do for you is let you decide what to do."

"Hello?" Jared says over an incredible din.

"Where are you?"

"Heather?"

"Yes. I can hardly hear you. Where are you?"

"We're filming in Chinatown's largest dim sum parlor."

"Can you meet me? To talk more?"

Jared is silent for the space of two breaths, and then says, "Can you meet me outside the Chinese restaurant on the southeast corner of East Broadway and Rutgers? I think it's called Wing Shoon, or Wing Shine, something like that. You can take the F train down there, and get off at East Broadway."

"I'll do that," I say, although I know I'll grab a cab instead.

★ ★ ★

"I wanted you to see this place," Jared says after a careful kiss on my cheek outside of Wing Shoon. "This was once the Garden Cafeteria. It's where Emma Goldman and John Reed used to eat. You know who they were?"

"I know. I had the hots for an anarchist once."

He smiles. "But of course you did." He coughs uncomfortably. "So. Has it been a week already?"

"Where can we sit?" I ask. "Do you want to go inside the restaurant and order some hot-and-sour soup?"

"Not kosher," he says softly.

Internally I roll my eyes.

We cross the street to the steps of Seward Park Library.

Jared stares back across the road to the tallest building on the block, about ten stories, with a clock on top. There's a Hebrew word carved over the parapet under the roof.

"Can you believe that's the old Forward Building?"

"What's that word in Hebrew?" I say, pointing.

"Yiddish. It says *Forward*. I took a walking tour once. I cannot believe it's being turned into condos too."

"What was the Forward Building for?"

"That's where they published the Yiddish newspaper that first put Isaac Bashevis Singer into print in America. *The Forward* is still going, but there's just not that many people reading Yiddish these days. They publish the paper daily in both languages, but most people read the English one. They moved the offices years ago to a nondescript building in midtown. Check out the four carved flaming torches that are symbols of the socialist movement. Those socialists would turn in their grave if they could see what was moving in."

"Do the new condos make you that sad?"

"I'm not sure. Should I even care about such things? No one else seems to."

We sit silently for at least a minute.

"Jared, I know we tried to talk this through. But I've thought a lot more about us, if you're still interested in hearing what I have to say."

"I'm here, aren't I?"

I start: "This kosher thing is a problem, huh?"

He pauses in thought and says, "In Israel, they wouldn't even recognize what American Judaism is. You are just a Jew. You keep the *kashrut* and the *shabbos* or you don't at all. There's no such thing as picking and choosing what works for you from Column A and Column B, like orders of beef with snow peas or chicken with broccoli at an old chop suey restaurant."

"You don't wear a *yarmulke*, so how much of a stickler are you?'"

"I told you, I didn't get film jobs with one," he says a bit angrily. "Anyhow, there's no Jewish law about wearing a *yarmulke*. There's an old Middle Eastern tradition of covering your head for a king. Jews probably starting wearing them because God was seen as the King of Kings."

"That sounds a bit fishy to me."

"Maybe I'm finding loopholes but—"

"So why can't we find loopholes when it comes to us?'

He looks at me and picks up one of my hands before he answers. "How so?"

"Say we tried being together. Let's even go a step further—say we move in together if all goes well. What if we were kosher inside our home? What I do out of your sight wouldn't matter, would it?"

"That's an interesting possibility—but would you go to synagogue with me?"

"I'm not sure. I could try it out. Honestly, it's not something I'd look forward to."

"But why? This is your own heritage. Why do you run from it?"

"The heritage I don't mind. I love hearing everything you have to say about the religion, about our traditions. Synagogue is a different story. Lectures from a pulpit have always turned me off."

"How would you know if you've never gone?"

"I'm a Jewish girl from New York. I've been to *bar mitzvahs*. I've been to weddings."

"That's not the same as seeking it out on your own. I think you'd be surprised how much focus going to synagogue could give you. You'd try it at least once?"

"Yes. But don't count on me. I really have a strong sense of what I'd enjoy."

"All I want is for you to try it."

"Like I said, I will."

Jared pulls on the tips of my fingers. "Tell me, what do you expect of me if—we gave it a go?"

"I just want to be able to feel I'm an autonomous individual who happens to be in a couple. If I want to stay home on a Saturday, I want to be able to. If I want to eat meat and milk, then as long as it's out of your house, I don't see why it should worry you. It's my own moral decision."

Jared stares at two Chinese toddlers racing toward the Seward Park kiddie swings.

"That's all well and good, but we're in our thirties now, babe, so there's no avoiding the big issues. What if we got married? What would we teach our children?"

"I don't have the answer, Jared. It's all so new. All I know is that I think—I like you a lot."

Jared breaks into a smile and scoops me into his arms for a hug. "Know when I fell for you? When you told that dumb matzo joke on day one. You have no idea how much sleep

I lost this week. I'd go so far as to say I think I'm in love with you."

"Love? Jared, we hardly know each other. We've had one date, even if it was an all-nighter, and then some. Don't get me wrong it was a *great* date—"

"Heather, why are you here? Why did you call? You must have strong feelings."

I burst out crying. "I just want to warn you—it's hard to understand who I am."

"I understand."

"No, you *don't* fully understand. It's not just feeling alienated from the kosher life. It's not just being a little neurotic about relationships. Being an heir comes with a lot of responsibilities. Being an heir really fucks you up."

"I hear you, it's a struggle for me too."

"What is?"

"Being an heir."

Is he playing with me? I wipe away a tear with my thumb. "To what?"

"Something that goes with matzo very well. Jewish horseradish."

It comes to me with a thump. "You're the *Silver* of Silver's Horseradish?"

Jared grins sheepishly. "One of them. There are many of us. Actually, I'm a double heir. To horseradish on my dad's side, and my mother is ball bearings."

I donkey-kick him in the shin.

"Ow! That hurt!"

"Why didn't you ever say anything? You don't think being a kosher-food heir isn't relevant information?" I kick him again.

"Stop!" Jared says good-naturedly but quite loudly. "Why does an heir not say anything? Would you be talking about your family on camera if it wasn't to save your finances?"

"Probably not."

"Look, I wanted to be sure you liked me for me."

"That's what you say to a poor person! I'm not after any money—"

"I was going to surprise you with this info at the seder, but then when Steve revealed a little more than I wanted to know—"

"I was hoping that whole night Steve and I spent together would never come up."

Jared reaches for my hand. "It's okay. We weren't an item yet, even if I said we were. It was just a little awkward, that's all."

"Thanks for understanding. But, mister, I'm not done with my shock of your birthright." Sarah's cryptic words at Second Avenue Deli come back to me. "Did Sarah know what family you came from?"

"Yeah. I took her to my parents' estate once, even though I knew she wasn't right for me."

"Then Steve must know, too?"

"Yes. As a matter of fact, he is richer than the two of us combined."

I snort. "Where's his money from, vinegar?"

"His great-grandfather started a shipping firm. He's used to keeping mum, so I whispered to him at the first shoot not to tell you my background." Jared pokes me. "Hey. This isn't about Steve. This is about us. Do you want to give *us* a shot?"

I nod my head enthusiastically.

FiFTeeN

That Time of Year (Again)

After weeks of discussion on striking a balance between fluffy and didactic filmmaking, Vondra and I still haven't settled on a new project.

"I think you should stick to women as your milieu, but try a historical angle," Jared says. "Don't get typecast, like I've been—I love working on indie films but unless there's food involved I can't get hired."

Jared's brushing the hair out of my eyes in the main exhibition room of Deitch Projects, one of the few remaining essential galleries in SoHo. We're halfway into the opening night of *Cocky!*—Pieter's first photography exhibit in New York.

My mother, clinging close to her only daughter and her only daughter's fiancé in a room packed to the rafters with *men men men*, overhears Jared's advice, and surprisingly, has her own strong opinion. "How about women in castles?" she says. "You could do a film on that."

"On what exactly, Mom?"

"A day in the life of a medieval woman. You could show an average day, not a coronation or anything."

"That's pretty clever," I say appreciatively. It's not such a far stretch from the BBC idea of a day in the life of a post-9/11 New Yorker. "What got you thinking about that?"

"I'm reading *Mrs. Dalloway*."

"You're reading Virginia Woolf these days?" I ask incredulously.

"Well, Pieter rented *The Hours* because he loves Nicole Kidman, and then Sol suggested we all read the inspiration. The movie only features women in the twentieth century. Don't tell your dad, but I'm also reading a castle romance novel at the same time."

"It's the high-low influence." Jared laughs, but that crack is wasted on my mother. She doesn't read art magazines.

I think for another second as I sip my red wine. "It would be a fun project, Mom, but what's the bite?"

"You and your obsession with bite," Jared teases. "You and Vondra will think of a novel feminist slant that has all the critics salivating. How many award nominations do you want? Let's just get as much travel in before we have kids."

I laugh. Jared has a right to spout off. The next film is supposed to be a *we* decision. Our company has grown: Jared is now our in-house cameraman, his chance to break free from his soufflé segments. We're changing our name to Two Dames and a Gent to celebrate his arrival.

"We'll have to talk it out with Vondra."

"If you like that idea, don't forget Scotland," Mom says. "They have castles and top-notch yarn."

I smirk. "Since when do you care about yarn?"

"I'm taking a knitting class at the 92nd Street Y," she says. "A cooking class, too," she adds with a wink.

"Try Stirling Castle, the childhood home to Mary Queen of Scots, my favorite queen," someone says.

I turn with a start. Where do I know that campy voice from? Charity Royall. And her British friend Natasha. In full drag.

We air-kiss.

"What are you doing here, girls?" I say.

"You inspired me to go to New York," Charity explains. "The way you stormed out to Amsterdam—and did what you had to do to get your father back—made me face what I really wanted to do. Live back in North America."

"I came along for a holiday and a look," Natasha adds. "First we came to see Stonewall and The Great White Way. Tomorrow we're going to Canada."

"The Great White North," Charity quips.

"But how did you hear about this exhibit?" I say. "It's bizarre that you're here."

"We missed *Cocky!* in Amsterdam," Natasha explains. "It caused quite a sensation there. So when we saw the same exhibit listed here in the *Village Voice*, we decided to take a look."

I lean in close to my friends and whisper, "The photographer is my father's boyfriend."

"Wonderful!" says Charity.

My mother tugs on my sleeve. "I've had enough of the art people. I'm calling Wilson to take me back to the safety of my living room."

"Wait, Mom—I want you to meet some friends from my Amsterdam trip. Charity, Natasha, this is my mother, Jocelyn Greenblotz. I met them before I found Dad, so, uh, they know the, uh, back story."

"You can't tell anyone," she says as a hello.

"Mrs. Greenblotz, the gay community is very tight-lipped," Natasha assures with a self-contained laugh.

Charity leans conspiratorially toward my mother, "So, the world wants to know. Which cocks are your husband's?"

"It's been too long," my mother says with a girlish giggle.

My father creeps up behind us—dressed by Pieter's new stylist in a vintage black cowboy shirt, black Levi jeans, and three-hundred-dollar sneakers from Jeffrey, a store in the hipper-than-thou meatpacking district. Dad slips an arm around my mother. "What's so funny?"

"Sol, these nice ladies asked me which cocks are yours, and I told them that I can't remember."

"What else have you said to them?" he says with a start.

"It's okay, Dad. These are the friends I made in De Amstel Taveerne before I tracked you down. They were very helpful when I was beside myself. Very discreet."

"Okay," he says, not entirely convinced.

"So what's the answer?" my mother says.

"All of them," Dad says sheepishly.

We all share a belly laugh.

"How was Pieter's show?" Vondra asks the next morning in our office. "I hope you told him I was sorry I missed it."

"I told him. It was a little uncomfortable for me, but I didn't let on."

"Is he talented?"

"I guess the photos were executed well, but it's hard to take note of talent when your Dad's penis is framed ten times around the room."

Vondra giggles loudly in horror and delight. "That's what the exhibit was? I came so close to taking my mother!"

"Well then, it's a really good thing you didn't come. I would have told you, but I just wanted to see your face when you walked in."

Vondra is still laughing when the phone rings. "Can you

pick it up?" Vondra asks, wiping some mascara from her laughter tears.

"Heather, it's Roswell."

"Hi," I say wearily. How many times is he going to apologize for jeopardizing the seder broadcast? It's been almost a year already.

"I'm just calling you to apologize again."

"It's yesterday's news. It's over with. So you learned one big thing, don't smoke weed on a shoot."

"Yeah, I'm going to make that a law on my film."

"What film?"

"That's the other thing I wanted to call you about. I wanted to thank you for kicking my ass."

"When did I ever do that?"

"Remember that conversation you had with me in the car to your cousin's house? You told me if I ever want to make a film I should start with what I know best. I had a long discussion with my parents about it, and I decided to follow Abdullah's struggle to stay in America. It's unbelievable the crap he's still going through."

"You know, that's a terrific idea. There are some great teen-filmmaking festivals I've heard of. I could probably give you some leads—"

"I don't think so."

I raise my eyes to the ceiling. Same old Roswell. "So what's your plan then?"

"You know Cecelia Neville over at HBO?"

Where is this going? "Very well."

"That's what I thought. My dad said to be aggressive because that's how he got ahead in the audio/video duplication business. So I used your name—"

"What!"

"I got right through to Cecelia, and pitched a film about Abdullah's problems with the Immigration Office."

"Shit, Roswell. You can't use people's names without checking with them first."

"No? My dad thought it would be all right with you. That you would be proud of me."

"Tell your dad he missed the class on corporate etiquette. I'm sure Cecelia was royally pissed off when she realized she was talking to an eighteen-year-old."

"Well, uh, not really. She said she was looking for the right project for the youth audience, and check this shit out—*Yo, Are You a Terrorist?* just got the highest advance ever for a first-time documentariat."

"Documentarian—or documentary maker."

"Whatever. Pretty cool, huh? I don't need to go back to my freshman year at Hampshire College anymore, man."

"Vondra," I say when I hang up the phone. "And just when you recovered, this will set you off—"

She has her back to me, and swivels around with a finger pointing to her cell phone. I can tell by her tone of voice that she is talking with Mahmoud. She must be still trying to work out some travel glitches for my trip to Cairo, where Mahmoud and Vondra's wedding will take place.

Vondra smiles at me when she's hung up the phone.

"Wait until you hear about what Roswell's done—" I start.

"No, wait until you hear about what Mahmoud's done. Forget about your other hotel. He made one phone call to the head of Oberoi, a luxury hotel chain in India, who called the manager of the Oberoi at the Pyramids, the Giza Mena House Oberoi. Everyone from Winston Churchill to Britney Spears has stayed there. You have the suite with the most stunning view of the Pyramids."

I smile. "Well done."

"Can we go over our arrangements for Israel now? Mahmoud's doubtful we're going to be able to go."

"You're both going to be fine."

"How can you say that? How is he going to get a visa? Even if he's a high-level diplomat, he's an Arab traveling from Egypt to Israel."

"It's not a problem. Jared and I took care of it." I should have left it at that, but I can't resist: "Jared called President Bush."

Vondra looks at me with a curious expression and says, "Jared knows Bush? Does his family know him? The president? I'm not even sure Mahmoud knows Bush."

"Of course."

I can't take the pained look from my one-upmanship. "I'm kidding." That was a bit cruel of me.

"Why would you joke like that? What did I do to you today?"

"Nothing. But honestly—you go on and on and on about Mahmoud and who he knows. Concentrate on your own considerable talents and achievements. You'd be a bit more fun to be around."

"You don't like him?" she says in an angry voice. And then after a visible pause, she adds, "You were no picnic last year, I'll have you know."

"I know that. I'm really sorry I just said that. But I need to get this off my chest. You used to be very, well, more yourself, and less Mahmoud's fiancée."

She glares at me.

I rise and give her a kiss on the cheek. "I'm sorry. I adore Mahmoud. And I love you. Look, it was so important to me that both of you could come to Jerusalem that Jared and I spent an hour strategizing how to get Mahmoud the visa. It took a lot of wangling."

"Okay, so how did you do it for real?" she asks softly.

"Luckily the man at the Israeli visa office said, 'Green-blotz like the matzo?' And I took that as a cue to proceed. I'd come prepared, and let's say, it's lucky Mahmoud knew Sadat."

I have Vondra's interest again. "He's been dead for what, twenty years now? How did Sadat help you?"

"I'd clipped the articles about Sadat's staff at the library. I showed him Mahmoud's picture. And I emphasized that one of the highest-ranking individuals with the U.N. would hardly be a problem. I'm just going to have to bring you two in to the Israeli visa office and ask for this guy. He's going to type in clearance on the computer system."

"That's amazing."

"Well, if Mahmoud had to have known one Arab for him get the clearance for Israel, Sadat was the one. But I should warn you that we're all going to have to fly back to Europe to enter Jerusalem. There's no direct flights to Israel from Egypt. And you should allow for a massive layover time for getting onto El Al."

"Are they that tough?"

"They strip-searched my grandma Lainie once when she went to a spa near the Dead Sea for her seventy-fifth birthday. She was so upset she nearly collapsed at the airport. And that's before all this chaos we've got going now."

"Did your grandmother have to take her bra off?"

"And her briefs. A woman checked, of course. My father thought they should change their slogan to *EL AL: So safe, we'll strip-search your grandmother.*"

Vondra laughs, if a bit reluctantly. I guess my earlier outburst is forgiven. I should have approached her still-chronic Mahmoud-worship more diplomatically.

"I was just thinking, Heather, will Amy Hitler have problems getting through Israeli customs with her last name? Or did she get married to Greg already?"

I shake my head no. "I didn't tell you this? She's not with him anymore. Greg's bringing his new girlfriend to Israel. Sukie from the seder."

"That Valley Girl he drove in as a favor to you? Isn't she about twenty years old?"

"She's twenty-six. Remember, she told Jared when he was figuring out who to ask the Four Questions?"

"Like, *Ohmi-gawd*, those pigtails confused me."

I shake my head no. "Don't typecast her like that. She's way smarter than you think and very sweet. Greg slipped her his number when he dropped her off, and the next thing I knew she was visiting him in Miami. She's closing Upsy Daisy because it isn't turning a profit in this recession. And apparently she got obsessed with the idea that her last name means she's from the priest class. She's found her religious roots. She's kosher now, and she's converting next month and applying to a progressive rabbinical school in Florida."

"Why does she have to convert if she's already half-Jewish?"

"Jared explained this to me. Judaism is a matrilineal religion. You can only truly prove birthright by the mother. If we didn't have that regulation we could claim Harrison Ford and Sean Penn as truly our own."

Vondra laughs, and closes the clear plastic lid on her Flatiron Sushi order.

I eye it ravenously as I down my second of two iced coffees I ordered at the deli downstairs—I have to keep alert with so much work on my wedding and new documentary arrangements. "You ate the cooked egg and you're leaving a crab roll, are you crazy? Give that to me this second!"

"I thought you'd gone kosher. Didn't you tell me shell-fish wasn't kosher?"

"Yes, but I also told you that, *in the house* I'm going to be kosher. That's the agreement. Outside the house, I do things my way. Do you listen to a word I say, bitch?"

"Occasionally," she says, and with a big grin, adds, "Bitch."

I grab the crab roll and grin right back at her.

"So tell me this. How is it you can make up your own rules like that?"

"Jared's not too happy about it, but he agreed."

"How did you convince him to cut you a break?"

"We negotiated. We live in America, I told him, and like it or not, that's the way Americans do things. We improvise."

As I sneeze loudly from my spring allergies, Vondra gasps. "Holy mackerel! Have you read this?"

"What is it? Read it to me."

You better sit down. "It's in the *New York Observer* under the headline 'Next Year in Jerusalem.'"

"It's not about—"

"'*We heard it on good authority that the two dames behind Emmy-winning production company Two Dames will be celebrating two unusual unions soon. First up is Vondra Adams, tying the knot with Egypt's magnetic United Nation's spokesman Mahmoud Habib in front of the Pyramids. And if that isn't Power Wedding enough, the team will then travel to Israel for what some are dubbing the Jewish Wedding of the Century.'*"

"What?" I scream from my seat.

"'*Last Passover brought the Food Channel some of its highest ratings when the Greenblotz family's Passover seder was broadcast nationally. It wasn't just the nation who was watching: the cameraman who shot the seder, Jared Silver, the quietly dashing heir to—Can you believe it?—Silver's Horseradish, will be married to cutie beauty Heather Greenblotz in Jerusalem shortly after a joint family seder. Among the special guests of both the seder and the wedding will be a bevy of award-winning film-makers and representatives of every major kosher-food company in New York.'"*

Vondra laughs uneasily when she is finished. "What is going on? Who is their *authority?* Is it one of your friends?"

"Couldn't be. Although that was scarily detailed."

"Could your mother have sent it in? You've been closer to her these days."

"Not a chance." And then it hits me. "The words *cutie beauty* have the scent of my therapist. This has to be a clip for her success-story file. Bettina has important clients in media that could have placed that for her."

"That bitchy English lady? I thought you stopped going to her."

"She's Australian. And I called her last week just to give her an update. I thought I owed her that after our sales report and my engagement."

I have to hand it to Bettina. Her methodology worked. I get along pretty damn well with my folks these days, and of course there's Jared in my life. And Marcy and Rebecca are withdrawing their knee-jerk lawsuit over the Greenblotz name at the seder without their permission. They're seeing more money in their silk-lined pockets because there was a sales increase of twenty-five percent in our family business immediately after the broadcast—nothing like hard cash to soothe hurt feelings. After all the figures from this year's busy season are in, Jake expects to announce an even greater boost at the next board meeting.

With HBO and Cecilia Neville's industry muscle behind us, Vondra and I garnered two more Emmy nominations for *The Grand Ladies of Sex.* We lost out to a former fast-food worker's scathing exposé on the industry's evils: the exploitation of children through advertising, cruelty to animals, anti-union low wages and deception of the public when greasy burgers and milk shakes are promoted as nutritious. But this loss was good for me and Vondra. After the Emmy ceremony was over, we agreed that *The Grand Ladies of Sex* didn't really have as much bite as the winner's project, or our own Riker's Island film for that matter.

I hate to bark at Bettina again, but she can't keep meddling in people's lives this much. I'm flattered by the article, but the spilling of news about Mahmoud's trip to Israel is a worry. We were keeping that quiet for security reasons. Doesn't Bettina believe in running anything past her clients? Even if I'm not officially her client anymore.

I call her number, which I find most unexpectedly is disconnected. Her beeper also gets no response. Where is she? I just spoke to her last week. I call the phone company. There's no forwarding info. I even call Oprah's production company and ask to speak to a booker.

"Sorry," says the show's booking intern. "My boss has the same number you have."

Maybe if I took a cab to Bettina's office I could ask her why she did this. Somehow in my gut though, I know she's gone. Did the weathercock point east as it did for Mary Poppins, a signal for this odd bird to vanish?

"No luck?" Vondra asks.

"This is bizarre. I can't find her anywhere."

Could Bettina have gone back to Australia, or maybe to another city where the very wealthy congregate?

I'd never know. But like Jane Banks after hard-ass Mary left with the wind, I knew I'd be fine without her.

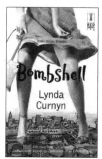

On sale in May from Red Dress Ink

A novel about exit lines—
and Ex Appeal…

It's Not You It's Me

by Allison Rushby

Charlie is off on the adventure of a lifetime,
and is pleasantly surprised when on the plane
she bumps into international celebrity and rock-star
sex god Jasper Ash—who also happens to be her
former best friend, flatmate and…almost-lover!
But "what could have been" ended with the classic
excuse, "It's not you, it's me." This will be a
European tour you don't want to miss.

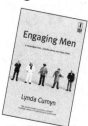

The Last Year
of Being Single

Sarah Tucker

**Just because he's perfect
doesn't mean he's Mr. Right....**

Torn between two men—her perfect-on-paper fiancé
and an intoxicating and flirty co-worker—twenty-
nine-year-old Sarah Giles writes a scandalously
honest diary of one life-changing year, and faces
the challenge of writing her own happy ending....

RED
DRESS
INK
TM

RDI11032-TRR